EVERYONE ON THE STREET WAS RUNNING AND SCREAMING.

Then I heard cars slamming into each other, horns blaring, alarms going off. Bikes lay smashed on the sidewalk as flat as tortillas; the pavement glistened with shards of glass from doors and storefronts and windows, between new piles of bricks and rubble. What the hell? An earthquake in Manhattan? A terrorist attack? The UN wasn't all that far away.

I looked down the block to see if I could figure out what was happening, and then I shook my head to clear it. No way could a troll, a red granite giant, be swinging his fists and other proportionately massive appendages as he—definitely a he—slogged down my narrow street. Parking meters bent so coins went flying; stair railings twisted into wrought iron spaghetti; the floor beneath my feet shook.

There he was, my Fafhrd, the creature I had just drawn. And no one saw him but me. I was not God, not Frankenstein jump-starting his creation with a bolt of lightning.

No, I was crazy.

Celia Jerome

TROLLS IN THE HAMPTONS

A Willow Tate Novel

DAW BOOKS, INC.

DONALD A. WOLLHEIM, FOUNDER

375 Hudson Street, New York, NY 10014

ELIZABETH R. WOLLHEIM
SHEILA E. GILBERT
PUBLISHERS

www.dawbooks.com

First Printing, November 2010
1 2 3 4 5 6 7 8 9

Chapter I

NEVER UNDERESTIMATE THE POWER OF imagination. Never overestimate it, either. Take me, for instance, Willow Tate. I'm thirty-four and I can almost support my family's Manhattan apartment and myself by writing and illustrating graphic novels for young adults. I'm good; they sell. I sign them with the non-gender specific Willy Tate, but they are all my work, my inspiration, my ideas. Sometimes I write not so good poems, too. And I've made candles, painted murals, built birdhouses, and strung beaded necklaces for friends. But that's creativity, not Creation.

Think about it. The screenwriter can create an entire new world and make it come to life in a movie, so real you think you are there on the desert or the mountain or some other planet. The artist can paint flowers you can almost smell. A romance writer can tell a love story so touching you weep into your hot chocolate. They all come out of thin air and active minds.

But neither imagination, nor creativity, nor great art can make something actual and alive. Fantasy simply does not translate into reality, no matter how lovely. You cannot move into air castles or subsist on pie in the sky.

Otherwise I'd have conjured up my own perfect hero long ago. He wouldn't need to be cover-model gorgeous, but he'd definitely be as noble, honorable—and hot—as the heroes of my action-adventure books. Maybe his only superpower would be making my heart beat faster, but that and a good sense of humor would be enough. And a steady job.

Instead of pulling a Romeo out of my hat, I am single, to my mother's horror, and the only man who gets my pulse thumping these days is Lou the Lout, the super of the brownstone building across from mine in the Murray Hill neighborhood, and that's adrenaline, not lust I feel. The old man terrifies me. He's never been aggressive or nasty, but he stares, even when he's sweeping the sidewalk, shoveling snow, or picking up after the pigs who don't clean up after their dogs. From my third-floor apartment—no elevator, no doorman, but a great midtown location on the East Side—I can see him looking up, into my window. That's what he does when he's not sweeping or shoveling or bagging garbage: he stares up from his place under the entry steps of his building, or from the barred window of the subfloor where I suppose he lives.

Both my parents tell me to close the blinds, which is about the only thing they agree on. It's easy for them to say, when Mom lives a block from the beach out on Long Island and has a garden in the backyard, and Dad has nothing but another high-rise senior citizen condo in his view.

Why should I block the sunlight and the scenery outside the walls of my apartment? I was raised in these same rooms, which is how I have an affordable rent-controlled unit. Mom got the summerhouse in the divorce. Dad got the Florida condo they bought for retiring. I got the city apartment. It works for all of us, except for Lou.

I spend most of my hours right here, working, sleeping, reading, or stringing those beads. I will not give up my view of the street, the pedestrians, the pigeons. I *need* that open space in the city. Besides, I refuse to let any old lecher steal my freedom. Okay, I won't walk on his side of East Thirty-Eighth Street, but that doesn't mean he's winning his war of intimidation.

The tenants of Lou's building don't seem to find him threatening, but to me he's like the monster under the bridge, waiting for unwary travelers. He's no cute gnomish old man, either, just a large, lumbering, and middle-aged troll.

. . . A troll.

Now there's an idea for a new series of books. No one does trolls. Vampires and werewolves are a dime a dozen. Dragons, witches, and psychics are done to death. Ghosts after death. But trolls?

I picked up my pen—red with a fine point—and a lined yellow pad I always keep on the round table by the window that's my office. (And dining room if company, or my mother, comes.) The 'puter and its drawing tablet are for later, once I know what I want. I took a sip of my green tea and thought, *Yeah, a troll.* I switched to a thin-line marker and started sketching. He'd be big, rocklike, wide-faced, with red skin. Green was overdone, and Lou was always flushed and angry looking, chapped in winter, sunburned in the summer. Even on a nice spring day like this one, I bet he dripped with sweat and smelled, but I never got close enough to tell.

I forgot all about him as I sketched and made notes for possible story lines. Should a troll wear clothes or not? Was he hero or villain, victim or avenger? He

needed a name. Or was he a she? Girls bought my
books, too. They might like a rough-and-ready female
character. Or not. Trolls with boobs? Trolls in love? I'd
have to run it by my editor after the weekend. For now
my character was Fafhrd, after the Fritz Leiber classic
fantasy hero, a gentle giant of a warrior, and best friend
of the Gray Mouser.

Ah, to be in the same realm as Fritz Leiber. Right
now I was flying on the wind of imagination. This was
what I lived for, what made it all worthwhile, the bad
reviews, the minuscule royalty advance payments, the
low print runs and lack of publicity. To hell with all that;
this was the fun part: the rush, the brain stimulation, the
euphoria of a great, new idea that a few brushstrokes, a
couple of lines, could make into something. That's the
creative high, the confidence, the glow, the near post-
coital satisfaction. No, this was more like the start of a
new relationship, fresh, exciting, full of tingly possibilities. Who knew how it would turn out, but this might be
The One.

I stopped to look at my sketches, my pages of plot,
conflict, and character. Damn, I'm good.

The tea was gone, along with a dusty chocolate kiss, a
stick of sugarless gum that lied about whitening teeth at
the same time, and most of the afternoon. Lined yellow
pages and pink sticky notes and drawings covered the
table; new files and folders appeared on the computer.
I could have gone on for hours; I was on such a roll. . . .

Which reminded me I'd missed lunch and my afternoon snack. Maybe I deserved Ben and Jerry's instead
of a banana. And I'd burn some of the calories by walking to the deli around the corner to get it. I'd been sitting
so long my neck was stiff and I could feel my rear end
spreading. I looked out the window to see if I needed a

sweatshirt, by checking what everyone on the street was wearing, but they were running and screaming. Then I heard the cars slamming into each other, horns blaring, alarms going off. Bikes lay smashed on the sidewalk as flat as tortillas; the pavement glistened with shards of glass from doors and storefronts and windows, between new piles of bricks and rubble. What the hell? An earthquake in Manhattan? A terrorist attack? The UN wasn't all that far away.

I looked down the block to see if I could figure out what happened, if I should flee the building or hide under the bed.

It was a good thing the mug was empty or tea would have been all over my carpet, I grabbed the table edge so hard. Then again, it was a good thing the table was there or I would have fallen over.

I shook my head to clear it. I'd been working too hard, that was all. And I was light-headed from hunger. No way could a troll, a red granite giant, be swinging his fists and other proportionately massive appendages as he—definitely a he—slogged down my narrow street. Parking meters bent so coins went flying; stair railings twisted into wrought iron spaghetti; the floor beneath my feet shook.

I squeezed my eyes shut, then opened them, figuring the daytime nightmare would disappear. It did not. Holy shit, that was a troll—my troll, Fafhrd—smashing the fire hydrant on the corner as if it were a plastic cup. Water fountained out and up, making rainbows in the sun, and floods in the gutters. The troll stood under the streaming geyser, gazing at the colors, splashing his size thirty feet and catching handfuls of water, acting like a child at the beach, or a kid with a bottle of soap bubbles. And then, and I swear this is true, he looked up at my window and grinned at me before disappearing around the corner.

My fingers were numb from clutching the table. I had to pry them off to reach for the phone.

"Nine-one-one? This is Willow Tate." I gave my address, but stuttered over my phone number. They had it on caller ID anyway.

"Just relax, ma'am. Take a deep breath and tell me what the problem is."

I took a deep breath, which did not calm me in the least. I tried to keep my voice from shaking, or screeching. "There's been"—a what?—"some kind of catastrophe on my block. An accident. Cars, buildings damaged, windows broken." On the second stories!

"Are you injured?"

"No, I am on the third floor. I cannot tell if anyone else is hurt. People are all standing around, some are crying. I don't see anyone on the ground." Crowds were racing toward the street from other blocks, jumping out of cars and rushing out of buildings.

"Yes, we are getting other calls."

I could see cell phones in everyone's hands. I'd guess the lines would be flooded. No, those were the streets.

"A fire hydrant is broken."

"We are dispatching ambulances and fire trucks. I'll notify the water authority. Can you tell me what happened?"

"A tr— A tr—"

"Calm down, ma'am. Help is on the way. Was it a truck?"

That sounded plausible. "Red."

"A red truck. Anything else?"

I could hear sirens already. "Big."

"Yes, thank you. I have your name and address. I am

certain an officer will want to speak to you later. Please try to recall as much as you can. You might jot down some notes, so you don't forget any details."

Details? They were all over my computer, my drawing pad, my table. I couldn't help myself. I grabbed for a pen as soon as I hung up the phone. Despite my shaking hands, I draped a scarf around Fafhrd's hips to cover his privates. Then I had to laugh. Okay, the laughter might be hysteria, but I had to smile at my own hubris, thinking for one second that I had anything to do with whatever had just happened. My burst of mental creativity had *not* given birth to a physical menace. Could not, should not, would not. So there.

I am good.

I am not that good.

CHAPTER 2

SOMETIMES I WISHED I DRANK. Or smoked, or had a stash of prescription or proscribed drugs. But my mother pops in whenever she feels like it, to go shopping, visit friends, find fault with my housekeeping. I know, I'm not a kid, and the apartment is in my name now, but she's still my mother. Too much alcohol gives me headaches, smoking would kill you, and the other stuff scares me. I may as well admit it; a lot of stuff scares me. And that was before a figment of my imagination wreaked mayhem on Manhattan.

I settled for some frozen yogurt with freezer burn. I'd had worse.

I tried not to look out the window, or listen to the sirens and the bullhorn orders and the beeping of tow trucks backing up. I also gathered all my notes into a manila envelope and locked them in the bottom drawer of my desk, along with the computer files on a disk. I don't *think* anyone can sue me for having a wild new idea. If they try, I can always say I jotted down my impressions after the fact.

After what fact? That a troll came from nowhere, created chaos, smiled at me, and vanished? Oh, yeah.

Maybe I should call *The Times* now. Instead I called Arlen, the guy I'm dating. He's not The One, the Happily Ever After, but he'd be better company than my thoughts, and maybe he'd bring some Häagen-Dazs.

"Arlen, something awful happened."

"I know. It's on all the news."

I should have thought of turning on the TV or the radio. "It was right here, on my block."

"They showed your building from the helicopter camera."

So that was why the building kept feeling like it was shaking. "Um, Arlen, if you saw that my building was in the middle of the mess, how come you didn't call to see if I was all right?" I mean, I would have.

"They said no one was hurt. And you said you'd be working all day, not out in the streets."

Arlen worked on Wall Street. He was very disciplined about work and had a hard time with my looser idea of scheduling. He could never understand a sudden need for a street pretzel to untangle a plot, or a quick walk to jar a character into shape. I'd never handed a manuscript in late yet, so what did it matter whether I worked from ten to three during the day or ten to three at night?

"Do you think you could come over, maybe bring in takeout? My treat." Arlen was also very careful about money.

"No can do. Your neighborhood is cordoned off. All of midtown is at a standstill. Maybe later. I'll call, okay, dear?"

I hate when he calls me dear, as if we are an old married couple. After three months? Maybe he calls all his girlfriends "dear" so he doesn't have to remember our names. But he's really nice, and good-looking, and likes movies. Of course, I would have found a way to get to him if he'd been traumatized. I would have found a sushi place, too, even if I like Chinese better. But I was desperate. "Later?"

"Sure. I'll listen to the news to see when the streets are open."

I looked outside. That wouldn't be for hours. They had the water turned off, at least, and a lot of the cars dragged away. Barricades and blue uniforms kept most of the crowds at a distance. One cop car was blaring that everyone should stay inside.

As if I wanted to go get trampled by a troll.

My best friends were unavailable. Sherrie was on her second husband; make that honeymoon. Daisy'd be at court all day. Ellen tutored after school. My family was hours away, the ground-floor neighbors spoke little English, the second-story groupies hate me because I complain about their music when I'm trying to write, the gay guys on the fourth-floor level work all day, and Mrs. Abbottini who has the rear apartment on my floor is nearly deaf.

I hated myself for feeling needy enough to say, "Please try," to Arlen, but I said it anyway. My thoughts were not going to be good enough company to erase that toothy, trollish grin. Independence is all well and good, but not when a fairy-tale ogre comes to life.

Arlen said he supposed he could tell the cops he was coming home after work so they'd let him pass through the barriers if they were still up in a couple of hours. He couldn't leave the office early anyway.

He wouldn't, he meant. Not for me and my jangled nerves. Maybe if I were bleeding or the building was evacuated. Maybe.

I went to visit Mrs. Abbottini, in case she was frightened by all the noise and commotion. She couldn't have seen what happened on the street; her apartment faces a tiny rear courtyard where the garbage cans are kept. But she would have felt the tremors from the helicopter, or maybe she was watching the news. Either way, she always had cookies and tea. I needed company more.

Mrs. Abbottini apparently remembered how mad she was that my parents gave me the apartment when they split up. She fought the realtor for the right to move to the front, but lost when I proved I had enough income to keep up the rent. Now she'd missed the biggest thing to hit the neighborhood since old man Mirabella brought home his "secretary," and had a heart attack working overtime. All she'd seen this afternoon was a cat tipping over the trash in a panic, and it was all my fault.

If she only knew.

She didn't offer so much as a stale Lorna Doone. The TV was loud enough to deafen the downstairs neighbors, but the commentators had no answers, only questions for people who hadn't seen anything but the aftermath, but wanted to be on the news. One carefully combed reporter said that seven victims had been transported to hospitals for minor injuries and shock, and the police were now interviewing them and every other possible witness. They'd have more information about the appalling hit and run for the six o'clock news.

"They're calling it a hit and run?"

Mrs. Abbottini didn't even look at me. "The driver didn't stop, did he?"

Now I was more confused. "What driver?"

She clacked her false teeth together, a sure sign of disgust. "If they knew who it was, it wouldn't be a hit and run, would it?"

"I better get back, in case anyone wants to ask me anything."

Mrs. Abbottini waved me away with a brush of her gnarly, spotted hand and a muttered curse, as if she could turn me into a toad and get my apartment. Yeah, right after the fairies flew by. Which, with my luck, would be tomorrow.

I did invite her to come to my place so she could look out. One of us could be polite in a crisis. Or desperate for companionship.

"I'll get a better view from right here on the TV. And your mother says your bathroom is dirty."

There was one hair in the sink the last time she was here. One dark hair. I have streaky blonde hair. I can't believe Mom told Mrs. Abbottini about Arlen's hair. Now the old bat thought I was a slob, besides a scarlet woman and an apartment thief.

I went back across the hall and looked out. The street was still filled with rescue vehicles and police and men in suits trying to look important in case a cameraman pointed in their direction. The pizza place down the block was boarded up already, so there went dinner.

The phone rang before I put the television on. Someone was concerned enough about me to call after all.

No, it was my mother. "Did you get to see any celebrities? They're interviewing everyone famous on the block. Maybe you should go plug your books."

Not was I okay, not was the building damaged. "Mom, why did you tell Mrs. Abbottini the bathroom was dirty?"

I could hear her sniff. "I should lie to someone I know for thirty years?"

"One hair, Mom, that's all it was. You know Arlen spends time here."

She sniffed again. My mother was a pro at the disapproving nose. Just ask her doctor who had to treat all the sinus infections she got.

"I was not upset that a man spent the night, Willy. You are a grown woman, and how you carry on without settling down is none of my business"—sniff—"but how could you entertain a man who expects you to clean up after him? I did not raise my daughter to be any man's maid."

"One hair?"

"And the toilet seat was up. What kind of manners does he have, anyway?"

Most likely the same as my father, which might explain why Dad lived in Florida, Mom out in the Hamptons. I gave up. "I'm fine, Mom. Thanks for calling. I'll talk to you later."

My mother never, ever gave up. "Imagine what kind of husband he'd be, wanting you to wait on him hand and foot. And you a successful author."

"Mom, I am not going to marry Arlen."

"Then why does he keep an extra toothbrush next to your sink?"

"It's easier."

"For that matter, if you are not going to marry him, why are you dating him instead of looking for someone else?"

I thought about giving the same reply: It was easier. But my mother took advantage of my hesitation to ask, "Is he coming over to be with you?"

Damn. "Later. The roads are blocked for now."

Mrs. Abbottini could have heard that sniff.

I called my father, my editor, and two friends, in case they'd heard the news and were worried. No one picked up or called back when I left messages on the answering machines.

I really need a dog.

CHAPTER 3

I WATCHED THE STREET AWHILE, then the news, but some athlete had tested positive for drugs and another Hollywood couple filed for divorce, so my block wasn't the hot topic anymore, except they were waiting for results of the investigation. I guess that meant no one had captured the troll. I couldn't imagine how he wasn't spotted. I mean, where can a ten-foot-tall, craggy red monster hide? Then again, how do you capture something that big, that strong, that hard-skinned? Bullets would bounce off him, tasers might tickle him, and I doubt if a polite request could encourage a troll to trot off to jail.

Mostly, I suppose, no one wanted to send the city into a panic by mentioning an alien invasion or something.

Which gave me pause. What if there was more than one of the creatures? I looked at the lock on my file drawer. I know I only wrote about one. Maybe they were like dust bunnies that multiplied when you weren't looking.

No. I did not call on some weird magic to animate an idea. I did not. Hell, I don't know any magic, not a single spell, no matter if people called my grandmother a witch. I kept my distance from the old bat, but sorcery had nothing to do with my staying away. And nothing to do with me.

After all, I'd written about a sea serpent, and no waterspout with eyes and fangs rose sixty feet to flood Ellis Island. Okay, so it rained a lot while I wrote the story, but that was all. My book before that, the one that won all the awards, was called *The Wild Child*. No feral female alien climbed out of the subway, only the usual young Lolitas who dressed like hookers. So I was not responsible for the troll.

To prove it, I cleaned the apartment. I mean, if I could wave a wand and produce a rock giant, surely I could cast a cleaning charm on three rooms.

I couldn't. So I'd do it myself. With a vengeance, to show my mother I was no man's servant, to show Mrs. Abbottini I was no slob, to show myself there were no bogeymen in the bathroom. Mostly I'd do it because this is my home: mine, safe, secure, needing no one or no thing but what I could provide.

Except today I missed a small smattering of human comfort and contact to show I mattered to someone else.

Damn.

I tied the tails of my shirt up in a knot, gathered my hair into a scrunchie, hiked up my low-riding shorts, and pulled on yellow rubber gloves. Luckily the intercom buzzer went off before I had to plug in the vacuum. Three short beeps—Arlen's signal that he was downstairs. He did come, he did care! I beeped back to unlock the lobby door, then hurried to kick the (still dry) mop and bucket back into the closet, throw the (unused) dust rags on top of it. The furniture polish can rolled under the couch, but who looked there? I threw the yellow gloves after it, then the scrunchie. I fluffed my hair into place as best I could, undid another button on my shirt, pulled the shorts back down to my hips, and opened the door before Arlen could knock.

The problem was, the man staring at my half-bared, bra-less chest was not Arlen. For one thing, Arlen wasn't as tall. Or as handsome. He never wore tight jeans, and he'd never have filled them so well if he did. Mostly, Arlen was not a black man.

This one had his right hand raised to knock on the door, his left reaching into his back pocket—oh, my God, he was going for a gun or a knife. He was going to kill me. If he didn't, my father would, for opening the door without looking through the peephole. Mrs. Abbottini would never hear my screams. She might ignore them anyway, figuring she'd finally get the front apartment.

"Miss Willow Tate?" the man asked. He looked angry, now that he wasn't looking at my boobs.

All I could do was nod, clutching the doorknob—after I buttoned my shirt right up to my chin.

"Do you always buzz open the lobby without asking who's there? Or open your door to strangers?"

"I, ah, I am expecting . . ."

His brown eyes dropped to my waist, which was exposed by the knotted ends of the shirt and the low rise of my shorts.

I untied the shirt and said, "No, I am expecting a friend. He was on his way over, and I thought . . . That is, he always buzzes three times."

He frowned and spoke sternly: "I buzzed twice, the same as I do at my grandmother's house so she knows it's me. She still waits to hear my voice before she unlocks the door."

He had a grandmother that he spoke of fondly. How bad could he be? Uh, who could he be?

I must have said that out loud, because he finished reaching behind him—I tried not to cringe—and pulled out a wallet, which he flipped open to show a police badge.

"Officer Donovan Gregory, ma'am. I was off duty when the call came out for every available man to help canvas the neighborhood. That's why I'm not in uniform. Not that you would have noticed, since you didn't look through the peephole."

A policeman! I wish I'd cleaned the apartment yesterday. I wish I'd combed my hair and put on makeup, too, he was so sharp looking in jeans and a loose jacket. "Please, come in. I'm sorry." I hoped he did not think I was apologizing for being afraid of him because he was African-American. The messy room, the stupidity, the wardrobe malfunctions, and thinking he was Arlen, *that's* what I was sorry for. "It has been a distressing afternoon."

"For all of us." He came through the door, glancing around. I'm sure he noticed the dust on the furniture and the cleaning stuff under the sofa, but he did not say anything. He went directly toward what had been my mother's dining alcove, which was now my office. Officer Gregory bent over to look out the window from the height of my chair. "You had the perfect view."

I still did. I'm afraid I stared at his butt as rudely as he'd stared at my boobs, until I realized he was looking at some drawings and notes on the table near my computer. I stood beside him, moving the pages away. "But I was working here, so I didn't notice anything at first."

He looked at the papers, sketches from an earlier idea. "What is it you work at, ma'am?"

I reached under the table to produce a copy of my latest book, *I'ver the Hero*. I kept a box there to give away. Sometimes I had to use them as tips for the UPS guy or the pizza deliverer, when I was out of small bills. "Here, maybe you know a kid who likes superheroes."

"The department doesn't like us taking gifts." But he smiled and said, "A lot of the guys at the precinct think they're superheroes already, and my grandmother thinks I can walk on water." He touched the "Willy" on the cover. "That you?"

"Yup. Boys don't want to read girlie authors, so I use Willy. That's what my friends call me, anyway, short for Willow."

He smiled again and tucked the paperback in his jacket pocket. "So you're a writer?"

"And illustrator."

"Great, then you must be observant. I sure hope so. We're having trouble getting a handle on today's events. So many people, so many bad descriptions." He took out a small pad from an inside pocket and flipped through a few pages. "You told the emergency operator you saw a truck?"

"I don't really remember what I said, I was so upset. Is that what it was? I couldn't be sure. I was busy, as I told you, and only looked up when I heard a commotion. At first all I noticed was the carnage in the street. I did spot something red going around the corner."

I stepped closer, and pointed to the right position.

"Yes, ma'am. Everyone saw the red. It's after that we have problems. Most of the witnesses say they saw a trolley."

"A . . . trolley?" Not a troll? "But . . . ?"

"I know. We don't have trolleys. But that's what a lot of them say they saw. An out-of-control, high, red trolley."

I didn't have to lie to say, "I didn't see anything like that."

"We're looking at a tour bus as a better possibility. One of those double-deckers with railing. Apple Tours or something, but no one mentioned passengers or a driver, and this street isn't on any sightseeing route." He looked back at me and flashed a really cute dimple on his cheek. "You're not that famous, are you?"

If great smiles counted, he'd be running the police department. I smiled back. "No such luck."

He flipped a few more pages of his notebook. "The report from the hospitals is that most of the injured suffered shock rather than actual injuries. One driver went into cardiac arrest, and several others needed stitches for cuts from the broken glass. None of them can remember anything, and they were right there on the street. Weird, huh?"

"Weird," I agreed. No one saw a troll? No one remembered an animated clump of rose marble rampaging thorough the street? Knocking signposts and parking meters down like a drunken adolescent out to get mailboxes with a baseball bat? Playing in the water from the broken hydrant like a city kid in the hot summer? Maybe the other witnesses were like me, too embarrassed to admit what they'd seen, because it couldn't exist. "Are you sure the others said a trolley? Like on tracks?"

Officer Gregory shrugged. "That's what they said. Only no one saw any tracks or overhead wires, so no one can explain how it could have gotten here or why it ran wild. And there are no extra skid marks or red paint chips on anything. Yet a lot of people swear they saw a trolley."

"Could it be mass hysteria?" I was thinking mass amnesia, if there was such a thing.

"You're not hysterical, are you?"

"No, but for one frantic instant during the crisis, I thought I saw a big red man."

"An Indian? He'd have to be one hell of a brave to do the damage he did."

I didn't correct him. "I know. I guess panic can do that to your brain, make it come up with a plausible explanation. I must have seen the back of the truck, trolley. Whatever. Like you said, a man would have to be over nine feet tall."

"That's what doesn't make sense. You'd think people in the cars would have seen what flattened them. There was a messenger thrown off his bike, a pizza parlor waitress standing by the glass window before it got smashed. Even a dog-walker who ended up hanging off a fire escape, with her dogs. None of them can say what hit them." He flipped through his pages. "I've got one more resident to track down. I'm hoping he can be more helpful."

I felt like apologizing again. Officer Gregory was so nice—and cute—I really did want to help him. He'd been called in on his time off and all, only to hear bullshit from everyone. But if no one else saw Fafhrd . . . ? My dragging in an impossible, otherworldly suspect could only make his job harder. And weirder. Untethered, unoccupied trolleys were bad enough.

"You might talk to the superintendent of the building across the street," I offered, trying to give him something constructive. "He's always hanging around, watching everything. If anyone saw what happened, it would be him."

"Lou?"

"You know him?" I *knew* the old man was a criminal!

"Sure, everyone knows Lou. Nice guy. He was the first to call in the accident, and he took a bunch of the victims into his lobby until help came."

While all I did was call 911 and fret from upstairs. I could tell I'd disappointed the cop again. But Lou, the Good Samaritan? "I find that hard to believe."

He turned another page. "Yes, I have a note that you'd called in a complaint once. Nothing came of it."

"He still stares at me."

"Lady, if you walk around in short shorts, your shirt tied under your ribs and your buttons open so it's obvious you're not wearing a bra, every man in the borough is going to stare at you."

I could feel the heat start under my newly buttoned collar and flood my face with color. "I don't— That is, I was—" I pointed to the cleaning supplies under the couch, as if that explained anything.

"But I guess," he continued, "that they'd stare no matter what you wore." He smiled again. "Great legs, Miss Tate. And the rest ain't bad either."

Oh, my.

"Sorry. I forgot I'm back on duty. You wouldn't report me for sexual harassment, would you?"

For making me feel attractive in my uglies? For admiring my book? For not making me feel like a total idiot? "Not at all. I, uh, thank you, I think. Would you like some iced tea, or coffee?" Or to pose for a portrait, maybe?

"Thanks, but I better get going to find some answers. But I appreciate the offer." He took a card from his pocket. "Here's my number if you think of anything else." He headed for the door, but turned and said, "Promise you'll be more careful about letting strangers into the building. I have enough to worry about with reckless drivers. I know this is a nice neighborhood, but you never know what kind of monster walks through the streets."

"Like trolls."

His eyebrows lowered. "That's a polite term for some of the berserkers I've seen, but I guess you being a writer it makes sense. Be careful."

"Thank you for caring. I appreciate it, especially on this horrible day."

I held the door open, because I couldn't very well ask him to stay. He was a policeman, a stranger. Maybe he was married. Maybe I was wishing, but he seemed reluctant to leave, too.

He flashed those dimples again. "And keep your shirt buttoned or I'll be citing you for obstructing traffic and causing civil unrest."

Damn my pale coloring for the blush I could feel spreading across my cheeks. "I'll be sure to do that. I was going to change before my, ah, friend came over."

"He's a lucky guy."

The devil made me say, "Just a friend."

And the devil rewarded me with another burst of sunshine from Officer Donovan Gregory's smile. "I'll let you know if I learn any pointers from your book," he said.

"Be sure you do that. I'll look forward to a review from a real hero."

"And they say this is a thankless job." He left, whistling.

I locked the door after him, then leaned on it, wanting to whistle myself. Then I ran to the window to see if I could spot him in the street. Instead I saw a reminder of the damage and destruction as haulers towed big dumpsters onto the sidewalks. Somehow I'd forgotten about the horror of the day.

I guess that's what everyone else was trying to do, by naming a trolley as perpetrator. I took my files out of the locked drawer and studied the notes and sketches. There he was, my Fafhrd, right down to the gap-toothed grin he'd sent me before disappearing, but with fewer lines on his face. The only other difference was the swag of fabric I'd colored in around his loins so I could get the library sales. This creature of mine had smashed parking meters like matchsticks, put a massive fist through glass storefronts, lifted a car by its bumper, squashed a bike like a bug, shoved people and street signs and garbage pails aside as if they were cobwebs.

And no one saw him but me.

I was not God, not Frankenstein jump-starting his creation with a bolt of lightning.

No, I was crazy.

CHAPTER 4

GOING CRAZY IS ANOTHER ONE of those things I'm afraid of. Nana Bess, my father's mother, went insane. I'm not certain she was ever *not* crazy, but she definitely got worse over the years when I knew her. She had pen pals all around the world by then. The problem was, she didn't have a pen, a phone, or the Internet. She just sat in her room, wrapped in shawls, talking to her distant friends. They answered her, too. She swore they told her things, which no one ever believed, of course, until they proved true. Coincidence, everyone said.

She got angrier and angrier that no one believed her, until no one—no one real—wanted to have anything to do with her. She'd shout and scream, then cry and grieve, so the relatives kept the grandchildren away from her. Finally my father and his brothers and sister found a place for her with a cousin in England. They told me she died in her sleep, content.

Which sounded a lot like what they told my cousin about her dog going to live on a farm when everyone knew the dog was put down after he bit the mailman.

Being like her, lost in your own world, with no one understanding what you're trying to tell them, scares me.

I know, so does Lou, and having strange men come to my door, and maybe trolls. And a lot of other things, which sometimes makes me wonder if I am already psychotic. I went to a therapist a couple of times. She said my fears were all normal. Like everyone in New York being afraid of the subways at night, or getting stuck on an elevator during an electric failure. And she swore that fear was a survival instinct, so avoiding molesters and marauders and rats was natural. So was the general trepidation of nuclear war, tsunamis that could wipe out Manhattan, and the return of the Black Plague.

I don't know.

Everyone worries about finances and health and family; that's a given. But fear is different from worry. Here are some of the other things that keep me awake at night:

What if I choke on a bone and no one will be around to perform the Heimlich maneuver and I'll lie here dead until the rent check is late? Or worse, my mother comes and finds me?

I'm afraid that I'll never have another good idea. Or I'll have a great idea but no publisher will buy it. I'll lose the apartment and have to move back to Paumanok Harbor with my mother and her mother. Oh, God.

Thunder and lightning, hurricanes, pit bulls—no matter how many nice ones I've met—are all on the list, along with snakes—and I've never met a single one of them, thank goodness. Speaking in public? I'd need a prescription. Going alone to a cocktail party? I can feel the sweat drip down my back now.

I'm terrified of getting sick like my cousin Susan did. She's had surgery and chemotherapy and radiation. And she still might die, with no hair. Then there's AIDS, not that I don't practice safe sex, but you can never be a hundred percent protected, can you? And Alzheimer's.

I fear taxi drivers with eye patches and gold teeth who don't speak English. I have nightmares about them, but the therapist said that's just insecurity about going new places. Also due to being shifted around as a kid.

I'm terrified of becoming like my mother, who spent her life trying not to be like *her* mother, but she is: interfering, demanding, critical, unless it comes to animals or herbs. My mother can do anything with dogs and cats, and her mother writes books about natural healing. They're both difficult, eccentric, and authoritative. Not that I don't love them, of course.

Falling in love petrifies me. I've never done it. Maybe I can't. Or if I do, what if he doesn't like my weird family? Or they hate him? Worse, what if he doesn't love me back? Or does at first then changes his mind, to love someone else? The therapist said many children of divorce have the same concerns, which didn't help me one bit. I stopped going.

You know what scares me worse? The idea of never falling in love at all. Watching my friends get married, have children, become part of a bigger entity outside themselves while I am left alone. On the other hand, I think wanting to be alone when you are with your supposed loved ones must be the worst of all.

I'm afraid I'll never have the right answers.

Like now. I'm almost sorry I asked Arlen to come over. I don't want to be by myself, but suddenly Arlen feels like a stand-in, a settling for something I haven't found. Which is cruel and conniving and something I am not proud of. I am not, in general, a user. At least I try not to be. I have principles.

I do like Arlen, and I do like being with him. Of

course, I liked him a lot better before he didn't come in a hurry when I needed him.

I liked Arlen a lot better before I met Officer Gregory, too. Ten minutes with the off-duty cop had me smiling and blushing and feeling pretty and feminine. And crazy, but that wasn't his fault. Now that he was gone I felt panicky again, which also wasn't his fault, but made me realize how starved I was for that kind of attention. Officer Gregory made me happier when he came, and sadder when he left. I don't think it's a good sign when a woman is more attracted to, and feels more comfortable talking to, a perfect stranger than a man she's been seeing for months.

According to my friend Sherrie, she of the second marriage, a woman never needs to stop looking at men, or liking them. Men keep looking, and lusting, married or not, so why shouldn't a woman? I have no idea if my father truly wandered before the divorce. His eyes did. My mother thought he did. Now he has more lady friends in Florida than I can keep up with. Marilyn cooks lasagna, Myra is a good tennis partner, Monique is teaching him French—and those are just the M's.

Maybe it's another relic of my parents' divorce, but I really believe in fidelity in a marriage, and even before. I mean, if you can't trust the guy you're sleeping with, why are you sleeping with him?

Well, for the sex and the companionship and movies and dinner out and someone to go to your friends' weddings with. Okay, maybe I am a user. But I don't date two men at once, not after the third or fourth date anyway. And not once we've established an intimate relationship. That's another principle.

Sometimes you have to overcome your fears. Other times you have to overcome your principles.

"Yes, I'd still like some company tonight," I told Arlen when he finally called. I took a shower. He brought sushi. He told me about his day. I asked him if he believed in the power of imagination. He asked if I wanted to be on top again.

That was about as far as Arlen's mind could travel into the unknown. But I admired his grounding, his stability. I thought we balanced each other. He thought sex would help me relax. Then again, he thought sex helped keep him fit and focused, centered. Like taking his vitamin supplements.

Tonight that suited me, pure arousal, an out-of-mind interval with no troubling thoughts. I should have known better.

Arlen knew all the right places to touch and kiss and caress. Except he smelled and tasted like seaweed. I ignored that and managed to fall into bliss without once thinking of eels. The problem was, what Arlen considered foreplay, was enough for me, for tonight. Now I thought I could fall asleep without nightmares. I was ready to drift off, pleasantly satisfied.

Arlen wasn't, naturally. Like a good camper, I tried to rise to the level of his, ah, ardor. But, damn, I shouldn't have thought of those eels.

"Arlen, you know, I don't like sushi."

He was grunting and kind of sweaty. He paused in his efforts. "Of course you do, dear. We have it all the time."

I grunted to show I was working with him. "But that's for you. You like it, I don't."

He raised himself on his arms and looked down at me. "Can we discuss this tomorrow? Better yet, you can get whatever you want next time."

I moved my hips and clenched my internal muscles.

That's only fair, not to ruin his mood. I even reached down and held his sac. I know how he likes that.

He was right back into the moment, pushing and pumping with vigorous intent. "Oh, baby. Oh, yes."

I squeezed a little harder. "Arlen, the next time my skull hits the frigging headboard, you can kiss these boys good-bye."

He put his hand on the top of my head to keep me in place. Now I felt kind of squashed and suffocated. This wasn't working, either, but I knew it was my fault—I guess I am too easily satisfied—so I moaned a few times, urging him on. Of course I did. The sooner he was done, the sooner I could go to sleep.

Afterward, he wasn't tired. He rolled over and turned on the light. "Why didn't you say anything about the sushi before?"

I tried to shield my eyes from the lamp's glare before I was wide awake again, but he took my arm so I had to look at him. "I wanted you to be happy."

"Past tense?" Of course he'd pick up on that, with his logical mind.

"No, of course not. I'll always want you to be happy."

"But you're not?"

"It's been a rough day."

"And you wanted something more exciting? What did you expect me to do, come up with whips and hand-cuffs?"

"Good grief, no." I couldn't imagine him going docile and subservient, and I have a better imagination than most people. I certainly wasn't into pain, which was where this conversation was leading. "I just—"

"You and your damned imagination. Can't you give it a rest?"

I was wide awake now. "What's that supposed to mean?"

"I keep thinking you want me to be one of your superheroes, and I never measure up."

"I don't—"

"You do. You live in some kind of fantasy world where people can leave their jobs in the middle of the afternoon, where they can fly over buildings to get to your side, where doodling and dreaming can pay the rent."

Well, my doodling was paying the rent, and the price of his damned sushi, since I'd said I'd treat.

"Let's not argue, Arlen. I've had enough upset today, what with the troll and all."

He was sitting up, putting his clothes back on. We both knew there'd be no invitation to spend the night. "The what?"

"The, ah, trauma of the traffic mess. I even had to be interviewed by a cop."

"Ah, that troll."

"No, he was nice about it."

He was dressed and ready to go. I pulled the sheet up so I wasn't the only naked one. He leaned over to kiss me good night. "I'll see you on the weekend."

"Uh, no. My cousin is coming, remember? She has a CT scan at Sloan early on Monday, so I invited her to stay for the weekend." Memorial Sloan-Kettering was *the* cancer hospital in New York. That's where you want your family, even if it was almost three hours away from where they lived.

"You hate your cousin."

"No, I don't." And even if I did, no one else was allowed to criticize my family.

"You always complained when she came in for chemo."

"I was upset at all the time it took from my work to go with her when her mother or father couldn't. And no, I wouldn't let her go by herself. She was a snotty kid, that's all, eight years younger than me, and tattling to her mother and my mother about every bad thing I did. I never figured out how she knew, except for snooping. Susan's older now. Besides, she has cancer. The least I can do is give her a place to sleep and a friend at her side when she comes for treatments and stuff."

"So you let her stay here because you feel sorry for her?"

"I *ask* her to stay because she is family. There is no question of her taking the bus back to the Hamptons when she's sick or tired."

"And I can't see you when she's here?"

"Well, I am not about to be making love with her sleeping in the next room over. Or go out and leave her alone when she might need help. I thought I'd take her to a museum, if she feels up to it, or the park."

"And I am not invited." That was a statement, not a question, so I did not have to answer.

"Well, call me when your new best friend leaves and you have time for me."

I figured we both knew that wouldn't be for a long while.

CHAPTER 5

I WAS OKAY WITH LOCKING THE door behind Arlen. Both ways. I guess Arlen was okay with it, too, because he didn't call to talk later, or the next day, either. I didn't call him, not even when my cousin left a message that she wouldn't be coming into the city until Sunday evening. There was a bachelorette party Susan wanted to go to at home in Paumanok Harbor, out at the edge of Long Island's South Fork. I was glad she felt well enough to go.

Mom was glad when I told her about Arlen.

"He was never good enough for you anyway. Once a pig, always a pig."

This came from my mother who trained dogs and sometimes fostered a couple of shelter animals. Ever since leaving my father and Manhattan, where no dogs are permitted in the apartment, her house at the beach was always full of dog hair and sand. One blot on the scorecard of my sink and Arlen was Attila the Hairy, an unworthy warthog.

But maybe I was judging Mom too harshly, because she went on, "And there was no smile in your voice when you talked about him, no sighs or secret whispers when I saw you together."

I was touched she noticed, but said, "Mom, I'm not in high school, giggling in study hall."

"You never seemed excited to be with him."

How could I be when I was waiting for my mother to go for his jugular? She insisted on being the dominant member of her own pack. That's hard enough for me to take, much less for a man who did not care for dogs. Which was another black mark against him in Mom's book. And mine, now that I thought about it. I'd have a dog in a minute, if I were allowed.

Anyway, my mother had gone on to her favorite topic, after the four-footed variety. "Now maybe you'll meet someone who'll push you out of your comfortable niche, who'll make your head spin."

I already had, but I don't think Mom meant a troll. To stop her before she could explain how it was my duty to keep the entire race from extinction, I told her, "Actually I met a nice guy this afternoon. A cop."

"A cop? Oh, that mess in the street."

"Yes. He came to ask me if I saw anything, and he was a real charmer."

I thought I heard Mom lick her chops like Georgie, a huge Bernese mountain dog she sometimes boarded. Before she started to drool, I said, "He's black. African-American."

Now I thought she said, "Jesusmaryandjoseph," but we're not remotely Catholic. Then she rallied, good liberal that she is. "Well, it's early days. And he must be a nice man or you wouldn't have mentioned it. Unless you want to ruin my day."

"No, Mom. He just showed me what I was missing."

"Well, good for him. And for you."

"Yeah, I think so." Then I decided to see just how open-minded my opinionated mother was. I knew her liberal leaning stood foursquare erect when it came to fidelity, adultery, women's rights, animal rights, and good housekeeping. "Mom, have you ever seen a troll?"

"The guy who brought me his Airedale might count as one. He had hair on his arms and growing out of his ears, big bushy eyebrows."

"The guy or the Airedale?"

"The owner. He treated his dog like shit."

"That's an ape, not a troll."

"What about the tourists in East Hampton, driving their Hummers and Jags? They don't stop for pedestrians when they're driving, but cross the street in the middle when they're walking, holding up one manicured hand to stop traffic. And they let their kids spit their gum on the sidewalk. Do you know what it's like to try to get that out of a dog's foot? And their poor pets—trophy dogs, all of them. I had to break one jerk's window before his fancy designer dog died of heat stroke inside his fancy car."

My mother could go on forever about dogs, and about tourists to the Hamptons. She lived in one of the last almost untouched villages of Long Island's peninsular tip, between Amagansett and Montauk, but on the "wrong" side of Montauk Highway. The south, or ocean side was where the money was. The north, or bay side used to be for farmers and fisherman, but the moneyed crowd was encroaching, to the dismay of long-term locals like my mother.

"I meant a real monster, not an uncouth Hamptonite."

"Come on, Willow. You're just trying to distract me from the black man. That is, the policeman. Is he going to call? Have you made a date?"

"It's not like that, Mom. He was just nice when he didn't have to be."

"Of course he had to be. It's your tax money paying his salary. Did he leave his card?"

"Yes."

"That means he wants you to call, so there's no hint of abuse of power or conflict of interest."

"What about fraternizing on the job?"

"That's for coworkers, isn't it? Call him if he was that nice."

"He only wants to hear from me if I remember anything else about what I saw."

"So make something up! You're a writer. Be creative."

That was the problem, not the solution.

I checked in with my father, who was more concerned with his bad hip ruining his golf game and his tennis matches than with me. He swore my mother's father had been a troll, big, ugly, and mean, but he made me promise not to tell her he said so.

My Fafhrd wasn't mean or ugly. Neither was the troll in the street, I decided. That is, if I was not crazy, if he existed. I went with that, instead of waiting for the guys with the straitjacket.

He hadn't hurt anyone, except for trying to push them out of his way. He'd been determined to get somewhere, it seemed, but I didn't think he was looking for water. The hydrant was an accident, then a happy surprise. Then he left. Why'd he come? Why'd he go?

I unlocked the desk drawer and looked at my sketches, then put the flash drive files back on my computer. I made some more notes, a list of questions, possible villains, a dramatic rescue. Fafhrd as Lassie? Maybe. He couldn't fly like Superman, or climb like Spidey, being much too heavy. But what if he could wink out of sight at will, the way the street menace had?

I worked on that until I had an outline I was pleased

with. I just didn't know if I should consider writing the story. It was definitely out of the box, and I couldn't afford to spend months on a project that might never sell. So I called my boss, Don Carr. As editor and publisher and majority shareholder of the whole company, DCP, he was always busy, but he picked up the phone for me.

"What have you got?" he yelled over the noise of his office. It was a big open loft, with artists and writers coming and going and tossing ideas and Frisbees and donuts back and forth. "That prima donna who writes the werewolf series is going to be two months behind schedule, one of my vampire bride writers decided to go on a honeymoon, and the ghost hunter guy joined his buddies in the afterlife. And I don't think he's going to be emailing any more books. So talk to me, Willy."

My next book wasn't due for another five months, so he couldn't mean that one. "Well, I have a new idea . . . "

"Great. I love it. How soon can I have it?"

"I want to talk to you about it first, see if you think it'll appeal to our readers."

"Come in Sunday morning. It'll be quiet enough to think then."

I knew Don often came in on weekends to catch up, and to get out of going to his in-laws with his wife and kids. Since Susan wasn't coming until dinnertime, and I had no date for Saturday night/Sunday breakfast, Sunday morning was perfect.

It was one of those rare clear, clean spring mornings in the city, with not much traffic making smog, no heat yet to raise the garbage stench.

DCP's offices were way downtown, near the financial district, so the streets and sidewalks were almost empty on the weekends.

The weekend guard didn't know me, but he had my

name on a list, so he let me up without calling first. Don must be desperate.

He had a box of pastries from the bakery, and a plastic container of fruit salad from his wife. I brought trail mix bars. The coffeemaker was on, so we were set.

Instead of trying to pitch the story out loud, I gave him my outline and sketches.

"You eat while I read," he said, pointing to a chair, but I was too nervous to sit. I picked a blueberry muffin from the box and a napkin and went to the windows that took up almost the whole front of the loft. The streets below were deserted, so I looked around and up. A building across the way was under construction, but no one was working on Sunday.

From what I could see, they were adding upper floors, which would block some of Don's light and view, but I wasn't going to say anything. I looked at him. He was smiling. Maybe at the jelly donut that dripped on my sketches. I hoped not. I put a napkin in front of him, but he kept reading. That was a good sign, wasn't it?

I went back to the window. Some of the new floors were framed out with steel beams, and a crane was waiting next to a bunch more, so I guess they were going higher still. I couldn't quite make out what the red stuff was on the existing roof of the building until it moved.

Fafhrd! My troll was climbing up on the steel girders, swinging like a spider monkey from beam to beam. Then he noticed the crane. I gurgled something, but Don just said, "Coffee's ready. Get some."

"But—"

"Shh. This is good, Willy."

Oh, no, it wasn't. Fafhrd—I didn't know what else to call him—was investigating the boom of the crane, snapping the chains and locks that held it in place. There've been a lot of crane accidents lately, what with so much building always going on, so the safety precautions were on high.

Not high enough for a ten-foot, rock-solid troll. Who, incidentally, was now wearing a black sash around his privates, the same as I had drawn on my sketches. I wouldn't think about that.

"Don, you better come see this."

Fafhrd had managed to loosen the crane and was climbing out on it, letting it swing away from the building, so he was dangling over the street. I couldn't tell if the noise I heard was Don gasping, the crane straining, or Fafhrd laughing as he rode the boom like a kid on a playground whirler.

"That's going to break for sure," Don shouted, reaching for his phone. While he dialed 911—not that there was anything anyone could do in time to save the crane, the girders it was striking, the other buildings it might hit on the way down—I beat on the window. "No. No, get down!"

Don hit the floor.

"Not you. Him."

"You see the guy tampering with the equipment?"

"Don't you?" I pointed, and Fafhrd waved back to me, just as the crane's tower separated from the carriage platform and went crashing down toward the street. The troll jumped off, back to the roof.

Don shook his head. "Poor bastard couldn't live through that. Not that it doesn't serve him right."

The poor bastard was looking down, shaking his head, too.

Don and I got closer to the window to look down at the wreckage below. Pieces of steel, parts of other buildings, a ton of rubble had landed in the street. A couple of cars were buried. "I bet they're going to evacuate the whole neighborhood."

Then: "Holy shit! That's my car!" He went flying for the elevator. On his way out, he yelled, "I love the idea. Really original, new, fresh. Write it. We'll talk money next week."

I could see people coming out of buildings, alarms going off. I could not see a troll.

I sat on the floor and ate a jelly donut.

CHAPTER 6

THEY DIDN'T FIND A BODY, of course. When I went downstairs to the street, with my proposal back in its canvas tote, a policeman was interviewing Don, who thought he saw trouble. Or a troop of truants. Or maybe a train. A red train.

"Yeah," the tired cop told us. "We're getting that from a couple of other witnesses. Makes no sense. We know it was trouble, but a bunch of school kids? A train on a building? Let me tell you, this is not what I want to hear on a quiet Sunday downtown." He turned to me. "What did you see, miss?"

"Something red. Definitely wearing red." I wiped at my shirt, where the jelly had dripped. "I saw the crane swinging. Mr. Carr saw it, too."

Don was on his cell phone, calling his insurance company. Heaven knew what he was telling them. He was *not* saying that a troll had used a multimillion-dollar crane as a jungle gym. So I didn't say that, either.

Two other possible witnesses nearby were muttering about a bunch of teenagers, or some nuts trying to sabotage the building because the renovation was to increase office space for an oil company. They all decided no one man could have wreaked such havoc by himself. Maybe the activists brought a red wrecking ball up to the roof, or something that looked like a train.

The cop scratched his head. He looked at me again, hoping for a reasonable answer, I suppose. "Are you sure you didn't see anything else, Miss, ah, Tate?"

I pointed back to the window of the publisher's loft. "I'm sorry, but I was too far away. And too stunned by what I was seeing, that crane swinging loose, to notice anything else."

I went home, a death grip on that canvas bag.

Later, I walked over to Thirty-Ninth and Third to meet my cousin at the Hampton Jitney bus stop. I'd forced myself to shop for a healthy meal for Susan, vegetables to stir-fry, salad, and fruit for dessert tonight; organic cereal and exorbitantly priced berries for breakfast tomorrow. It turned out she couldn't have breakfast in the morning before those fancy scans, and all she wanted for supper was a pastrami sandwich from the kosher deli on Third Avenue. She'd been looking forward to it all week, so that's what we got, along with a couple of bags of chips and some cookies and more ice cream. And chocolate-covered raisins. Raisins made it healthy. She could eat the vegetables tomorrow.

Back in the apartment, Susan took a good look at me, screwed up her face, and said, "You've really done it this time, haven't you?"

"How did you—? That is, I haven't done anything wrong. And if you tell my mother, I'll never let you stay here again."

She took another bite of her sandwich. "You'd never be that mean. Oh, can I stay until Wednesday?"

"Sure, how come?"

"I see the doctor then, and hear the results of tomorrow's tests. I was going to go home and come back in with my mother and father, but Pop thinks he's coming down with a flu or something and I shouldn't be near him. It's most likely Lyme disease—everyone's got it this year—but I can't take the chance. Lowered immunity, you know."

"No problem." Of course it was. That meant I had to go with her and hear her future. Damn, we were talking life and death here. Tomorrow's tests were to see if the chemo had worked, if the cancer was gone. I didn't want to be there when they told her! I hated being at the hospital altogether, seeing all the suffering. I know they do wonderful things at Sloan, but it's still sad. And scary. There but for the grace of God, etc.

"I have a new project, but I can take time off for whatever you want to do."

"Shopping." She took the baseball hat off her head. "My hair's coming back and I want to talk to a stylist."

I doubted she meant the woman across the street who cut hair in her kitchen in return for my babysitting her daughter once in a while. But I could see what Susan meant. She had cute little brown curls on top of her head, but some straggly mousy strands on the sides.

"I might have to buzz it all again, but I really want my hair back."

She sounded so wistful, I would give her mine, if I could. "It's coming. We'll find an expert for advice. I promise."

"You know, you don't have to look so concerned. I'm going to be all right. Grandma read my tea leaves and said I'll be fine."

Her grandmother was my grandmother, and I didn't believe a thing the old witch said. I'd heard that a positive attitude was important to recovery, so I wouldn't say anything to Susan, but I'd sure as hell have more confidence in what my doctor said than in some back-yard herbalist. If Grandma was so good, how come she couldn't cure the cancer in the first place?

What I said was, "If Grandma said it, then it's true. Besides, you've got the best specialists in the field."

"Right." Susan left her sandwich to look over my DVD collection. "I'll be happy to stay here and watch movies while you work. I still get tired, from the chemo and stuff."

I had another handful of potato chips. Sweet potato chips, which had to have more nutrients, didn't they? I mumbled something about renting something she hadn't seen, around a quiver in my throat. Hell, she was still my baby cousin.

Instead of picking a movie, she asked, "So when are you going to tell me what's going on?"

Shit, she was still my pesky baby cousin. And far too knowing.

"I split up with Arlen."

She blew dust off the DVD player. "I already heard that. Besides, you wouldn't be half so twitchy over a dickhead like him."

So everyone knew he was a dickhead but me? I took a bite of the sour dill pickle, which was just how I felt. And made myself stop rocking my chair on its legs. "There've been a lot of strange incidents in the city."

"There are always strange happenings in the city. In the Harbor, too. You should hear about the rich guy who's renting Rosehill this summer. A movie producer. He says he's looking for a new kid star, untrained and natural. Every mother's trotting her son past the estate, or wherever the big shot goes in town for coffee or dinner with his current starlet. We have a texting hot line for when they're spotted."

I wasn't really listening. "What's going on here is scary, peculiar."

"Like the crazy trolley car no one can find?"

"Yeah, and today a crane fell off a building roof."

"That's not so unusual."

"It is when people think a train pushed it. Like a little red engine shouting, 'I think I can.'" I looked out the window to see the sky darkening with nightfall, then asked, "Have you ever seen a troll?"

"Yeah," she said, so I turned back, to see her flipping through my portfolio, the empty tote bag in her lap.

I grabbed it away. "Damn, you always were a snoop. Some things are off-limits, Susan."

"Sorry." She didn't look the least repentant, there with her cherub curls. "It looked like a fun story."

I didn't feel like confiding in the brat. She might be twenty-six years old, and with a sickly pallor to her complexion, but she was still a brat. And she stared too hard at me, as if she could read my mind. Maybe she could. In my family, anything was possible. Luckily the door buzzer beeped.

This time I wasn't expecting anyone, and hoped it wasn't Arlen, who could only make the situation more awkward. I pushed the intercom. "Who is it?"

"Van Gregory, Miss Tate. Officer Gregory. May I come talk to you?"

I'd wondered what his friends called him, Donovan being too long and, I don't know, pretentious, for what seemed a nice guy. "Sure. Come on up."

I made certain I checked in the peephole this time. Yup, it was the handsome cop, in an NYPD sweatshirt this time, with the same tight jeans. I hoped he didn't notice me staring, or notice that I'd forgotten to lock the door when we carried all the deli bags and Susan's suitcase up.

I made the introduction to my cousin, who looked embarrassed that she didn't have her scraggly hair covered.

"Don't worry about it," Van—that's how I was thinking of him—told her. "My grandmother just went through chemo. Her hair's coming back better than ever. You look great with short curls."

Susan smiled, and I gave Van a grateful look. A real hero, right in my doorway. "Come in, come in. We're having dessert, and there's plenty to go around."

"Thanks, I will. I'm on my way home, but I heard you were at the scene of another incident today."

Susan moved to the other side of the sofa to make room for him, but she glared at me. "You were there when the crane fell and you didn't tell me?"

"I was downtown at DCP. That's my publisher," I explained to the policeman. "Don Carr Publishing. I met my editor there to talk about a new project."

"That's an amazing coincidence, don't you think?" Van helped himself to a Mallomar. "I haven't had one of these in ages."

"Do you know you can't buy them in the summer?" I wanted to change the subject.

Susan wasn't going to let me. Her mouth was screwed up at one side, and not from the pickle. "That's too weird."

I sighed, knowing she was like gum on your shoe when it came to curiosity, or nosiness. "I thought so, too. That's why I didn't say anything."

"And you saw nothing that could help identify the perps?"

I dished out ice cream so I did not have to look anyone in the eye. "I did not see any train."

Van chose the rocky road, and crumbled an Oreo cookie on top, which showed the man had taste, besides looks. "We have no idea where that one came from, or the trolley. Do you know that one of the cars that got flattened downtown belonged to your friend Lou?"

I almost spilled the chocolate syrup. "Lou from the building across the street?"

Susan took the bottle from me and drowned her pralines and cream. "Isn't he the old coot who stares at you?"

I nodded, but demanded to know, "He was there?"

"His car was. We don't know where he is. That's one of the reasons I'm in the neighborhood. You didn't see him anywhere, did you?"

"No. God, he wasn't injured, was he?"

"No bodies were found at the scene, and they've sifted through all the rubble. And checked nearby hospitals. No injuries that we know about. But he's not at home either. You didn't travel downtown with him, by any chance?"

"I wouldn't get in a car with him. Do you think he's involved in the accidents?"

He reached for the chocolate syrup. How the hell did he stay so slim? I ate my ice cream plain. Of course, I ate out of the container.

Van licked about a million calories off his spoon. "It's beginning to look like the two incidents were no accidents."

"I told you he was up to no good."

"The computer boys are looking deeper into his background now. But someone would have seen him tampering with the crane. You didn't, did you?"

"No. I wish I could say yes, but no. I only saw a troll."

Susan laughed. "She's working on her new book," she explained to Van. "It's going to be great. A big red creature lands in New York City. You must have got that idea from the red trolley, huh?"

Maybe I did, somehow. Maybe the troll was my unknown inspiration, not my creation. Before I could explain, or try to, someone else knocked on the door. I checked, and made sure the cop saw me do it, then opened it to Mrs. Abbottini. She took one look around, at the black man, the ice cream, the potato chip bags and cookies, the cozy scene on the couch with Susan's pants unbuttoned, Van's shoes off. She crossed her arms over her gravity-lowered bosoms, and snorted. She actually snorted like one of the carriage horses in the park, the ones my mother is always fighting to get retired. Then the old lady who'd known my family most of my life, snarled and said, "Your mother would be ashamed of you, Willow Tate."

CHAPTER 7

IF MRS. ABBOTTINI'S EVIL EYE didn't kill me, embarrassment would. About a million years of collective shame shot through me like when the toaster oven had a short. The bias, the prejudice, and the discrimination this brave, kind man must suffer! Here he was trying to keep the streets safe, for a bigot like this nasty old lady. How could I ever apologize? Worse, how could I ever hope he'd come back?

Van put his ice cream bowl down on the table and wiped chocolate syrup off his lips. "I guess I better be going."

But Mrs. Abbottini wasn't finished embarrassing me. "And your grandmother would be having heart spasms. How could you feed your poor sick cousin that junk food? No matter what your mother says, it is a good thing you don't have children. You'd lose them in the parking lot, daydreaming the way you do."

By now I was ready to throw the half-empty jar of maraschino cherries at her, doing my best Lady Macbeth: "Out, out, damn liver-spotted snoop."

Once again, Susan saved me. Maybe she wasn't so bad after all. "But this is just what I wanted, Mrs. Abbottini, so don't blame Willy. She bought fruit and vegetables, too. But I lost enough weight that I can splurge, and why shouldn't I? I figure I deserve whatever I want."

I almost applauded.

"Besides," Susan went on, "Grandma Eve says I am going to be fine."

Now Mrs. Abbottini made a gesture that was half a cross and half a high five. I took it to mean from Grandma's mouth to God's ear or vice versa. "That's all right, then. I just came by to ask what I could make for dinner tomorrow. Rose"—that's my mother—"says you are staying over for a couple of days."

Of course no one had thought to tell me Susan was here until Wednesday, not until Susan herself arrived with a big suitcase.

"So do you want sausage and peppers or lasagna?"

That was healthy?

"I'll make enough for your young man, too," she said.

So maybe she wasn't so bad, after all.

We left early for the hospital. Susan couldn't eat breakfast so I didn't either. I figured I could get a croissant and a fruit cup from the kiosk in the lobby while Susan had her tests. Except they didn't call her for her nine o'clock appointment until after eleven. I was starving. The waiting room was mobbed, with people from lots of nationalities and languages and conditions. No one was real friendly, most were nervous. The acoustics were dreadful, with names being called and doctors being paged and people on their cell phones, despite the signs. There was no way I could concentrate on the new book.

Susan thought I had almost an hour to kill once they called her. She had to drink some crap, then sit by herself before they injected more radioactive stuff that could show contrast. According to my cousin, who ought to know, cancer cells appeared on the screens as a different color.

I got a buttered roll and an orange juice, and a bottle of water for later, then found a stone ledge outside the hospital where I could sit down to eat. Now I could breathe the exhaust from the street traffic and the smoke from the workers and patients—good grief, the cancer patients—who weren't permitted to light up inside. The weather wasn't as nice as yesterday, kind of overcast and dreary, but the atmosphere was better than the heavy miasma of the drab radiology waiting room with too many anxious bodies and sporadic air conditioning.

I looked at the blank pad I carried, but had no new inspirations to write down or enthusiasm for reworking the outline. The hospital depressed me, I guess. And I had to get back upstairs to be cheerful for Susan, so checking my watch broke whatever concentration I might have managed.

When the hour was almost up, I left time to find a ladies' room. The one near the nuclear medicine waiting room wasn't real clean, and I had second thoughts about all that radioactivity that had to go somewhere. I went up a floor and followed the signs. This bathroom was less crowded, with two women talking at the sinks, two of the five stalls occupied.

I put enough toilet paper on the seat to make my mother happy. I still couldn't wait to wash my hands. The problem was, a troll was bent over the sink before me.

Wrong, wrong, wrong.

First, this was the ladies' room.

Second, a woman nearest the door was nonchalantly drying her hands on paper towels as if pink soap wasn't spurting across the room.

Third, there were no such things as trolls.

I flattened myself back against the stall door. "You do not belong here!"

The woman gave me a dirty look. "What, you own the john?"

"Not you. Him." I pointed. She looked right at Fafhrd and shook her head, muttering something about a psychiatric ward and slobs. She went out.

"Go away!" I tried to whisper, so the women in the last two occupied stalls wouldn't hear.

Fafhrd obviously wanted to get the water to keep flowing, but the sinks had that industrial device that only kept the water on for enough time to wash maybe one hand. He kept pounding the spigot part, which only broke the metal piping.

Before he destroyed anything else, I edged toward the sink farthest from him and turned the faucet handles. Maybe he only wanted to wash the pink soap off his hands. And his chest, his neck, his hairless skull.

Fafhrd smiled at me and splashed the water at his smooth, stony abdomen. Then someone flushed a toilet.

Uh-oh. The sound got his attention. He stood up, bashing a hole in the ceiling, and cocked his head in the direction of the stalls.

"No!"

A middle-aged woman with a name badge came out, gathering her purse and her jacket. "Are you all right, miss?"

No!

The troll walked right past her and knocked the door off the stall. I could hear splashing, then thumping, then the water flushing again. He must have figured it out, except the toilet wouldn't refill fast enough.

I heard an explosion that turned out to be the porce-

lain toilet being wrenched off its foundation. Now the
water kept running.

The woman in the other stall cursed, then ran out, the
hems of her slacks wet. I'd throw them out, myself.

The first woman started to open the door to the hall,
shouting for a maintenance man, just as the partitions
between the stalls began to go down like dominoes. The
second woman pushed past the first one, yelling that
the building was collapsing. She held her hand over her
head, as if that could protect her from the walls and ceil-
ings caving in, which they did not, because Fafhrd hadn't
finished his washup.

Now staff workers and patients started to peer in
the open bathroom door, in time to see Fafhrd, big red
Fafhrd, pick up another toilet bowl and toss it across
the room into the sink. Water gushed everywhere, to
his grinning delight. He pulled out the soap dispensers,
making himself a bubble bath. The water ran off, though,
when he tried to lay down in it, no matter how his huge
hands tried to gather it back.

With every fixture in the ladies' room spouting tor-
rents, Fafhrd's bath puddle turned into a stream, then a
river, flowing out the door, to the corridor and down the
hall, where people were screaming.

I was too stunned to move, even when the rushing
water—from who knew where—covered my sneakers.

Porcelain kept smashing, the water level kept rising,
and the people were yelling about the torrent, not the
troll.

"Get out!" I shouted, kicking up a tidal wave myself.

"What, is someone trapped in there?" A janitor type
person rushed past me—with a mop. Now there was an
optimist.

"It's . . . it's . . . "

"Another bowl shattering. Must be shock waves from that new atomic disintegrator they're testing downstairs to fragment tumors."

To disintegrate tumors? This kind of force could disassemble an automobile. Heaven knew what it could do to a person.

Then I saw that Fafhrd was trying to float the toilets like rubber duckies. "Stop that!"

"Yeah, lady, I would if I could." The janitor dragged me out into the corridor.

Alarms were going off, and other men in the same uniform were on walkie-talkies, shouting at once so I doubt anyone could hear what they were saying over the sound of the water and the screams from the people running toward the exits.

"Shut the frigging water off at the main."

"Evacuate the building?"

"Assess damage to the floors below."

"Break a hole in the outer wall to let the water out onto the street instead of letting it seep through to the basement levels."

"And for Chrissake, don't let anyone use a toilet!"

I wouldn't say there was panic in the hospital. After all, these people were used to disaster, and this was only water. But the corridors were full. Someone had sense enough to shut down the elevators before the electric lines got wet, so people were bunched up at the stairs and emergency exits. They were all wet, all angry, all bitching about the budget cuts that left the building in disrepair. No one mentioned the monster that pushed through the wall to leave the rest room.

People ducked.

"Get down. It's another bursting bowl!"

Fafhrd blew me a soapy kiss and disappeared.

I had to wait, my feet getting waterlogged in my sneakers, because the stairwells were jammed.

Announcements came over the PA system that all nonessential personnel from the upper floors were to assist people below out of the building. Emergency exits were flooded but passable. All maintenance men report to the water main. Operations were canceled. Hand washing was canceled. Appointments were canceled.

What if they had to cancel treatments that might save someone's life? Or a respirator's plug got wet? Fuck!

No new admissions. No usable bathrooms. No lights in the wing below except for the emergency overheads.

Wheelchairs were directed to the other side of the building where the elevators and lights were still operating. I thought I got a glimpse of a familiar face helping a man with an IV pole, but the crowd was pushing me toward the stairs. I didn't think there was a danger of being trampled, but the climb down wasn't comfortable, not with water cascading at our feet, and too many bodies. At least if anyone slipped, they'd be cushioned by the crowds.

"Proceed slowly," a voice called out. "There is no emergency. Repeat: the building is not in danger of collapse. There has not been a terrorist attack or a bomb or a mishap in the laboratories. Repeat, this is merely a water pipe malfunction. There is no emergency." Unfortunately, the last message was "Repeat: all staff evacuate."

What, they were abandoning ship?

Most people on the stairs kept going down, to the street. I pushed my way into the nearly deserted nuclear waiting room where I was supposed to meet Susan. It had windows, so it wasn't as dark as the halls.

Susan was looking dazed, uncertain what she should

do, fumbling with her cell phone. Thank goodness she was done with her tests before they shut down the electricity to that side of the building.

"What happened?" she wanted to know.

"A transported bowl," a nurse shouted, rushing past. Susan had more questions, I knew, but I pulled her down more stairs and out of the building, into a gypsy cab just as fire engines turned the corner.

I avoided answering Susan by listening to the driver, who was on hand because his wife's mother's boyfriend worked in the cafeteria there and called to say there'd be a lot of business. The streets were already clogged; midtown would be impassable in ten minutes. We were lucky to be out of the mess.

My pants were wet up to the knees. My shoes were destroyed. I told Susan to make the salad, with chicken and cheese for protein, while I showered and changed and bundled my clothes into a plastic bag for the garbage. Then I found the card Van had left with me.

I left messages at the precinct, his private number, and his cell.

He got back to me in minutes. "Tell me you didn't have anything to do with the floods at Sloan this morning," came before hello.

I couldn't say that, so I kept quiet.

"Shit."

That, too, by now, with the sewage lines busted.

"But I might have seen Lou helping someone."

"He volunteers there once a week. Listen, we're going crazy here. Is the invitation still open for Mrs. Abbottini's lasagna tonight?"

"Of course."

"I'll bring dessert. And wine. I think we all need it."

He brought a friend, too.

Chapter 8

V AN WAS HOT, BUT HOLY HORMONES, Bat-girl, this guy sizzled. He was about forty, I'd guess, with dark hair just long enough to fall into his eyes, with a touch of silver at the sides. And what eyes! They were a clear, startling blue with a black rim. Nothing baby blue about these, not with a gaze that felt as if he was checking the lace on my scanties. He wasn't as tall as Van, nor as broad, but you could tell he was fit by the way he stood, confident and relaxed. He was wearing a gray mock turtleneck, a loose black jacket that had to be Armani, and black trousers. Oh, my.

"I think you'll want to talk to Grant," Van was saying. "He's Federal now, working with us on the Manhattan incidents."

"Federal?"

The stud spoke: "My department is actually attached to Scotland Yard, of course, but we are working with your CIA and the Office of Homeland Security."

James Bond on my doorstep? Was there anything sexier than an English accent? I looked to see if Susan was as impressed as I was, but she was busy taking the wine from Van to chill. This Grant guy must look too old to interest Susan. He looked better than Mrs. Abbottini's lasagna to me. In fact I could use a little cooling myself right now.

"I did not mean to intrude on your dinner, Miss Tate," he said. "I'll come back later, shall I?"

"No, that is, please stay. We have enough food for ten people, and if you can answer my questions, I'd be thrilled." Well, I was thrilled already, thinking what a great addition he'd be to my life. That is, to my story. Here was Fafhrd's partner, the Gray Mouser of Fritz Leiber's books, a lean, lithe swordsman extraordinaire, clever and charming. That worked for me. "Please, come in, Mr. Grant."

Van made formal introductions as we sat down. Mr. Grant was actually Agent Thaddeus Grant, but he preferred Grant, nothing else. As in my wish was granted? I wondered. I said I preferred Willy to Willow or Miss Tate, especially since we were already on a first name basis with Officer Gregory.

Grant asked that we not discuss the recent events until after the meal, with a significant nod to Susan and the policeman. That was fine with me, too.

I'd cleared the table of my computer and supplies, bills, lists, magazines, phone books, et cetera, stashing everything under my bed. I wanted to throw a real dinner party, with a tablecloth and candles and everything, in case Mrs. Abbottini peeked in to take notes for my mother. Thank goodness for the occasional Martha impulse, and the dread of another nagging phone call. Now I almost wished my neighbor would knock on the door, so she could report about the two handsome, intelligent, important men I was entertaining.

Well, Susan was doing most of the entertaining, telling the guests about Paumanok Harbor.

Neither of the men had ever been out that far on the Island, although Grant had visited East Hampton once on unspecified official business. My curiosity was running rampant, but I did have a modicum of manners, so I let my cousin talk.

The Harbor sounded a lot better than it was, the way Susan told it, all beautiful scenery, quiet off seasons, and friendly small-town neighbors, half of them related. She didn't mention the eccentric characters who knew every detail of everyone's life, the isolation in the winter, the never-ending wind, the traffic, or the prices raised for tourists' pocketbooks. Then there was the near impossibility of making a decent living there unless you served the wealthy summer people.

I was dying to ask about Grant's work, if he carried a gun, what the investigation had uncovered, and if he was married. Instead I had to listen to Susan recite the chamber of commerce brochure.

She explained that she'd been cooking at one of her uncles' restaurants after culinary school, but she had to take a leave of absence for treatments. It was unpaid leave, but Uncle Bernie kept up the medical insurance—under threat from the whole clan. That led to a conversation about medical care here and in Britain, and the comparative costs of everything.

We had wine and salad and crusty garlic bread to go with the lasagna, and an apple pie Susan baked this afternoon while I was cleaning the living room. The men said everything was delicious, and proved it by asking for seconds. I could have been eating half-defrosted frozen peas—yeah, I've done that in an emergency when I was out of ice cream—for all I tasted, waiting for my chance to find out what was going on.

While Susan and I cleared the table, Grant handed

Van a credit card and asked him to take Susan to buy flowers for the cooks, Mrs. Abbottini and Susan, and for the hostess, me. Thoughtful, tactful, generous—the guy was near perfect so far.

Susan reached for a scarf to tie around her head, but Van wouldn't let her. "Come on, Curly, you're a survivor. Be proud. And you look as good as that apple pie tasted."

Yes, Virginia, there really are decent men out there. Arlen would have looked away from Susan and kept his distance, as if she were contagious.

After they left, I made coffee and Agent Grant and I sat in the living area, me on the couch, Grant on the old leather chair that I'd covered with a quilt from a flea market.

I didn't know where to start, so I sipped my coffee and just watched him. He made for nice scenery, except he was watching me.

Finally he said, "Peculiar goings-on, hm?"

I laughed. "You can say that again!"

He did not laugh back. I realized he seldom smiled, unlike Van, who flashed his dimples often, and to good effect.

"And far too coincidental," Grant went on, eliminating any urge I had to chuckle, "that you've been at each of the troublesome events. One of the first rules they teach in detective school is there are no such things as coincidences. Look for the common threads, find a pattern, locate a common denominator."

"Me?" I squeaked.

"We're not sure."

I did not like the way the conversation was going. "Who is this 'we' anyway? You never said what agency you actually work for."

"It's called DUE. Department of Unexplained Events. There's a much longer, technical name for it, but that's the one we prefer. DUE is less troubling to the average citizen."

Good grief, he was talking UFOs, X-Files, Men in Black. "You think this is something extraterrestrial? That I am an alien?"

"Oh, no. We know where you were born, what doctor delivered you, where you have that charming birthmark. You are no alien."

The birthmark was on my ass, for heaven's sake! "I cannot believe this!"

"Do you believe in trolls, then?"

I choked on a swallow of coffee.

While I sputtered and dabbed at the droplets on my nice shirt, he said, "I know what you have been working on."

Ohmygod. "How? How could you know? Only my cousin and my boss know. Maybe Van, too, by now."

"I am sorry, but we've had to establish access to everything. Your computer, your apartment's video camera, your phone lines. I swear no one listened to or recorded anything not pertinent to our investigation."

Suddenly he was not the cherry on top. He was the worm in the apple. My conversations, my ideas, my life? "How dare you! I insist you stop right now. I'll get a lawyer, a court order. A . . . a new cell phone."

"We have a warrant, not that it's any consolation knowing that your privacy has been breached. We intruded as little as possible, and then only because of the grave threat to the security of the entire world as we know it."

"You think I am a danger to the entire world?" He

was crazier than I was. And I was alone with him. With my luck, he did have a gun. And who cared if he was married or not?

He crossed his right leg over his left knee, getting more comfortable, while I felt like I was suffocating. "More coffee?" I asked, thinking I could leave via the fire escape.

"No, thank you. But let's start over again, shall we, with the facts, as we know them. Maybe you will understand better, and forgive us. And me."

He described the street scene. "A trolley. On your block."

The falling crane. "A train, a troop of teenagers. Outside your publisher's window. And today, at the hospital, a bowl. A trolley, a train, a bowl. What's the thread? What do they have in common?"

"They were red?"

He nodded, as if congratulating a really slow first grader. "What else?"

"Me?"

"That too, but a trolley, a train, a bowl. As if people were trying not to say what they really saw."

I gave up. "A troll. No, wait. There's another common denominator. A man named Lou was at all those places, also. Why aren't you talking to him?"

"I did. He's one of us."

"One of you? You who?"

"Lou is DUE, too."

I just had to laugh at the absurdity of the whole thing. Trolls, silly acronyms, threats to the universe, 007 sitting on a threadbare quilt accusing me of being a WMD. What was next, He Who Shall Not Be Named?

This time Grant laughed, too. A nice deep laugh. "I

know, I know. It's pure nonsense. Utter drivel. Folderol. But you've seen the damage, and you understand this is no laughing matter."

"You are wrong. I do not understand any of it."

He came to sit beside me on the couch, and took my hand. He held it between both of his, and I forgot the anger, the distress, and the confusion. He looked me in the eyes, with that gorgeous blue gaze and said, "Let me help. Trust me."

The last man who'd said that stole my credit cards. I took my hand back.

Grant stayed beside me on the couch. "Very well, let me tell you a story, a fairy tale, if you will."

I reached over for the quilt to throw over my lap after I folded my legs under me, in the sofa corner farthest away from him. "Very well, I am ready for a bedtime story." I realized what I'd said, and added, "Not that I am going to bed, or suggesting anything."

One corner of his mouth lifted. "Of course not, although . . . "

"Although . . . ?" He'd be interested? He'd run in the other direction?

He did not answer those questions, either, but I thought I saw a certain gleam in his eye. He cleared his throat and began with: "Once upon a time." But I could tell what he was going to relate meant more to him. He believed it.

According to Agent Grant, the world, our world, Earth, was once populated by all kinds of magical creatures. Fairies, centaurs, mermaids, leprechauns, selkies, all the enchanted beings of folklore and myth.

"Vampires?"

"They are not real. Please do not interrupt."

I hid my smile. Vampires weren't real, but fairies were? "Go on."

According to him, all the various factions got along, more or less, with little in conflict and enough space between them. Then Man started to intrude. Perhaps to compensate for not having magic at their fingertips, or for not being as long-lived as the others, humans could reproduce much more quickly and prolifically. The humans also had ambition and dreams, unlike most of the other folk, who lived more in the moment. Since they couldn't conjure up a meal out of air, or change the weather to keep warm and dry, men needed to hunt, which upset the forest creatures, and farm, clearing land from the woodland dwellers, and build houses, permanent dwellings that interfered with the Earth's lines of power. And they claimed territories that had once been shared by all. Worse, they started to destroy the land with their inventions, their cities, their need for metals and fuels.

"Ah, a story with a green message. How politically correct. I bet pollution and fouled waters are next."

"Hush."

The very worst came when the men started to fight among themselves. No amount of wizardry could get them to stop, or listen to reason. Instead they started trying to kill everyone with magical powers that could be used against men. Finally it was decided by all the long-lived ones to separate themselves from the world of men. Not move, not disappear from existence or go extinct, just shift.

Grant picked up a pen lying on the end table and twisted the barrel so the two halves were not quite aligned, but they were still connected.

"Parallel universes, if you will. They called it the Day of Unity, because it required every single being, every bit of power to shift the worlds. While we cannot to this day cooperate to end famine, disease, war." He shook his head and went on.

One world held the humans, one held the eldritch, and they were never to mingle again except in ancient memory. Hence all the tales of pixies and sea serpents and sorcerers. If, by some chance, humans caught a glimpse of the magical realm, they would not recognize what they saw.

"They'd see trains and trolleys and flying bowls instead."

"Exactly."

I frowned. "That's mind control. Mass hypnosis."

"It's better than mass hysteria, isn't it? Think of witch burnings."

All right, his story might explain some of what happened. "But then how come the line got crossed?"

"Not everyone obeys the rules, do they? But there's more."

Before the split, he explained, as if giving a history lesson, not a theory of high fantasy, there was some inbreeding, experiments if you will, an effort to assimilate the poor weak humans into the magical world. The mixed breeds were not successful. Some could not reproduce; others were pitied by the glamour folk, feared by the clannish humans. Some of them got to stay in Unity as halflings, some stayed with the humans.

"Most of what we consider psychic powers comes from those mongrel ancestors. Some of those who trespass now and again are remnants of the mixes. They come from curiosity. Or worse."

My creation was a hero, not a plunderer of lesser universes. I knew it in my heart. "Fafhrd is not evil."

"Trolls seldom are. You do not want to mess with ogres. And fairies can be impossible to deal with, their minds flitting as fast as their wings. Trolls are not usually curious creatures. either."

"So how did Fafhrd get here, and why?"

"We think an EG called him up. An Evil Genius from this side, a descendant of the interbreeding, someone with enough talent and understanding, and ambition. There's great power in the Unity world, great wealth, too."

"You do not think I am the Evil Genius?"

"No, you are the Visualizer. Somewhere there is the Verbalizer. But there's a villain, too, taking your talents and combining them with his as an Enhancer. Maybe he is not acting intentionally, and maybe he is just experimenting. We have no way of knowing."

"Wait a minute. I do have talents. I win awards and get paid for them. I can draw and tell stories, a better one than this bullshit. Fafhrd is my creation."

"Ah, but your ancestors were some of those half-breeds. Many settled in England and Ireland. A large group eventually came to the colonies. They preferred living together, to avoid those witch hunts and the like. A branch of a famously psychic English family emigrated to Long Island."

I knew what he was going to say, so I said it for him. "To Paumanok Harbor."

"Exactly."

That would explain my crazy grandmother Bess who talked to spirits, and my mother's mother with her herbs and predictions, and my own mother's uncanny dog-whispering. Then there was Mrs. Terwilliger at the library who always knew what book I wanted before I asked. And Susan, who knew if I'd gotten into mischief. Mrs. Ralston could guess the sex of an unborn baby, and the harbormaster warned boats of coming storms long before they showed on radar. And it never, ever rained on the Fourth of July parade.

Yeah, Agent Grant's fable explained a lot. Or it would if I believed half the manure he was shoveling.

CHAPTER 9

I WASN'T BUYING IT. Grant told a pretty story, and God knew he had a pretty face to go with it. As my grandmother Eve—who was *not* a witch—always said, handsome is as handsome does, and this one had crossed the line when he or his ridiculous agency had put spyware on my computer. He expected me to swallow hogwash about an Evil Genius? That was straight out of one of my books, no, out of a lot of them. I often used that title as a placeholder until I constructed the perfect bad guy. This charlatan was using my notes, using me—but for what purpose? To get a plate of Mrs. Abbottini's lasagna?

I was glad when I heard Susan's key in the lock, but she just popped her head in to say they'd heard Mrs. Abbottini's TV from the hall, so she and Van were going to bring the flowers over. She handed me two other bouquets, one of roses, one of orchids, to put in water.

"The orchids are for you," Grant said. "The rarer beauty."

How could you throw out a guy who said things like that? And he was looking at me with such compassion and understanding, longing for me to believe his tall tale. I sat down again once I'd fussed with the flowers, but this time on the leather chair, away from him.

"No matter how odd my family and friends are, they are not witches and warlocks and creatures out of Tolkien. They are normal, everyday loonies, trying to raise families, make a living, and find a measure of satisfaction and happiness doing it. No one is out to destroy the world. They are just like everyone else."

"Except they are not." He brushed a dark curl off his forehead. "The world may think so, and they try to behave as if it were so. Some of them"—he nodded in my direction—"might not even realize how special they are. But you and your neighbors are far different from the average citizen."

"No, they are just small-town eccentrics making wild guesses, playing the odds, counting on coincidence. I do not believe in any psychic hocus-pocus. My own father's warnings and portents never made any sense."

"Tell me, have you ever heard of the Royce Institute in England?"

"Of course I have. Everyone in Paumanok Harbor has. The Royce people adopted the Harbor as a kind of sister city. The mayors visit back and forth, and there are always a few Brits teaching at the local schools. They offer free college to any graduate from the high school; free prep school if a junior high kid passes the tests. Room, board, travel expenses, tutoring, the works."

I ought to know. My parents met there. My grandmother pushed for me to go, but I insisted on art school. Besides, it sounded like one big matchmaking operation. Nearly everyone who went got engaged or married. Grandma Eve swore the tea leaves said I'd never find my soul mate except through the institute, never be a complete person. So far she was right, but that didn't mean she wasn't wrong in the long run. We fought over it a lot before and after college. I guess she is still disappointed in me, but we don't speak much.

I did not want to talk about some fancy foreign university, but Grant was determined. "Well, here is another story, more a history lesson, but this one is easily proved. You can check online."

As if everything on the Web was true. Hell, the Easter Bunny could have a MySpace page.

"The institute's full name," Grant began as if I were eager for a lecture, "is not generally made public. The university is open to everyone; the Royce-Harmon Institute for Psionic Research is known to a large but select group. It was founded by a family of British noblemen and their offspring, the males of the family all possessing a unique trait: they could tell if someone spoke the truth or lies."

Kind of like Susan, I thought, but did not say. She'd gone to England the summer after high school. I never asked what she did there.

He went on: "Some of the daughters developed the family gift also, so it was carried through the female line as well, not just the heirs to the earldom or their male cousins. One Earl Royce had an illegitimate son, the Harmon in Royce-Harmon, who married a Gypsy woman. She came from a family of fortune-tellers and horse-tamers, and possessed what was called 'the sight.' The Rom were definitely descendants of the Unity world. Close breeding among their narrow circles kept the magic in their clans. The same with the Royces, the Harmons, and the other connected families who married second or third cousins, or in-laws to relatives by marriage. They bred well and often, widening the gene pool."

Grant continued, and I was interested despite myself

to hear that, with vast wealth, the Royce tribe started a foundation to keep track of their heritage. They knew little of genetics, at first, of course, but they did everything they could to nurture the "gift." The institute was a way to foster the shards of magic wherever they found it, according to Grant, while keeping their members safe from harm. Which meant secret. They taught the students how to control their talents, and how to assimilate themselves in society.

"That's why they wished every child from your hometown, which their descendants had settled, to come to them for training, for shelter, and for testing, to keep the records straight and complete. A different form of your No Child Left Behind program. Yes, they do encourage selective breeding, to wed power to power and widen the gene pool. No one is ever forced or coerced, but psychics seem drawn to others like them. At Royce proximity takes over, matches are made; new talents are given birth to. You are the result of one such union."

"Which was wretched for both of my parents."

"Love matches the world over end in divorce. No one promised happily ever after, only similar understandings and possibly exceptional children, like you."

"I do not see where I am anything special. And I do not believe I was preordained to be a . . . whatever you called me. I think the students at the school are brainwashed, that's all."

"But the institute does much more than study genetics of the original families. Students from around the world come, anyone who appears able to foretell the future, read minds, control the weather, cure by touch. Swamis, shamans, witch doctors, fakirs, dowsers, you name it. Some of them would be hated in their own milieus, the way the half-breeds were despised and feared before the worlds split. People tend to distrust what they cannot understand."

Like I did not trust him, not at all. But I listened.

"Psychics, though, can accept one another and work together. Great things have come from the institute's laboratories. We haven't lost a ship to the Bermuda Triangle in decades. The Loch Ness monster has been shrunk to manageable size for photo ops. Two asteroids have been moved before they posed danger to the planet. The lines between our world and the other have been kept impenetrable. Except now the labs have sensed a disturbance, centering around you."

"All I did was write a story about a troll!"

"You visualized him. Perhaps from reversion memory. Perhaps he called to your subconscious mind. You never went to the village school and you never came to England to have your potential assessed. The deans are not certain what you can do. They have strict codes about not interfering unless the subject is a danger to him or herself, or the group, or the world."

Just what I needed, someone else telling me I was not living up to expectations. Once again, Grant was insinuating I was a loose cannon, a single-handed wrecking ball. Well, screw him. Not literally, of course.

I fetched the last of the wine. I needed it, even if it gave me a headache. And how long could Susan and Van sit with Mrs. Abbottini anyway? Didn't old ladies and cops and chemo patients need their rest?

Grant turned down a glass, making me feel scuzzy for wanting a drink. I took one sip and set it aside. "It's growing late," I hinted.

He ignored the hint. "Do you recall a few years back when a young woman from Paumanok Harbor got pregnant?"

"Which one? Paumanok girls get knocked up regularly." Which was another reason I didn't have high regard for the place where I'd spent every summer of my life.

"This one would have been younger than Susan. Her name was Tiffany. Tiffany Ryland."

"I remember the story. She claimed she'd been drugged and raped, but they never found the guy, so no one believed her. Typical backwoods small-town thinking."

"According to the record, she decided to have the child, but her parents refused to support her decision, or an infant. Relatives in Montauk took her in. Tiffany gave birth to a son, but the baby was not right. Nicholas did not thrive, he would not play, and he did not speak. Social services had him to speech therapists and specialists. They declared him autistic. But he understood when spoken to, and he developed a language of his own, one no one else could understand. Tiffany's mother tried to get him declared a ward of the state because Tiffany was so young, but Tiffany was a good mother."

"Better than hers was," I said, outraged on that poor girl's behalf.

Grant ignored the interruption, too. "Then someone's great-aunt from Ireland, over for a wedding, heard him babble. She thought she heard traces of Gaelic, which neither he nor Tiffany nor the Rylands had ever spoken. She talked to one of the transfer schoolteachers, who convinced the young mother to take the boy to England, to the Royce Institute. People there searched every old record and document, and sure enough, Nicholas spoke a smattering of Gaelic, but mixed with the ancient eldritch tongue. No one alive had ever heard it spoken, or understood its nuances, but the child was obviously a crossbreed. The children of Unity are born speaking their language, understood by all without the divisive dialects found on our side. The scientists recorded every syllable little Nicky spoke, in hopes of establishing a vocabulary, a primer, a way to communicate better with him and others like him. What if autistic children were not defective, but were atavisms, or products of some hidden DNA? But the boy was kidnapped before the research could produce any results."

"Most likely by some animal rights organization, for treating the boy like a lab rat."

Grant frowned at me. "Nicky was treated like a prince. His health improved, and he learned to laugh and play. He was stolen away from the car crash that killed his mother."

"Now that you say it, I did hear about that. 'Local handicapped boy disappears while abroad.' The accident made the nightly news."

"It was no accident. The car had been tampered with. Someone wanted that child."

"I think the authorities questioned my grandmother and my aunt about Tiffany's mother in case she had him."

"No, Alma Ryland did not want anything to do with the boy. She called him a freak, a disgrace. She'd not have stolen him, and I doubt she knew his value as a ransom prize. The woman did not grieve for poor dead Tiffany, letting the Royce Institute pay for burial in England. She did accept a big check from them, to renounce any familial rights to the child, should he be found."

"I think she moved to the trailer park in Springs. Mom saw her name once in the local paper. DUI." I

don't know why my mother thought I'd be interested in
the local gossip, but it was something for us to talk about
without arguing.

"We keep an eye on her," Grant said. "She quit AA
years ago."

I pushed the wineglass farther away.

"The boy is not there." He reached into his jacket
pocket and took out a picture of a little boy, perhaps
three or four years old. Then he showed me a drawing
of what Nicky Ryland might look like now that he was
eight. "We're been looking for him for five years."

Both pictures depicted a waif, a thin, pale child with
big, sad eyes, the kind you wanted to pick up and hug, or
ask if he was lost. "The Verbalizer."

"Precisely. You see the troll, but Nicky Ryland can
speak to him. Maybe he called your Fafhrd because he is
so unhappy in his captivity. Maybe he was forced to send
a message? We do not know. The only clue we have is
from one of the telepaths, a missing person locator who
has worked on the case for years. She thought Nicky
might be in Manhattan. That's when we started paying
more attention to you."

"I still say Lou is the bad guy. Maybe he has the boy
locked up in that basement apartment of his. I never see
anyone else come or go."

"Lou does not have any children, and he was placed
here to watch you."

"He stares."

"He foiled three attempts to kidnap you in the last
seven months."

"And no one told me?" I refilled my wineglass and to
hell with the guaranteed headaches. To hell with what
Mr. DUE thought.

"Your father tried to tell you how dangerous the

city was; your mother keeps urging you to England, or back to Paumanok Harbor where others can watch over you. Your grandmother adds a dash of protection to the herbal teas she sends you. Others who smell danger live nearby, but publicly unnamed for their own safety. As a final precaution, we asked Mrs. Abbottini to let us put a camera in her hallway. We tried to let you live your life."

"And now?"

"Now you'll have more observers, not that you'll notice them, waiting to see if the Enhancer approaches. We need to know who he is, what he wants. We need to rescue the boy."

"How?"

"We'll figure that out once we know where he is. We think you're the key. The boy, the troll, and you are all connected, so we find one, we'll find the others, and the bastard who stole Nicky."

"And save the world."

His mouth twitched, almost a smile. "And save the world. So I stick to you like glue."

My mind drew a really good picture of him plastered to me, naked of course, our bodies touching in all the right places, his strength to my softness. And he'd damn well be smiling.

He couldn't be psychic or he'd be blushing right now instead of explaining that Lou was watching when Grant wasn't. Everyone had pictures of the boy, to be on the lookout. No one knew about the troll. "No one," he repeated. "Other than in your story."

My mind was not following his directives, only his lips moving. "You stick to me like glue?"

"As much as possible. I fought hard for this job."

"You had to fight to be assigned this case?"

"Of course. I could wrap up the kidnapping, bring a

valuable wild talent back to the fold, destroy a major threat, and rescue a gorgeous maiden, all in one shot. That's what I call worth fighting for."

He thought me gorgeous. And worth rescuing. I was touched, until I thought to ask, "How many of you are there in your DUE agency?"

"Actual agents, as opposed to the thousands of Institute graduates who are always ready to lend their talents? Eleven in the city right now. Five are women, three are married, one is gay. That leaves me and Lou to watchdog you."

"You must have fought hard. Lou hates me."

He shook his head. "Lou admires you. You fought for what you believe, without giving in to family pressure. You've made the most of your talents without even knowing them. And you know martial arts. You foiled one would-be kidnapping yourself, by kickboxing the skeg in the, ah, privates. Unfortunately he got away before Lou could question him. But Lou buys all your books for the kids in the neighborhood. He thinks you hung the stars. I'll settle for the moon."

Wow. "Um, how do you intend to stay close?"

He put the pictures back in his pocket, not looking at me. "Well, I could move in."

"Not in this lifetime."

"Every day is a new life. Just ask your cousin. But you got rid of the dickhead just in time for me to play your new boyfriend. That way no one could question why I'm hanging around."

That idea would be bad for my heart. There was no getting past the fact that the guy turned me on. He had to feel that spark when he held my hand, or when our fingers brushed over the photograph. Pure animal magnetism, I told myself, which I did not intend to encourage like a mare in season. Unless, and here was a new danger, he was using mind control on me. I wouldn't put it past that whole Royce abracadabra academy to use some kind of hypnosis to bend me to their will. Sure, once we were lovers, I'd be more pliable to whatever shady purpose Grant intended.

No way was that going to happen, attraction or not. This guy was a wanderer, if not a con artist. He was not the steady, reliable, no fooling around kind of man I wanted. Why, if Grant didn't have a girl in every tele-port, I'd— No. He was crazy, that's all.

"Or I could move in with Mrs. Abbottini, claiming to be a long-lost nephew."

Definitely crazy.

"Just think about it all. Call me in the morning."

I couldn't find a pad or pen to write down his phone number. They were all hidden under my bed.

"Don't worry. Just think about me and, poof, I'll appear."

My jaw must have dropped because I could hear the joints crack.

"Just kidding." He produced a card and put it into my hand. "Until then, think about what I said. And please, try not to think about the troll. If you do work on your story, just don't put in any more creatures of fantasy. Remember, ogres are hell to deal with. And dragons— Well, there's no way we could stop the panic then."

So I dreamt of dragons all night, blue-eyed flame-throwers that made me burn.

CHAPTER 10

F OR ONCE SUSAN DIDN'T ASK any questions
the next morning. I'd gone to bed by the time she
and Van got back from Mrs. Abbottini's last night. She
called out something about a tie ballgame that lasted
twelve innings, but I pretended to be asleep, so she tip-
toed off to her own bedroom.

Maybe Van had told her not to make too much of the
British agent's visit. Grant had asked me not to mention
him for security reasons, the same reason he'd given for
why I shouldn't discuss the boy, the troll, or any part of
the fantastical yarn he'd spun. As if I would. Who'd believe such a pack of lies?

Maybe Susan was subdued because she was too concerned with the results of her tests to care about my involvement in an international investigation, or my part
in the Manhattan mayhem. Maybe she just knew I'd lie.
Either way, I was glad not to have to answer her probing
queries. Lord knew I was doing enough mental gymnas-
tics myself.

I wish I'd thought to make Grant jump through a
couple of hoops last night, when I might have gotten answers, but I was too bemused by the man and his, well,

manliness. What seemed possible, even logical at night appeared foolish, implausible, unbelievable by the light of day. That or whatever spell he'd cast on me had worn off.

I should have asked exactly what his connection was to the Royce Institute. For a government agent, a public servant—although I could not imagine him as anyone's lackey—he seemed to know a lot about the workings of a private, secretive, mind-warping organization.

I also wished I understood why I was so attracted to him, knowing he was bonkers and deluded, if not outright crooked. I wasn't happy to be so fickle, either. A few days ago I thought Van was hot. Now I did not mind that he and Susan seemed to be making a go of it. Watching twelve innings of baseball? Give me a little more credit than that. I knew Mrs. Abbottini fell asleep by ten o'clock every night.

Susan was a big girl now, so if the cop made her happy, that was fine. She deserved a good time. And if he hurt her, I'd break his kneecaps.

Before Van entered the picture, I was mostly satisfied with Arlen, who did not complicate my life in the least, just the way I wanted a relationship.

Talk about complications! Just thinking about Grant tied my stomach in knots and put my brains in a salad spinner. Now I did not trust my taste, or my hormones. Or him. The guy turned me on, okay? That did not mean he told the truth. But why would he weave such a convoluted, bizarre story, and why pick on me?

If, and I was only speculating, if half of what Grant said was true, then I was not losing my mind. If, again supposing this Unity thing occurred, neither of us was ready for Bellevue. I was not merely imagining a troll that no one else could see; Fafhrd really existed, al-

though in the wrong place; and Agent Thaddeus Grant
was going to save the world.

Sure.

Setting aside my skepticism, I had to ask how? I was
in novel-plotting mode while Susan hogged the only
bathroom in the apartment. I had to ask the what-if
questions to see where they led. What was the troll here
for? To rescue the boy who'd called him? To find a play-
mate? Fafhrd was young. I realized I'd never considered
the maturity of my troll, just assuming the species never
grew older. But they had to have been children once.

Thinking of how Fafhrd played with the crane and
splashed in the puddles made me lower his estimated
age. So if a troubled friend called out to him, kind of like
Facebook across the ether, in his own language, then
he'd break laws and cross boundaries, like any adolescent with a new driver's license or a forged ID.

He had to be brave to do what he'd done, if foolhardy.
He did not seem terribly clever, but, hell, he was a troll, a
young one, and all kids were reckless idiots.

On the other hand, what if he had been dragged into
this non-magical sphere willy-nilly by Nicky's words and
my drawings? Damn. That meant I was responsible for
getting him back to where he belonged.

He liked water. Why? Didn't his homeland have
streams and rivers? Or did Fafhrd feel dirty in the city,
with the grit of the streets on his stony skin? Or maybe
he thought Nicky was thirsty, or near water. The East
River wasn't that far away from my block.

Grant thought the boy had to be close to me for the
barriers between the worlds to disappear. Whoever stole
Nicky knew that, too, if the Department of Unexplained
Events theory was correct, and if I'd been targeted for

kidnapping in fact. The plotter knew where I lived, what I did for a living.

Thinking about the Evil Genius was too scary. Besides, I would have known if someone tried to stuff me in the trunk of a car or anything. And I would have noticed a strange kid talking in ancient elf or whatever Grant called the language. Besides, if the plan had been to get a troll to cross over, or get the barriers down, the goal was already accomplished, but centaurs weren't moving into Central Park.

So the whole theory fell apart like a house of cards. It was not true, none of it. The troll sightings were hallucinations, creativity gone wild. Like Arlen said, I had too much imagination. The whole mishmosh was a giant hoax. Literally.

That was it! I bet Arlen put Grant up to it, out of spite. There was no such agency, no threats to my safety or sanity. Hell, the English accent might be a fake, and Lou was just an old curmudgeon. Now that I thought of it, I'd never seen Officer Donovan Gregory in uniform, either.

While Susan was in the shower—still—I called Arlen to complain.

"Me? Hire an actor to play a cop? Listen, Willow, you're not that special." He hung up.

I should have known Arlen'd be too cheap to spend the money on such an elaborate scam. At least I wasn't his dear anymore.

No matter how much I did or didn't believe of Grant's witches' brew, the fact was that a little boy had disappeared after the supposed car accident. If he was still alive, Nicky Ryland deserved to be found and returned to his rightful family. If not that awful grandmother, then people who would love him and care for him and help him cope in the only world we had.

I took a drawing pad out from under the bed and drew Nicky into my story. I changed the police sketch some, gave him longer hair and higher cheekbones. I dressed him in a school uniform, but he didn't look right, so I put him in jeans and sweatshirt. No. Pajamas? A soccer uniform? A kilt? Damn, the bastard who stole him couldn't be hiding him as a girl, could he? I settled on loose clothing, as if whoever bought the clothes did not really know the boy or his size. I made Nicky skinny, short for his age, with big eyes that had fear in them. Poor baby.

Why can't you talk to anyone? I asked the final sketch. Why don't you go to the authorities?

Grant said Nicky understood English, but only spoke in what was now known to be one of the most complicated languages ever studied. The experts in England thought half of it was in mind-to-mind communication, so of course no one could translate. That was it. Nicky was speaking English, but only to people who could receive telepathy.

Sure. Still, I tried to concentrate, to listen for him, but all I heard was my shower running out of hot water.

When Susan was finally ready, I put my drawings and notes aside, hurried through my own preparations to meet the day—and any good-looking secret agents who might be acting as bodyguard.

I took Susan to a fancy Lexington Avenue spa for the works. Hair, face, feet, body wraps, massage. On me. It took most of the day, and most of my month's income after taxes and rent, but it was worth it. She looked fantastic with the trim and guaranteed safe highlights in her hair. The makeup, which cost more than I spent on mine in a year, put the color back in her complexion that the long winter of treatments had leeched away. She felt better, too, which we celebrated by buying tops for both of us in that new bamboo fabric. Soft and organic and sustainable—what more could a concerned consumer ask? I asked for a cream-colored one; Susan chose blue.

She wanted to cook a meal for Mrs. Abbottini, and Van, I suspected, so we shopped the produce stands for fresh ingredients and the gourmet delis for everything else. I did not see Lou following us, or anyone else who was supposed to be sticking like glue. Then again, no one accosted us either.

On the way home, we passed one of those tiny vest-pocket parks between two buildings. This one had a waterfall and a pond and some benches. I knew the benches were always filled at lunchtime when workers came to eat outside, but now they were empty.

"How beautiful," Susan said, putting down her shopping bags to admire the view.

I did not find the view all that appealing. A troll's ass is still an ass, only less hairy. Fafhrd was bending over in the pond, washing the breechclout wrap I'd given him on paper.

"Oh, look, they have trout."

"Oh, hell."

"What, did one of the bags break?"

No, Fafhrd had turned to wave to me. "Put that on!" I yelled, forgetting where I was.

"You're right," Susan said. "I need to keep my hat on and the sun off my face and hair. That's what the cosmetologist told me."

Fafhrd was climbing out of the pond, walking toward me. "No, you stay there. Be good."

I must have shrieked that last because Susan said,

"It's only a little terrier. Your mother would have it eating out of her hand in a second."

A trout, a terrier, what was the difference? She did not see the troll.

I dragged her away.

At home I called Grant. I hadn't intended to. Not ever. His presence added to my confusion and my angst over the whole mess. On the other hand, he had the only workable theory, the only understanding shoulder. "There was another, um, event this morning."

"It's not on the police blotters yet or the TV news. Our man didn't report anything."

"A man was watching me? I never saw him."

"We're good at what we do. But the field agent did not report seeing anything suspicious."

"He wouldn't, would he, if what you say is true that no one else can see Fafhrd?" Then I said, "I thought you were going to stay close." I tried to keep the disappointment and, I am sorry to admit, resentment out of my voice. I guess I failed, because it sounded like a whine even to me.

"I wish I could, but I spent the day faxing Nicky's pictures to every school in the city with Special Ed programs. Public, private, and parochial. Then I had to check out the first replies."

"He could be home-schooled, if his captors want to keep him out of the public eye."

"Yes, I thought of that, but home-schoolers have to register with the Board of Ed, so I was in touch with them, too. I have a list of supposedly functioning autistic boys of the approximate age. There are a lot of them. I'm waiting for an ESPer to look it over to see if any name sticks out."

Why didn't he cut open a chicken and read its entrails? "The troll didn't have him."

"I am afraid to ask, but what did he wreck today?"

"Nothing that I saw. I told him to be good, then hustled Susan away."

Grant sounded excited. "You can speak with him? Does he understand? How does he communicate back?"

"I never tried to talk to him before. Usually he waves and smiles."

"And what did he do when you told him to behave?"

"He mooned me. He turned around and wiggled his butt in the air. He understands, all right."

Susan yelled out from the kitchen wanting to know if I had a mandolin.

"Sure, right next to the harmonica." I told Grant I had to go face another crisis.

He said, "Don't worry, we'll figure it out better when we get to Paumanok Harbor."

"But I am not going to the Harbor."

"I think you are."

"Now you're claiming to be a psychic, too? You can tell my future?"

"No, but that's where the power lies, where the boy and you both came from. It's where you need to be."

"You cannot force me, and I don't care what esoteric agency you work for."

"If you go, the perp will follow, with Nicky, to keep the two of you in proximity. And the troll will be on your heels, where he can do less damage."

"He can wreck my mother's house!"

Grant ignored my complaint, rightfully, I suppose. What was one house to a city block, a skyscraper or two? To say nothing of how many more people could be in Fafhrd's way here if he decided to play kickball with Kias or something.

"The countryside will be better all around. With the layout of the South Fork, we can shut down the only highway out of the Hamptons if we need to set up a roadblock. And, remember, most of that power in Paumanok Harbor will be on our side."

"No. As soon as Susan leaves, I am getting to work on my book. That's how I make my living, you know, not by drawing twenty-dollar bills and cashing them in."

"We need to talk about this. Can I come over?"

"I don't think that is a good idea." I did not want to spend one more minute with a man whose voice on the phone had my pulse racing, or whose far-fetched story was beginning to sound a little more convincing. Besides, I was afraid that I wanted to see Grant more than I cared about sending Fafhrd home.

Mrs. Abbottini was thrilled to be invited to dinner with Susan and me. She brought homemade sangria, that lethal stuff posing as an innocent fruit drink. We all got tipsy. She declared that one of us ought to snabble up that charming policeman. We encouraged her to make a try for him.

She fell off her chair, so we both walked her back to her apartment.

Later, Susan was still uncharacteristically quiet. I worried that she was worried about tomorrow, and the talk with her oncologist. Her parents kept calling, and my mother, and various aunts and uncles. They all wished her luck, as if luck could change the results of the CAT scans. Maybe it could. Luck, prayers, wishes, whatever. Hell, if a bunch of fairy-tale folk could move an entire world, maybe the weirdos in Paumanok Harbor could cure cancer.

And Grandma had promised.

Right.

I'd have to talk to the old bat about her prognostications giving Susan false confidence without foundation. I wanted to speak to her about the Royce Institute, too. She'd attended the college, I knew, and believed wholeheartedly in the whole heredity shtick. That was all she used to talk about, besides her gardens: lineage, succession, carrying on the family traditions, as if we were royalty. She claimed that with great power comes great responsibility. Or was that Spiderman?

I fought my whole life against her and her pushing me where I did not want to go, chasing something I did not believe in. If I had, I might make more sense of Fafhrd and the Gray Mouser. Or I might be more filled with conundrums.

I did not want to know those pseudo-psychic secrets. I was not going to the Harbor, and that was final.

Chapter II

I WAS GOING.
   Here's how:
   We took a bus up Third Avenue then walked over to
Memorial Sloan-Kettering, then waited an hour past Susan's appointment to see the doctor. So far, I'd caught
no sight of Grant, Lou, or anyone who wasn't a patient
or with a patient. They all looked concerned, not wary
of predators.

   They did not see any trusses, trumpets, or troglodytes,
either, thank heaven.

   Thank heaven, and whatever deity you chose, the
doctor declared Susan free of cancer. Nothing showed
on the scans; the CA-125 blood tests had low numbers; and he found no new swellings or symptoms.
Susan had an eighty-five–percent chance of staying
healthy, the doctor said, with the odds getting better
every year she stayed cancer-free. New discoveries
were leading to more effective treatments, too. He
predicted a long, happy life for Susan. He sounded
like my grandmother; I wondered where he'd gone to
school.

   Susan seemed unaffected and unsurprised about the

whole thing, while I had to wipe my eyes and blow my nose.

While she waited on line to make an appointment—not for three glorious months!—and another to settle her current accounts, I went out to make phone calls. I had to leave a message for Aunt Jasmine, Susan's mother, and our mutual grandmother, but my mother picked up at the first ring.

"That's great, Willy, but we were expecting no less. I have some bad news elsewhere, though."

My mother's usual bad news was about some rescue dog that arrived sickly or mistreated, so I wasn't worried. Instead I heard about my father's heart attack.

"It was mild, so don't panic. I told him all those chippies would kill him eventually."

My father's retirement community lady friends were all in their sixties, at least. The chocolate chip cookies he loved must have done more damage.

"He's going to have heart surgery tomorrow."

"Should I go down to West Palm?"

"I'll go. You don't know anything about sick people. And what if he needs a bed pan or a sponge bath?"

"He has friends," I started.

"Hah. If they could be trusted to watch his diet and not let him overexert himself in that heat, he wouldn't have keeled over on the golf course."

"But, Mom, you'll only fight. That can't be good for him in his condition."

"Nonsense. He thrives on it. People stagnate without a little conflict now and again. Besides, I swore to stick with him through sickness and health."

"Those were the wedding vows. You got a divorce."

"One thing has nothing to do with the other. I do not go back on my word."

Logic wasn't a high priority in my family. "Okay. When do you leave?" I figured I'd call every other hour, to make sure sharp words were the only weapons they used.

"There's a problem."

Yeah, my father had a heart attack, I was seeing stone giants, and Prince Charming was a fork-tongued finagler.

No, this was a real problem, according to my mother. Another one of her cousins, Lily—I told you, nearly everyone in Paumanok Harbor is related—has a daughter in New Jersey, Connie, my third cousin, I think. Connie was having high-risk, premature labor, so she was in the hospital. Connie's husband could not get leave from the Army, so someone had to go take care of the couple's two-year-old daughter.

"Me?"

"Don't be foolish. You know less about toddlers than you do about middle-aged men. And whose fault is that, I ask?"

So I wasn't being asked to go to a scary situation in New Jersey, but I was still concerned about my father. Should I go to West Palm anyway? Mom might need someone to take turns with Dad, or run errands. Or keep them from killing each other.

But Cousin Lily was the housekeeper for Rosehill, the biggest estate in the Harbor. I remembered Susan saying something about a movie mogul renting it this winter. Lily worked for the estate, not whoever rented the place. She had an apartment of her own in the big house. "So? Mr. Mogul can mop his own floors for a week."

"But his dogs are there."

I should have known, talking to my mother, that a dog would appear sooner or later.

"Mr. Parker leaves them with Lily, instead of dragging them back and forth to the city or to California. They're nice dogs, standard poodles, obedience-trained. Both are black males. One is—"

"Mom."

"What? Oh, yes, well, I agreed to stay with the dogs when Connie had the baby. I would have brought them here, but I already have two rescue dogs at home, senior citizens. Besides, that little Pomeranian I told you about is still here."

Mom wasn't worried about the Pom; she feared for the poodles. The six-pound furball had three legs and a nasty temper. No wonder it was found abandoned.

"Send him back."

"They'll put him down."

Which was unthinkable in my mother's world. Nipper could be adoptable once my mother did her magic, which was a bad choice of words for today.

"So ask Grandma to keep him at her cottage."

"He dug in her garden."

Which was just as unthinkable, in Grandma Eve's realm. The ankle-biter was lucky to be alive. "Then let Aunt Jasmine fill in for Cousin Lily at Rosehill. Or ask Susan. She's feeling better and can use the money."

Neither of my suggestions was feasible. Susan's father was sick, but no one was telling her how seriously until she got home. They thought he had babesiasis from the tick bite, and they were on the way to Stony Brook, the nearest big hospital to the Hamptons. And no, Susan couldn't stay with the dogs, because her uncle Bernie needed her at the restaurant as soon as possible. His cook eloped with a Portuguese tuna fisherman, and the under cook sliced her finger off. Oh, and the poodles suffered from separation anxiety. They'd chew the furniture, chew on each other, chew holes in their feet if left alone too long. They were already on puppy Prozac, which my mother did not believe in.

And they said things were quiet in the country.

"So you're going to Florida, Aunt Jasmine's going to Stony Brook, Cousin Lily is going to New Jersey, Susan is going to cook, and you want me to watch some over-bred, neurotic animals?" Suddenly my life was sounding like an Abbott and Costello routine.

I reached for a different script. "I don't cook. Or clean."

"The owner's hardly there, and we're hiring a service for the rest."

"Then hire a dog-walker, too."

"They need more companionship. And I need you to look in on the shelter dogs and your grandmother, none of which are getting any younger."

"Grandma hasn't brewed an herbal potion to cure old age yet?"

"Do not be sarcastic, darling. It is not becoming." She sniffed and went on: "And Nipper needs care, too, to make him feel more secure. He'll be fine at home if you go over there a few times a day. He has pee-pee pads."

Ugh. "If the movie guy is so rich why can't he get his own temporary serf?" I never liked the class system at a summer resort and never would.

My mother sniffed again, and not from allergies. "Because he is a movie guy, Willy. And because he just might take an interest in one of your books if you happen to leave them lying around."

Hmm. "But what about my work?"

"It's not like you go to an office or answer to a boss. I'm sure you can think just as well here as in the city.

Better, without all those mishaps going on in Manhattan. And we do have a library."

One room, two computers, and an ancient librarian.

"The family needs you."

I sighed. What could I say, other than to ask how soon?

Grant found me outside the hospital's covered entryway. He was the fittest looking man in sight, including doctors, orderlies, and taxi drivers. Women headed toward hospice stared at him. So did I.

Today he was wearing khakis and a polo shirt, with a navy blazer. I'd figured out he did not remove his jacket over dinner that other night because he had a weapon under it. Which meant he thought the situation was scarier than bedpans and babies. Maybe I'd be safer out of the city, after all.

He took one look at my face and asked, "Bad news?"

I shook my head, but said, "Yeah. Paranoid poodles and a three-legged attack Pomeranian."

"Notes for your new book?"

"No, messages from my mother." I tried to explain some of the twisted strands of fate that had me swinging in the breeze. "Maybe there is a conspiracy theory, after all."

"You do live an interesting life, Miss Tate."

My life was getting more interesting by the moment when he broke into a smile, a real smile. Strangely enough, I felt better about everything, seeing the humor in the situation because he did. He wasn't laughing at me, either, but for me.

"I am going to Paumanok Harbor."

He leaned over and kissed my cheek, then he stepped

back and looked around. "I am terribly sorry," he said in his most formal Brit. "That was unprofessional. But I am delighted you see things my way."

I was seeing stars. Wow. If a friendly brush to my cheek could start fireworks, I wondered what a full lip lock would do. Then a horn honked, and I was back in the middle of the covered walkway.

"I'm sorry, but it's not your way; it's my mother's." This time I made better sense of explaining about my father, Cousin Connie, and the rich guy's pets. "Oh, and Susan got a good report."

"Wonderful. How about if I take both of you out to dinner tonight to celebrate? I need it. I've been in and out of special needs schools all day. I never knew there were that many handicapped kids out there."

I could hear the sorrow in his voice. Here was a problem he couldn't fix, and that bothered a take-charge guy like Grant, not because of pride but because of caring. His remarkable blue eyes were shadowed by concern.

I asked about the one boy we maybe could help. "Any trace of Nicky?"

"No, nor from the real psi-pros in the field. We called in everyone we could, with no results so far. We're checking on the home-school kids tomorrow. I won't be able to follow you to the Island for a couple of days. But we'll have people there, and I'll be in touch. It should take the perp a day or so to realize you've gone, before he follows. Hopefully, with the boy. Whatever his plan, he needs both of you. He cannot accomplish much beside local havoc with one troll. So . . . dinner?"

I accepted for both Susan and myself, but when she appeared she had a young man in tow. She'd met Toby Kellerer in radiation, then had the appointment after him five days a week for a month, long enough to become friends. He had good news, too, so they wanted to celebrate together, but quietly at the apartment over pizza, if it was okay with me, so she could keep checking on her father. She saw no reason to rush home when her parents weren't even at the Harbor, so she'd go east with me tomorrow.

I wasn't sure how wise it was for me to have dinner with Grant on my own. Did it count as a date? Or was it just more brainwashing business? More likely he just wanted to stick close to me in case Fafhrd came out to play. But Grant did kiss me.

I ought to say no, what with having to get myself ready to leave town for who knew how long. I'd need to ask Mrs. Abbottini to bring up my mail, and call Don at DCP so he didn't send any page proofs or copy-edits while I was gone. I ought to stay in with Susan, but she and Toby did not seem to need company, not with all they had in common. And Grant did kiss me. So again I asked how soon.

Seven. If I tried hard, I might have my hair and my clothes and my makeup passable in the five hours I had until then. Maybe I could lose those five extra pounds if I jogged the fifteen or so blocks home. Nah, Grant wouldn't notice, not when he was looking for Fafhrd.

Toby was on his cell phone, calling his family in Connecticut, when Susan asked if it was all right if he spent the night.

I checked the timer for my hot-oil hair conditioner, then looked at my old couch. "It's not real comfortable."

Susan gave me a look she must have learned from Grandma, the one that said, "I wonder how an idiot like you grew on our family tree."

Oh. "But what about Van? I know he is on duty tonight, but I thought you two . . . ?"

"Van likes you. And baseball. Yuck."

"But are you sure?" I mean, she never mentioned Toby before.

"I can't get pregnant, from the chemo. He can't father a kid. Testicular cancer. Both of us have had so many blood tests, we couldn't have any STDs, but we'll use protection anyway. So why the hell not?"

I thought of Grant. Why not, indeed?

CHAPTER 12

GRANT BROUGHT THREE BOOKS about trolls. I think they were about trolls, but I had a hard time taking my eyes off him. Tonight he wore a black cashmere turtleneck and gray trousers. His black hair and black-rimmed blue eyes were that much more distinctive against the dark colors, not that he needed anything to make him more distinctive. Looks, power, money, intelligence—what was a poor girl to do but drool?

He smiled in appreciation of my own looks, and took a deep breath that said something better than "You clean up nice." So now maybe I could stop holding in my stomach.

I'd finally decided on a red silk blouse and a short but not indecent black skirt with a slit up the back. I had good legs, I thought, especially in the Gian Todaro strappy high heels. I had to hope he didn't suggest we walk any farther than the corner or I'd trip and show off my red satin thong. But it would be worth it, for that azure-eyed gaze that started at my shining hair and ended at my red-polished toenails.

While he politely asked Susan about her father, and

engaged Toby in conversation about his job at Chase, I glanced at my gifts. The man has class, knowing how I love books, while not giving any secrets away to Susan and her friend.

The trolls pictured were hairy, stooped, mean-looking. That isn't how I saw trolls. Mine were clean-cut and athletic, looking more like marble sculptures than moss-covered rock dwellers. "Fafhrd isn't ugly," I said, without meaning to interrupt Toby's narrative about the banking industry and his future there. "Or mean. He's just young."

Toby was confused, but Susan laughed and told him: "My cousin really throws herself into her books. She's working on one with monsters now."

"Fafhrd isn't a monster, not in a bad sense, anyway." I was more resolved than ever to make him a hero. I knew from Toby's confusion that I was going to have a hard time rehabilitating the reputation of his species. Why, those computer malware makers were called trolls now, and so were the blog bullies who relish ruining people's lives and stealing their privacy, if not their identities. "I am going to change the opinion of trolls, I swear."

Susan laughed again. "Willy is such a good writer, her characters come alive."

Grant cleared his throat. I decided it was time to leave. I'd spoken to both my mother and my father in the Florida hospital, and everyone had my cell number. "You'll call if there's any news?"

"Of course. Go have a good time. And don't get into any more trouble," she warned, as if I could help myself.

A silver Beemer was waiting at the curb, and the driver got out to open the door. Lou whistled at me.

Lou? He had a suit?

"Good evening, Miss Tate. You look very fine, if his lordship hasn't mentioned it."

I turned to Grant. "Are you a real lord?"

He helped me into the front seat. "Lou is a joker."

Lou had a sense of humor? He grinned and started the car as soon as Grant was seated in the back. We drove uptown and to the west side, a neighborhood I did not know well, and pulled into an alley next to a sign that proclaimed "Skip's Fine Dining." Lou handed the keys over to a valet and we went in through a frosted glass door.

For all I was worried about dinner with Grant, I lost my appetite when I realized Lou was eating with us. Me and Lou, on the same side of the table. I never even walked on the same side of the street as him before. This wasn't quite the strangest thing to happen this week, but it was right up there with trolls and telepaths.

We waited at the bar for our table to be cleared. Lou ordered a beer on tap; Grant went for some micro-brewed English style ale. I had ginger ale.

After ensuring that no one was close enough to over-hear the conversation, they started discussing the logistics of keeping watch out in the Hamptons. That's why Grant invited me to dinner, I finally realized, so they could pick my brains about Paumanok Harbor. And I'd plucked my eyebrows for that?

I tried to explain that they ought to set up operations in Montauk if they wanted to remain unnoticed. Called The End because you couldn't go any farther east, Montauk had all the motels and crowds, while much smaller Paumanok Harbor had two inns, a bunch of bed and breakfasts, and a couple of cabin colonies like my family used to own. This early in the season, with school not yet out, the summer people hadn't even arrived. Right now the Harbor would be filled with year-rounders, returning snowbirds, second-home owners on weekends, and fishermen. Nice, ordinary, hard-working folk. The Harbor also had its share of drunks, dopers, and frontiersmen types. Either way, strangers were easily spotted, especially during the week.

"Good. I don't need to stay undercover. I'll be in plain sight," Grant said, "as a friend of the family if you still won't let me play your significant other."

I sipped my soda without comment.

"I know a couple of others there from university," he added, "so no one will question my presence."

Then they wanted to know more about Rosehill, but I hadn't been to the estate in years, so I couldn't tell them much about it, except that it was on a hill with a view of Gardiners Bay and Block Island Sound. And it was fenced in.

My mother's cottage, I told them, was a few blocks from the beach, down a dirt road. It was part of a summer resort my grandparents used to own, with a dozen family cabins and a big communal clubhouse. When Grandpa passed on, my grandmother decided she'd rather be an herbalist than an hotelier. She razed half the cottages, then joined the rest into houses for her two daughters and their families, and a combination potting shed, drying room, and garden center. She kept the clubhouse for her own home. We spent every summer there and long weekends when I was a kid, so I used to know a lot of the locals and some of the other summer people.

"No, I never met the man whose house I'll be watching." And with luck, I never would. As soon as he arrived to coddle his own pets, I'd be back in the city, even if I had to take the cranky Pomeranian with me.

Lou said he would check the security system Rosehill was bound to have. He was looking forward to playing tourist: fishing, golfing, swimming. My mind could not wrap itself around the image of Lou in a bathing suit, so I was relieved when he mentioned ogling the celebrities in East Hampton. He was a world-class ogler. He'd be arrested.

He finished his beer and got up to leave, shaking my hand. "A pleasure meeting you, miss."

So now Grant and I were alone. I couldn't decide if that was a good thing or not. I looked around, rather than at him.

"You don't see your, ah, friend, do you?"

"No.

"You look unsettled. Is your drink all right? Do you dislike the restaurant?"

"This is a lovely place. Everything is fine."

And soon it was. Grant opened up a little, talking about himself for once, about his family in England, his education. Yes, he had gone to Royce Institute, but only because his father was on the board of trustees. He hadn't studied anything more arcane than history and linguistics. Then he'd taken a master's degree in criminology, with another in forensics in the States. Again, he had not specialized in psychic investigation.

"But you believe in it?"

"I have seen too much not to believe."

I still didn't believe half of what I saw.

He was going to order the fish, but I told him it likely came from Montauk and Paumanok Harbor, so he ought to wait to get it fresh. I ordered the pasta, when the waitress stopped staring at Grant enough to remember to ask me.

I felt confident enough now to ask if he had a lady friend. A fiancée, a wife?

"No, I've been traveling too much for any steady relationship. I suppose I'd change my ways for the right woman. What about you?"

I tried to laugh off the fact that I'd never been close to getting married, or in love. "According to my mother, I'll wither into a cranky old maid with too many cats. My grandmother says there's only one true love for me and I am wasting my life not going to find him. She is a great believer in destiny."

"And you are not?"

"I think a person has to make his or her own choices."

"But what if the choice were preordained?"

"How would we know? So we have to act as if we have options, not wait around for some extrasensory GPS system to tell us what road to take."

"This must be hard for you."

"Having a delicious meal with an interesting companion?"

His lips quirked up in a half smile. "Living in Harry Potter's world."

"Spending an evening with Merlin."

Now one of his eyebrows rose. "You think I am a wizard?"

"Tell me, do you have anything to do with all the trouble in Paumanok Harbor? To get me there?"

"Now you are the one looking for conspiracy theories. Do you think I caused your father's heart attack? I thought you said it was chippies?"

"No, my mother said it was chippies, not me. But you said you did not believe in coincidences. My uncle is seriously ill from a tick bite, Cousin Lily has to leave town, my mother is going to play nursemaid to a man she says she hates, and Rosehill is empty except for two needy dogs, to say nothing of Uncle Bernie's restaurant. Don't you think it odd that all of that happens at once?"

"When you put it that way, it does seem peculiar. But I cannot see how anyone could manipulate the varied events. The baby was going to come sooner or later. Men your father's age do get ill. Cooks fall in love and elope."

"And the other one slicing her finger?"

"Weird, but that places Susan at the restaurant, not you."

"Susan needing to cook means she can't watch the dogs. My mother won't trust just anyone with a creature under her care."

His blue eyes clouded as he considered the possibilities. "As they also taught in cop school, shit happens. It would take a mighty big spider to weave such a web, to draw you in."

I shrugged. "Or a rampant persecution theory, to go with my other delusions."

"I don't think you are delusional. In fact, I am certain of it."

He was staring over my shoulder. I turned to look.

"Do you see him?" I asked Grant, while I tried to shake my head and silently mouth a big "No!"

"No, but I see a Pole holding a big red candle up to the ceiling to set off the—blast it! My new jacket."

And my silk shirt and splurged-on designer heels. That was two pairs of shoes destroyed, counting the sneakers from the toilet bowl incident, and I was getting tired of tossing my footwear in the garbage. "Stop," I shouted.

Luckily, people thought I was trying to halt the arsonist, who was running past me through the sprinkler showers. He snatched a vase of flowers from another table and tossed the cymbidiums at me, with another handful of water.

Two waiters and a cook were hot on his trail, but

he'd already disappeared. The maitre d' and the hostess rushed around with fire extinguishers, but there was no fire, just sirens to alert the fire department. A lot of the diners had already raced for the doors, but we crawled under our table, in case Fafhrd came back.

Grant was angry, but not over his jacket. "Damn, I was hoping I could see him once I knew what to look for. I couldn't, even knowing he was there. You are amazing, to be strong enough to overcome such a binding spell."

I wiped my face with the dry edge of the tablecloth over my head. I was hoping I never laid eyes on Fafhrd again.

"Did he say anything to you?" Grant wanted to know.

"No. He just brought me these." I held up the extra flowers I was still clutching, heaven knew why. They were more than a little crushed from fingers the size of my forearm. "But I think he looked a little sheepish, as if maybe he's growing a social conscience. No one got hurt this time, did they?"

"Only the restaurant and some of the patrons' clothes."

"Mine, too." What wasn't destroyed by the water was ruined by my squatting in the puddles.

"Too bad. You looked fetching tonight. You still do, with your hair going all curly that way."

Fetching? Who said that these days? The old-fashioned compliment almost made up for the soles on my heels coming apart and the hours I'd spent getting my hair straight. Almost. "Where do you think that devil goes when he flashes out of sight? Home? Or just elsewhere, a sphere between the two worlds?"

"I have no idea. That's a question for the theoretical philosophers at Royce."

Someone shut the sprinklers off while we waited, but

the restaurant was in shambles. Skip himself hurried around to anyone who hadn't fled, offering rain checks for a free dinner.

"Now I know why they call them rain checks," Grant said, helping me up and out from under the table.

My hair must look like Medusa's locks by now. Heaven knew what my makeup was doing, and my silk shirt was plastered to my chest—to the busboy's delight. Grant handed over his jacket. As wet as it was, I felt better being covered. I inhaled his cologne, and admired his physique in the cashmere sweater. Now that was fetching, as in fetch me the smelling salts, Maude.

He did not have a gun at his waist, which comforted me, too. Weapons scare me. I've heard too many stories of the wrong person getting shot. Although I wasn't sure about waiting for a taxi in this neighborhood.

Grant spoke to the owner, and Skip himself called for a town car to drive us home, for free. Neither of us was presentable enough for another restaurant.

We picked up pizza and took it up to my apartment. All was quiet behind Susan's door, so I did not call out to announce our return.

She stayed in my old room, on a single mattress with a trundle bed for sleepovers. I'd moved to my parents' bedroom when I took over the apartment. I rearranged all the furniture, got a new king-size mattress, and colorful quilts instead of my mother's white chenille, but it still took me a long time to feel comfortable having a man in the bed where my mother and father slept.

I am not a slut. I know, morals these days aren't the same as they were for my parents. I take that back. Mom and Dad lived through the Sixties. But I don't sleep around; don't bring strangers to my parents' bedroom. No one-night stands, no morning-after hangovers, won-

dering who was next to me. Been there, done that. Most
of all, I did not have complicated, self-destructive rela-
tionships, which explained Arlen.

So now I ate pizza with the most complicated man
I'd ever met and wondered what was going to happen.
There was no question that I was attracted to the point
of idiocy, but he was so . . .

"You still don't trust me, do you?"

"Are you sure you're not a mind reader?"

He reached over to catch a string of cheese on my
chin. "Sorry, I failed that course at Royce."

"They really have courses in mental telepathy?"

"The curriculum is very liberal arts, including the so-
called ether arts. Mostly the psionic courses offer general studies, like how to enhance existing talents, how
to recognize them in others, the honor codes to prevent
abuse. Royce is a huge community, you know, a whole
small city of its own, not just the schools. Seminars, dem-
onstrations, and surveys go on constantly for whoever is
interested. Then there are the occasional witches' tour-
neys."

"You're kidding, right?"

"No, they do hold games, but again for the sake of
studying, with independent, objective judges. You'd win
most power contests, hands down. No one that I know of
has actually been able to see a creature from Unity, except in dreams. Think of Royce as the psychic equivalent
of the Mormons' genealogy library. They keep track of
births, deaths, and marriages. And inexplicable events."

"DUE."

He turned serious, not that he was ever a lol kind
of man. "That's where we come in, yes. I know this is
hard for you, but I cannot emphasize your importance
enough. I don't know how to earn your trust, and I sup-

pose it's not very professional of me to even try to win your friendship, but I don't want to see you hurt. I like you."

"I like you, too."

That was easy. Saying good night wasn't. I felt as awkward as the shy, introverted geek I was in high school. Yawn as if I were tired so he'd leave? Take his hand and lead him to the bedroom so he'd stay? I wanted him, no waffling there, but did I want to mess with a wizard? No matter what he said or didn't say, I knew Agent Grant had to have some psychic skills himself. How else could he be assigned to that department? I suppose it was impolite to ask. I did anyway.

He avoided the question by pretending to think. "Do I have paranormal talent? Hmm. Well, I'm a very good lover."

"That's paranormal?"

"You'll have to see for yourself."

I couldn't tell if he was teasing or not. He had on the expression I was coming to think of as the lord of the manor, distant, unaffected, stiff upper— He shifted in the chair. Stiff something, anyway. So he was not quite as unaffected as he pretended. He felt the spark between us, too. From the look he was giving me, he was willing to start the fire.

I was still undecided.

CHAPTER 13

"ICE CREAM?" I was stalling, and we both knew it.

He did not push the issue. "Sure." He relaxed back on his chair. "Need help?"

I needed one of his Gypsy fortune-tellers to tell me what to do. Not that I would believe a soothsayer any more than I believed my grandmother's doom and gloom predictions. Everyone has his or her own agenda. Grandma's was to get me to become one of the Royce cultists, bred and wed for the group's goals. I still did not know Grant's.

I found out that he preferred butter pecan to chocolate, and he liked to dip a cookie—he called it a biscuit—in the melted ice cream. I was pretty certain James Bond never dunked his desserts. Uri Geller might. P. T. Barnum might have invented the habit to sell more cookies. That was Agent Grant, cool, smooth talking, and downright weird.

So I tried to understand his worldview better. "You said vampires aren't real. Trolls are, but vampires aren't? Fairies, ogres, elves, but no vampires?"

"Hmm," he said around a soggy cookie. "Physically

impossible with different blood types and Rh factors and all. And legend has it that fae blood is poisonous to other creatures. So how could vampires live when there were few humans? They'd wipe out their own meal tickets."

"What about werewolves?"

"Another impossibility. Aside from mass differentials, you cannot mix the DNAs for man and beast. Lions and tigers can mate; zebras and horses. But not dogs and cats. Not men and wolves, or women and leopards."

"But I thought magic could do anything, like when witches transform princes into toads."

"Yes, quite powerful beings, witches. But the toad is magic-wrought. It cannot reproduce. Neither can a werebeast. So no, one or two might exist if some being of great talent goes mad, but not as a race."

I let my own ice cream melt some, but I did not try to lap it off a cookie, although watching his tongue catch the drips was definitely appealing. I went back to asking my questions. "How can you be so certain about all this stuff? I mean, if it's supposed to be so secret, how come you know? And what if the whole rigmarole is nothing but supposition, and what the Royce people want you to think?"

Grant set down his bowl and shook his head. "I do not know why you have it in your head that Royce is an enemy, but it's just another institute devoted to preserving and promoting knowledge, this time knowledge ignored or repressed through the ages. They've studied so many ancient texts that yes, they are certain of their premises. As in having the precise dates when shape-shifting entered the lists of fey talents known to man. Vampires and werecreatures are relatively modern inventions. Most likely they evolved from another forbidden crack in the barrier centuries ago, interpreted by humans as best they could. The notions stuck. Our predecessors needed something tangible to fear, something they could put a name to, rather than a dangerous unknown entity they could not really see or understand."

That made sense, in the way "better the enemy you know" makes sense. That was the problem. What Grant said had way too much logic, but the logic itself was built of dreams on top of a mirage. I shook my head. "I have enough things to fear without inventing new ones."

"Are you afraid of me?"

The ice cream was done. Now it was time for honesty. "Some. I think you'd do anything to attain your goals." I think he could break my heart, but I did not say that. Too much honesty is not good for anyone's soul.

He replied, "But one of my goals is to keep you safe."

"Do you have protection?" I blurted. "That is, do you have a weapon?" My cheeks must have been scarlet, 'cause I could feel the heat rising. Had I really said that?

He reached for his wallet—I wished the floor would open up and swallow me. But no, he reached behind him to his waistband and pulled a small revolver out from under his sweater. I'm no expert, but it looked lethal. So did the long knife he unsheathed from an ankle strap, and the thing that looked like an ice pick up his sleeve. He showed me a tiny taser on a chain in his pocket and something that could have been pepper spray on his key ring.

"I can't tell you what my watch can do. It's top secret. So are a few other items in my possession."

I felt less safe, somehow. Now everything seemed more real, more immediate, more dangerous. Crazed people really were trying to kill me or kidnap me? People with similar arsenals?

Besides, there was the man himself. I mean, a house-breaker didn't stand a chance, but what if I pissed him off? I didn't know if Grant had a temper, if he turned surly with alcohol, hyper with sugar—I took the plate of cookies away—or just had a mean streak. I was tired of the not knowing, tired of the indecision, tired of wanting what I didn't want to want, if that made sense. It did to me, so I said, "Get naked. No weapons."

He laughed and said, "Lady, my body is a weapon." He started to lift the turtleneck over his head.

He must have a black belt in mind control, because I didn't care about the dangers anymore. I'd committed.

I should be committed. Susan could come out. Or Toby. I changed my mind again. "I mean, your clothes must be wet." I'd changed my damp outfit for a T-shirt and sweat pants. "I have a bunch of my father's old shirts. I keep them to paint in. They'll do until your sweater dries." I was surprised the cashmere didn't go up in smoke from the heat I felt rush through me at the sight of his bare chest. All flat planes and ridges, he was, with a narrow band of dark fuzz arrowing under his waistband. Oh, my.

"We could go back to my hotel where I have dry clothes."

All coherence gone, I pointed to my bedroom, meaning I'd get him a shirt.

"I knew you were a woman who knows what she wants. Luckily, it's just what I want, too. I don't think I could wait for a taxi." He threw his sweater on the floor.

I guess I hadn't told him I changed my mind. Before I could say it, he leaned over my chair and kissed me. This time, the kiss was no gentle brush of his lips. Oh, no. This was a whole body kiss, a seduction in suction, a tongue touch that promised fireworks, if not the whole Fourth of July. I didn't care anymore if he swept the pizza box off the table and made love to me there, in the front window. Or on the floor. Or on the couch that I'd told Susan was too narrow.

So what if I'd only known him for two days or so and half considered him a con artist? I'd never known a kiss to be such a turn on, that and his damp skin, his firm muscles, his cologne and his tongue. Did I already say his tongue? His hands stroked my back, my neck, the side of my ribs and my rear end. In two minutes I was going to fall over the edge and miss the main event. I pulled him into the bedroom. I didn't have a mind left to change.

Turn on the lights or leave the room in darkness? Find a candle? Find a nightgown?

His hand found the bottom of my T-shirt and raised it up and away. In seconds my bra was gone and his hands were cradling my breasts. I stopped worrying and pressed my body to his.

Was there anything more sensual than bare skin to bare skin, for the first time? Now I could feel his need, too, hard and thick, straining to get closer yet.

"Why don't you—?"

He held a finger to my lips, and whispered, "Shh."

I nipped at his finger, but he stepped away. I thought he was going to finish undressing. I mean, he still had his shoes on. I was in a hurry, but not for wet shoes in my sheets. Instead of kicking off his shoes or unfastening his belt—which my fingers were itching to do, to unwrap my birthday present—he found the light switch.

Okay, he needed to find the condoms.

Under my night table?

I was admiring his ass as he bent over, but the mental fog of arousal was being blown away by his weird ac-tions. Maybe I should rethink this whole thing, now that I could think again. "What are you doing?"

"Just disconnecting this." He held up a thin wire, with a thin bud on its end, which he untwisted from the cord. "No one needs to listen to us."

Now a red haze of fury replaced that former glow of sex. "A microphone? You had a microphone planted in my bedroom?"

"We had to be prepared in case someone broke in at night."

I could barely speak. "In my bedroom?"

"Where else would a kidnapper look for you at night?" He started to unbuckle his belt.

If he took that belt off, I swear I'd strangle him with it. "You listened to me and Arlen? And when I talked to myself?"

He took his hand off his zipper. "No, not me."

"Lou?"

"We have a central headquarters. And no one actually listened to it, just listened for distress or a call for help or a window breaking."

"You put a microphone in my apartment?" I couldn't get beyond that. I reached past him and yanked the whole thing out from beneath the night table. The clock radio fell on the floor.

He picked up the radio and checked to see if it was working, as if that was the issue here.

"You bugged my bedroom!"

"Actually, there are several of these devices. I explained before. We have a warrant, so it's all totally legal. The Patriot Act, you know."

"Which is a bucket of bs. You know I am no threat to national security! How dare you?"

He held up his hands. "I didn't do it. I didn't even give

the orders for it. I just got to New York five days ago, after spending a month at revival meetings, listening to the congregants who spoke in tongues."

"What, so you could invade the wackos' homes and seduce them?"

"Willy, come on, be reasonable. I'm good at languages and had some recordings of Nicky's speech. I was listening to hear if anyone spoke in similar patterns or sounds. It's part of my job. And this"—he indicated his bare chest and mine; damn, I was half naked—"was not part of any investigation. Sex is seldom on anybody's approved list of interrogation procedures. I am not a spy, just a man."

I found a bathrobe, an old ratty one that had no belt. "Screw you, you bastard."

"I swear my parents are married, and I thought you wanted to—"

"Say it, and I'll find that ice pick of yours."

He must have remembered the armory in the living room because he came back with his sweater in his hands but bulges in his pants from hardware, not a hard on. "I guess this means I am not invited to stay?" He looked longingly at the king-sized bed, with its colorful quilt and lots of pillows.

"I don't share my bed—or my body—with bastards. That's what you are. Not telling me my home was bugged. I know about the phone and the computer, and the surveillance cameras in the hall and the front door, but this—"

Words failed me again, so I just pointed to the door.

"I am sorry, you know."

"Tell that to the poor fools in Guantanamo. Or are you sending me there next? Or somewhere else, calling it protective custody? That's what my grandmother al-

ways wanted to do, have me sent away for testing. Hah."
I could tell he was getting mad, but I didn't care. "Brain-washing, arranged marriages, and fiends like you who . . . who use people."

"I swear I did not. I like you. I want to be with you. I work for DUE, but that does not mean I cannot feel attraction for a beautiful woman, or want to touch her skin and her hair, and learn her body's secrets."

"Then listen to the tapes, you pervert. Get out. And do not follow me to Paumanok Harbor or I'll have you arrested as a stalker. The chief of police is my father's friend. They played poker every Monday night for years."

"I can't be arrested. I am assigned to your federal government, remember?"

"Then I'll have you disbarred or defrocked, or what-ever. For . . . for abuse of power." I realized I was near hysteria, but it was either yell or cry, and I did not want this slug to see me weep over him. "No, I'll tell everyone you're crazy, and dangerous, and that you see monsters everywhere."

"But I don't see them, Willy. You do."

"No, I do not. I'll deny it. Besides, I am a writer. Ev-eryone expects us to be nuts. I refuse to do this. I won't listen to your bull anymore either. I am going to Pauma-nok Harbor to help my mother. To walk dogs. Nothing else. None of this crap will follow me, and you won't fol-low me, either."

His lips were pursed, but he nodded. "Someone will be watching out for you."

"Just like Big Brother."

"Damn it, I am not the bad guy here!" he shouted back.

Then Susan and Toby were peering in my bedroom

door. Toby was wrapped in one of my old single bed sheets I never saw the need to replace. Susan looked from one of us to the other, then blamed me, as usual. "What have you done, Willy?"

I pulled my robe tighter around me. "Nothing. And you are no one to talk with your friend there wearing ballet slippers on a sheet."

Susan's eyes started to water up. Shit. I was trying hard enough to keep my composure, but if she cried I'd lose it entirely. "Do *not* cry, Susan. And I apologize. This is your happy day, and it will be happier when Mr. Grant here leaves."

"But you need him!"

"I do not need anyone! I am a mature, independent woman. I live alone. I know karate."

Susan turned to Grant and said, "She'll feel differently in the morning."

Now I did not feel so bad about making the traitor cry. "I do not need anyone answering for me either." I threw Grant's jacket at him.

"Will you call if you need me?"

"Yeah, when hell freezes over. And I suppose you'll blame that on me, too."

CHAPTER 14

I SLAMMED THE DOOR BEHIND HIM. Then I marched into my bedroom and slammed that door, too. I did not want to talk to Susan. I did not want to see a skinny young man in ballerina sheets either.

I refused to cry.

So I called Van. He liked me, according to Susan. I liked him. I thought he was an up-front, honest kind of guy. I've been wrong, but he was my best chance for finding someone who understood the situation and who might take my side. I thought of calling Daisy, my lawyer friend, but I did not want to admit to anyone else that I'd been declared a national security risk. Besides, she was a divorce attorney. I doubt she could help me now.

Van returned my voice mail in ten minutes. I knew he was working, I said, and I did not want to disturb him, but I thought he ought to know that I was leaving town for a few days. That way, if anything happened to me, I'd decided, someone would know who to blame.

He asked about Susan, which made me feel better about calling him. He cared enough to remember she was going to Sloan this morning. So I invited him out to Paumanok Harbor. "If you have time off, a long weekend or anything. You said you'd never been. I can show you the Montauk Lighthouse and the docks and the fancy estates in East Hampton. I'll be staying at one of them, but there's plenty of room at my mother's." Then I explained about my father and the poodles and the pregnant cousin.

He didn't say anything for a minute, so I naturally assumed he was seeing someone else. "That's okay. I'll be busy with the dogs anyway. And helping my grand-mother."

"I'd love to visit," he finally said. "A bunch of cops are renting a place on the beach next week for them and their families. All they're talking about is fishing and golf and barbeques. I didn't want to go because I'd be the only single guy there. It would be great to be nearby, and with you, but I can't."

I waited again. His grandmother needed him, he didn't have vacation time, he didn't want to hang out with white folk?

"I'm not supposed to see you. Or talk to you. I'm off your case, and out of the loop."

"But I'm asking you as a friend. Not police business."

I could hear him mutter something a cop shouldn't say. "I've got orders. The Feds have taken over. They don't want anyone local involved. Very need-to-know only. I shouldn't even have answered your call."

"Especially since my phones are likely still tapped."

Now he didn't bother to mutter. "Shit."

"Yeah. That's what I thought, too. I'm going to go buy a new cell phone in the morning. One of those where you pay for the time up front."

"They still ask for a credit card."

"I'll pay cash." I made a note to get to an ATM first thing in the morning.

"I think they ask for your social security number."

"Even the sleazy, going-out-of-business electronics places around Broadway?"

Silence.

"Okay, you're not going to aid and abet, or whatever you call it. I understand. I really do. I wouldn't do anything to jeopardize your job."

"Thanks. Maybe we can get together when this is over?"

"I'd like that. You take care."

"You, too. You're in good hands, at least."

Yeah, my own.

I'd lost my peace of mind and my privacy. Now I couldn't even have a friend. I was too angry to sleep, not to mention the itch of sexual frustration I would *not* take into my own hands, so I packed my clothes and books and supplies and a box of Mallomars for the almost three-hour bus trip, and for facing my mother.

I never got to buy that new cell phone. My mother decided, without consulting me or my schedule, that we should be on the early Jitney bus so we'd get out to the Harbor by midday. She was leaving for Florida the next morning, when my father should be out of recovery, and wanted me to get acquainted with the dogs before she left. Which meant hours of instructions and dinner with Grandma Eve. I put my hidden stash of emergency chocolate in my bag. Besides, I remembered that half of Paumanok Harbor was in a dead zone for cell reception.

I had to call Don to tell him I'd be out of town.

"You'll keep working on the new story?"

I was not sure how wise that was, just in case my pen actually was mightier than some sworn magical oath. I saw no reason to ruin Don's day, too, so I assured him

I'd be working. "What else do I have to do while dog sitting?"

"Good. Send me chapters and a sketch so we can start on the cover. I thought a troll coming out of a waterfall. Very graphic, colorful."

Very likely, knowing Fafhrd. Only I'd draw him going back into the place behind the water, leaving, just in case I did have any influence over his motions. I couldn't recall any waterfalls around the Hamptons; the land was too flat. But I thought there was one at Splish-Splash, the big water park in Riverhead. The panic he could cause appearing at the top of a plume ride or a wave pool would get a lot of people, kids, especially, trampled or drowned. Nope, not a waterfall. Which meant, damn it, I was buying into the DUE theory after all. I tried to convince myself I was just taking precautions, playing the what-if card, without believing the woo-woo stuff. On the other hand, I would not dare go to Atlantis, the aquarium that was also in Riverhead. Fafhrd and all those huge glass tanks? Sharks getting loose? No thanks.

"How about him in a lonely salt marsh," I suggested, "with the moon rising behind?" I know tons of isolated places where no one goes except for clamming during the day. "I'll be right there at the shore to get it right. Big yellow moon, big reddish creature, nice reflections in the still water."

"Eh." That was New York for "I like my idea better, but I'll look at yours."

"I'll do a couple of sketches for you to see. I don't know if Mom's got a scanner, and mine's too big to schlepp, but I'm bringing my camera so I can email a picture for you to look at."

"Good, good. Oh, and I hope your father's okay, Willy. And the rest of your family."

"Thanks. You have a good time while I'm gone. Don't work too hard. You don't want to end up with a heart attack like my father."

"What, playing golf all day, playing with the ladies all night? That doesn't sound half bad to me."

"You'd die of boredom. And your wife would get mad."

"Maybe. Call me in a couple of days, all right, so I know how you're doing?"

"Sure. Thanks for caring."

"You bet I care. The Willy Tate name sells more books than half the hacks I have on staff."

Next I got Dad on the phone before his surgery. He sounded tired, or tranquilized. If I were going to have people messing with my heart, I'd need a lot of meds, too. He told me not to worry, he'd be fine. But I was to watch out for all kinds of danger. My father always saw threats everywhere, and I usually ignored his worries. But now I wasn't so sure. He'd been to Royce, too, where he'd met my mother. His family came from Paumanok Harbor originally, breeding grounds for espers, according to Grant, although Dad was born and raised in Manhattan. If I could animate a troll, maybe my father had some trace of psychic talent. Maybe he was clairvoyant.

And maybe he'd been warning me away from those phantom kidnappers. I should have paid more attention.

"What kind of danger, Dad?"

"Mmm, everywhere. Everybody." He yawned. "My head's kind of foggy. Just be careful, baby girl. I love you."

"I love you, too, Dad. Don't let Mom aggravate you."

"Maybe she's out of practice."

"Don't count on it. I'll come right down if you need me."

"I know you will, whippoorwill. I'll come visit as soon as I feel better. I miss you."

"I miss you, too, Dad." And now I felt guilty I hadn't visited since Thanksgiving. Damn, what if he didn't get better? What if—

I ate the emergency chocolate while Susan was saying good-bye to Toby, in my old bedroom.

Next was Mrs. Abbottini, though I needn't have bothered. My mother had already called her.

As soon as we left, my old neighbor was on her way to church to light a candle for my father, Susan's father, and Cousin Lily's pregnant daughter. She'd been lighting one every day for Susan, and it had worked, hadn't it?

Who was I to argue?

Of course, she said, she'd get my mail. And read it, too, I supposed. And water my plants. She overwatered two African violets to death when I went to Florida in the fall, but I had no idea how long I'd be gone this time, so I had no choice.

"Oh, and if anyone comes asking for me, could you say you don't know where I am, or when I'll be back?"

"Heaven knows I have no idea when you'll come home. Your mother couldn't say. But I know exactly where you'll be. Rose gave me the number for that fancy mansion."

"Yes, but I'd prefer not to have unexpected guests or too many phone calls. I'll be, ah, working whenever I'm not out with the dogs. Thinking about my next book, you know, so I don't lose my train of thought while I'm away."

Her dark eyes narrowed. "You're not getting up to any hanky-panky your mother won't like, are you? In someone else's house?"

I jumped on that. "Not at all. I don't want my friends dropping in there, once they find out I'm house-sitting at a place overlooking the beach. It's got a pool and a sauna and a tennis court. You know how people push themselves for an invitation to summer houses."

She ought to. She'd been coming out to my mother's place for a week every summer since my parents split up.

"What about that nice man you had to dinner?"

I wanted to ask which nice man, but I just said, "He knows where I'll be."

"Maybe he plays tennis?" she hinted.

"I don't." And I wouldn't play with him anyway. Tennis or hanky-panky.

CHAPTER 15

THE HAMPTON JITNEY IS TO a Manhattan crosstown bus what Maidstone Beach in East Hampton is to Coney Island in Queens: another world. The big city weekend wanderer's transport of choice has a bathroom, a hostess, free water or juice, *The New York Times*. They even take reservations. There are fancier ways of getting to the Hamptons: helicopter, private car, limo, or the pricier Luxury Liner bus that has reclining bucket seats. There are less comfortable rides, too, like the Long Island Rail Road, which leaves from chaotic Penn Station, involves a change of trains, and often has standing room only, broken air conditioning, and erratic schedules.

People with their own cars, of course, choose to drive, making the already inadequate Long Island Expressway the La Brea Tar Pits of the East coast, and that's without the horrifying length of the Queens Midtown Tunnel. Tunnels being only slightly less scary than bridges, and Manhattan being an island accessible via one or the other, I do not own a car. I could not afford to garage it, or afford the time to find alternate side of the street parking every day.

Best of all, the Jitney's last pickup is just a few blocks from my apartment. Susan and I got to Fortieth Street early, despite our reservations, and hoped the bus wasn't filled when it arrived from uptown so we could sit together. Not that it was going to matter; Susan hadn't taken her iPod out of her ears, so I guess she was still mad at me.

I was still mad, too. Mad enough to resent the six other people at the corner before us.

In the true summer season, especially late afternoons after work, the Jitney had to put on extra buses and divide up the routes, which caused scrambling around on the sidewalk, and a lot of grumbling. Today was early June, and a Tuesday, so we had no trouble getting on. Susan went ahead of me, while I handed my bags to the driver to stow under the bus. She picked two seats together near the back, which was not my favorite place because you could smell the bus exhaust from there.

Susan didn't seem to care. She pulled out her ticket and tucked it in the slot in front of our seats without a word. The Jitney gave free rides to needy medical passengers, showing there was still some heart left in the East End. Susan had claimed the window seat, without asking me, so she could lean her head against the glass, cushioned by her sweater. She shut her eyes, ignoring me, the people trying to stuff their carry-ons in the overhead racks, and the couple in the seat across the aisle who were eating something that reeked of sausage and peppers.

I guess she needed the rest after her night with Toby. I was exhausted, too, but I could never sleep on the bus, especially not until we were through the tunnel, which might cave in if I wasn't watching. After that, the first part of the Long Island Expressway was too stop-and-go for a nap, with construction here, a fender-bender there, too many cars and trucks everywhere.

I tried to sketch, but the ride wasn't smooth enough. The beach grass I penciled in the salt flats looked like lightning, which was too eerie for the story I wanted to write. I wondered if Fafhrd liked rain.

Once we cleared most of the city traffic, I leaned back and shut my eyes and tried to shut my mind down, too, with the steady engine noise and motion. I'd just about nodded off when the hostess came to collect tickets and money. So much for my rest.

Past Mineola, the highway was half empty and the bus seemed to be flying. I flipped the page on my sketch-book and drew my troll with his hands out, standing in a downpour, looking up and smiling. The scene wasn't dramatic enough for the cover, but not bad for a first pencil drawing. And not dangerous to anyone else.

Then we came to a sudden stop and my pad went flying. I looked ahead and saw nothing but red brake lights in front of us. Our driver was on the phone with his home base or other drivers, I supposed, getting in-formation on the snarl, and what exit to take to avoid it. Then he got on the intercom and announced that an accident had just occurred, right before the next exit, so we had nowhere to go until the road opened again. All eastbound lanes were shut down. We could see police cars with sirens and lights passing in the HOV lane or on the shoulder. Fire engines and ambulances, too, which looked bad for the accident victims.

We sat for what seemed like an hour, with the ex-haust fumes feeding through the bus, and the couple across the way eating the second halves of their sausage and peppers, which ought to be banned from buses.

I was beginning to feel nauseated. So I had a Mallomar and called my mother. A big sign in the front of the bus asked passengers to limit cell phone use to one call per trip, of short duration, to be considerate of others. Nice, but no one followed the rules. Everyone I could see was on the phone, loudly warning their friends and family that they'd be late, or conducting business that couldn't wait the extra time the trip would take.

I left a message for my mother, who'd said she'd pick us up. She must be out with the dogs, I figured, so I tried her cell. I left a message there, too, even though she never had figured out how to retrieve her missed calls. She did not text, either, but that was the best I could do. If she was smart, she'd call the Jitney office and ask if we'd be on time or late. Knowing my mother, she'd have tea with Grandma Eve, who'd tell her when it was time to go.

After another twenty minutes—I worried we'd run out of gas, idling so long, but was happy for the air-conditioning—we moved a couple of inches. One lane must have opened.

Police set up cones directing the three lanes to merge over to the HOV lane on the far left, keeping the high-way and the shoulder open for emergency vehicles. Some drivers had pulled off to the grass verge, so they had to push their way into line, too, which made for slower going. And everyone wanted to see the accident, ghouls that we were.

We traveled in lurches and bus-length leaps, which did nothing to settle my insides. I had another Mallo-mar. Susan slept on, somehow.

I couldn't see ahead, not from so far back in the bus, but when we got close, I craned my neck like everyone else. The driver was cursing over the forgotten intercom. The hostess shook her head.

I shoved Susan awake and indicated she should un-plug her earpieces. "What?"

"There's an accident in the right lane. What do you see?"

She put her face against the glass, blocking my view even more. "Oh, boy, it's a mess. There's a red fire truck on the grass, on its side. It must have been a water tanker, because the road is flooded. Other fire trucks are hosing it down in case the fuel tank was damaged, I guess. There's water everywhere."

"What did it hit? Can you tell?"

"A trooper, I think."

"An Isuzu?"

The man from across the aisle was leaning over my shoulder, breathing garlic in my face. "No, it looks like a State trooper. Or maybe that's just a first responder. It's hard to say with so much equipment around. What do you see?"

I saw a troll, hands out, under the streams of water, just like in my sketch, right down to the smile.

He couldn't see me. He'd certainly never hear me, and I doubted if he ever understood me. Grant said the language of the alternate world was half thought trans-ference, so I tried to let my mind speak. I squeezed my eyes shut and concentrated. *Go home*, I repeated over and over, half demand, half prayer. *Go home, Fafhrd.*

He never looked at our bus. I'm no telepath, no em-path. Maybe a sociopath, but hey, I was the Visualizer. I grabbed my pad and pencil again and wrote, "Go home" on it.

Could Fafhrd read? Did he know English? Damn, he was a troll, a species not known in folklore for its mental prowess. He did not know his own strength, much less the alphabet. The Visualizer had to do better. Sure.

How the hell do you depict "go home" in a sketch? I flipped back to the picture of Fafhrd in the rain, then started to erase it as fast as I could with the little eraser on the back of my pencil.

When I looked up, he clapped his hands and disappeared under the fountains of water. We crept past the accident scene. The man with garlic breath sat down; Susan popped her earphones back in and shut her eyes.

I stashed my sketch pad and pencil back in my tote, but my hands were shaking so hard I dropped a Mallomar. I bent down to get it and bumped my head on the seat in front when the bus picked up speed.

The driver spoke on the intercom again: "Sorry about the delay, folks, but I'm happy to report that no one was hurt. The ambulances and rescue equipment are all returning to their stations."

A few of the passengers applauded, whether for the good news or the fact we were finally on our way at highway speed, halfway to our destination. I felt too limp to cheer. And I had a lump on my forehead. I asked the hostess for something cold to put on it, which dripped, so now my shirt was damp and the air-conditioning chilled me.

No, the idea that Agent Grant was right chilled me. I was starting to believe the unbelievable. How else could I explain Fafhrd's appearance, just like my sketch, or his disappearance once I erased him? The snake was also right that Fafhrd would follow me to Paumanok Harbor, getting into trouble along the way. I vowed to do another sketch as soon as we got to the Harbor, showing Fafhrd leaning against a tree— No, he'd topple it over; if the blasted tree was one of Grandma Eve's, I'd never hear the end of it. I'd have him sitting on the beach—by himself—with a book in his hand. He'd be learning to read English, damn him, so we could communicate. Then I'd tell him to get the hell out of my life.

I suppose I should call Grant. What for, to tell him he was right? He was still wrong to bug my apartment, wrong to make me think he cared about me. He was wrong *for* me. Besides, if he was so smart, he'd already know Fafhrd was with me. Let him figure out the rest.

The Jitney stopped at Manorville, but no one got off. We switched from the Expressway to Sunrise Highway and made good time to the Omni on the Southampton bypass, the base for the Jitney. The hostess got off, the driver changed, and half the passengers left, some for a different bus to take them toward Sag Harbor. We got onto Montauk Highway, an absurd relic from the days of the Model T, if not horses and wagons. It was one lane in either direction, with a turning lane here and there, bumper-to-bumper with landscapers and pool trucks and pickups with surfboards hanging out the back. The road was perfect for the sleepy summer resort the South Fork used to be, not what it was today, a playground for the rich and famous and wanna-bes.

The bus stopped at Watermill, a pretty little village with the worst traffic jams on the East End. Bridge-hampton was next, another main street filled with an-tique shops and small stores and restaurants. It would have been quaint, except for the Kmart shopping center two blocks before it.

A couple of people got off at Wainscott, a between-village place that had its own post office, a gravel pit, and a commercial strip.

East Hampton was next, and you could feel the dif-ference. Towering elms arched over the road, elegant swans floated on the town pond, gardens appeared to be painted, rather than grown. Nothing was out of place except maybe a dented old Nissan with Jersey plates.

We passed Guild Hall, the library that used to make residents of the other villages pay—even when they had no libraries of their own, and we all belonged to East Hampton Town. But this was East Hampton Village, an incorporated community with its own government.

Past the restored farm and schoolhouse came Main Street, which was trying to be Worth Avenue or Rodeo Drive, with Tiffany's, Ralph Lauren, Cashmere this, Starbucks that, and real estate offices. You couldn't buy thread or a loaf of bread.

The only reason I could see to visit the place was the movie theater in the center of the street, but with no parking except blocks away, that was a pain in the neck, too. This was everything I disliked about the Hamptons, the conspicuous consumption of stuff no one needed, at prices no one could afford but the haves and the have-mores. Even on Tuesday, Main Street and Newtown Lane were filled with tourists carrying shopping bags and trophy dogs, buying Coach pocketbooks like they were donuts. This was the beach. Why the hell did anyone need three hundred dollar sandals? Of course East Hampton had its own beaches requiring its own parking stickers, lest the plebeians from Montauk or Springs trespass on their hallowed sand. Why, the bookstore in town didn't even have a romance paperback section, although everywhere else romances sold twice as many as all the other paperbacks combined. And they did not carry my books.

No, I did not admire snobby, elitist, East Hampton Village, except for its beauty.

Amagansett was a much friendlier little town, with

bakeries, pizza places, pubs, and a pet store mixed in with the galleries and ubiquitous real estate offices. We got off there, near the Farmer's Market, which sometimes even had local produce. We left the Jitney, because the bus went on to Montauk without making detours to Springs or Paumanok Harbor.

My mother was waiting on the sidewalk, pacing. "You're late."

As if it was my fault.

Maybe it was my fault.

Chapter 16

I STARTED TO SAY THAT I'D TRIED TO CALL. Actually, what I was going to say was if my mother ever bothered to check her messages or learned how to use the damned phone, she would have known the bus was late. But that was confrontational, and I was no rebellious teenager but a woman grown. And I'd just arrived.

Instead Susan said, "There was an accident. Willy thinks she caused the whole thing."

I never told my cousin that, not once. I refused to believe she could read my mind, because if she could, the little shit-stirrer would be running in the opposite direction.

"Willy always thinks she's the center of the world," my loving mother announced, helping Susan with her one bag and leaving me to manage my two suitcases, tote bag, and laptop. "What does she care if the dogs have to be fed?"

I never was the center of my mother's world. The dogs were. Any dogs. Anywhere. Right now two enormous poodles panted in the gated back of Mom's old white Outback. So all the bags and suitcases had to sit next to me in the backseat. Susan, of course, sat in the front.

The dogs that were soon to be my new best friends did not appear eager to meet me. They kept looking through the bars at my mother, whimpering. They were both black, but at least they had respectable haircuts, short curls instead of pom-poms like some ridiculous show dogs trying out for cheerleading squad.

"The one on the left is Ben," Mom said, making an illegal U-turn across Amagansett's main street. "The other one is Jerry."

I couldn't tell any difference between them, except Jerry was drooling more, over the seat back and on my shoulder.

Instead of watching the road, my mother kept looking in the rearview mirror. She saw me pull out a tissue and wipe at my shirt. "Jerry's not a great traveler. That's another reason Mr. Parker leaves them here most of the time. They're a little too high-strung for the city, but I've been working on that."

High-strung? Ben was trembling, Jerry wouldn't let me touch him through the bars of the dog gate, but he did drool over my hand. "I thought standard poodles were supposed to be calm, intelligent animals."

"These are inbred, of course. The AKC ought to have better control."

Coming from someone who was born and raised in Paumanok Harbor and related to half the population, that was almost laughable. Mom and I never did see humor in the same situation, though, so I held my tongue. I did that a lot around my family.

She sniffed in disapproval anyway. Must be for the Kennel Club, I decided, because Mom knew what animals were thinking, not people.

"Have you heard how my father is doing today?" Susan asked.

"He's still on intravenous antibiotics. They're working, because the fever is down and he's complaining about the food. Your mother is staying again tonight at a motel near the hospital. The drive back and forth is too long for her, with all the traffic, and they have appointments with specialists in the morning. Jas hopes to be bringing your father home by the end of the week. Grandma Eve says you can stay with her if you don't want to be alone in the house."

It was okay for me to be staying alone with these nervous dogs in a strange place, acres from the nearest neighbor, but Susan was invited to Grandma's instead of staying across the driveway in her own home. Not that I was resentful or anything. I was older, stronger, and more independent than Susan. And smarter.

Susan turned around and gave me a dirty look.

"What? I didn't say anything." But I did vow to stop whining to myself, like poor Jerry. Or was that Ben? "What about Dad?" I asked. "Have you heard anything? I didn't want to call the hospital from the bus."

Mom passed a loaded dump truck without looking in her rearview or side mirrors as far as I could tell, until she looked back at me. Maybe that's why the dogs were so anxious, driving around with her all day.

"I spoke to the doctor," she told me, still looking backward instead of at the road ahead. "Everything went well. No problems. The old coot needs to watch his diet and cholesterol. He'll be fine."

"Great. Then you won't be gone long." In fact, maybe she did not need to go at all.

"But he must need someone with him for awhile," Susan offered, helpful as always.

"A week, anyway, the doctor said. No lifting or bending. No stress. I'll do the driving."

No stress? Oh, boy. I hope whatever stitches they put in were tight ones.

"By the way, Willow, I spoke to him after you did this morning, before the operation."

"He was kind of groggy already."

"He wouldn't let them take him to the OR until he gave me a message for you. One of the nurses had to dial."

I leaned forward, so I could hear her over Ben's whining. Or was that Jerry? They kept changing places, pacing around their small enclosure. As soon as Mom was out of sight, I intended to put different colored ribbons on their collars. For now, I hoped they were only hungry and worried about getting home in one piece, not about to be sick. "What was the message?"

"That he remembered what he wanted to warn you about. He always was one for putting the fear of God into you. I swear that's why you—"

"What did he say?"

"Something about looking out for the undertow. As if you were stupid enough to go swimming in the ocean at this time of year. The lifeguards aren't even on duty yet and the water is still frigid. Do not take the dogs swimming, Willow. The salt is bad for their skin and makes them itchy."

"Weren't poodles meant to be water dogs?"

"Ben and Jerry don't like it. Or the pool. Chlorine is worse for them. You'll need to hose them down if they do get wet. No, use the shower at the pool cabana; it has hot and cold water."

Mother was going on about what else was bad for the dogs, but I was thinking about the undertow. I remembered the kid in *The World According to Garp*, how he interpreted the word as the Under Troll, the monster ready to suck him out to sea.

Did Dad know about Fafhrd? If my mother got the message straight, he hadn't said to beware of the under-tow, but to watch out for it. Which could be like watch out for that speeding car with the drunk driver, or watch out for your baby cousin. I didn't think Fafhrd was any danger to me, but how was I supposed to look after a stone giant? If, of course, my father was clairvoyant.

"Did Dad say anything else?"

Mom waved her hand, which wasn't a great idea on the narrower road leading to Paumanok Harbor. Luck-ily not many cars were going the opposite way. "Your fa-ther is always finding things to worry about." She sniffed to show her disdain. "He'd do better to worry about his heart and his health, the old fool, instead of rattling on about vague threats, just to unsettle a person. He told me not to eat anything on the plane. The cheapskates don't even serve food anymore. Oh, and he mumbled something about you not going out in a boat."

I almost never went out on boats. If the bus could make me sick, imagine what a boat could do. So much for my father's prophesies of doom.

We drove through the center of town, where the li-brary, the new arts and recreation center was, our own police station and firehouse, the post office and gen-eral store, a pharmacy, gas station, bank, and a couple of shops. The one real estate office was in someone's house; the beauty parlor was, too. Oh, and the general store sold thread, bread, and rubber flip-flops for less than five dollars. And bait. There were a few more stores and restaurants and bars—and bait shops—on the way to the docks, but we turned off before then.

Mom took the left onto our narrow street as if she owned it, right down the center at forty miles an hour. Well, I suppose Grandma did own it, since our family complex was up a private dirt drive, but customers used it, and occasionally a tourist made the wrong turn for the beach, one block north. The sandblasted sign at the corner listed Garland Farms, Eve Garland, Proprietor. That was my grandmother, with her herbs, preserves, and potions. Of course she did not call them potions, only special teas and cordials. Nor did she advertise tea leaf readings, but all the locals came for advice. She was the nearest thing Paumanok Harbor had to a shrink. Or a witch.

The next sign, this one from the sign maker in Montauk, advertised Rose Tate, Animal Behaviorist. She even had a degree in it. That was Mom, and people came from three states around with their maladjusted, misbehaving pets. If any of them—the owners, not the dogs—drove on Garland Drive the way Mom did, she'd double her fees, after lecturing the city-ites about children and dogs and stirring up dust on Grandma's crops. Then she'd lecture them about buying the wrong puppy, then ruining it. For some reason, they kept coming back. No, the reason they came back was their dogs were better behaved and happier after a few sessions with my mother.

The last sign was hand-painted and said J and R Richardson. Those were Susan's parents, Jasmine and Roger. Aunt Jas was a schoolteacher, and Uncle Roger managed the fields and the farm stand under Grandma's supervision.

I sighed. "I suppose I'll have to help at the farm until Uncle Roger gets better." I'd done it every summer of my younger life, weeding, picking, sorting, then weighing and bagging at the shop once I was old enough to make change. I hated it. Worms, ticks, prickers—and Grandma—then heat and sun and boredom waiting for customers. My nose peeled all summer, no matter what foul-smelling stuff she forced me to put on it. But Grandma was in her seventies now, and I couldn't refuse to help.

"No, she hired some high school kids to mind the stand once school is out, and a handyman to do most of the heavy fieldwork. He needed a place to stay, so she's trading the attic room and meals for chores until Roger recovers."

"She hired a stranger to live on the property? Grandma?"

"She read his leaves. And the dogs like him." Those were enough for my mother. If the dogs liked an ax murderer, he couldn't be all bad.

"You'll see for yourself," my mother said, taking the turn into Susan's driveway on two wheels. "We'll all have dinner at Eve's tonight."

Susan declined the command invitation, the lucky dog. She claimed she wanted to get started at the restaurant to help Uncle Bernie. That was the least she could do, she said, after he'd kept up her insurance payments all these months. And she'd straighten up her own house before her parents returned; fix some meals for them to have while she was at the Breakaway. Maybe she'd drive to Stony Brook tomorrow if they weren't coming home.

"Or that man of Eve's could drive you."

Sure, why not? Then Grandma'd most likely conscript me to pick strawberries, in between picking up dog poop. Grandma Eve adored Susan, always had, always would. She thought my cousin's cooking was a noble vocation, especially when Susan used the fresh ingredients from

Garland Farms. She thought what I did was like feeding pig swill to children, rotting their minds.

We dropped Susan off at her house, then kicked up gravel as we left, without stopping at Mom's or Grandma's. "You can visit the Pom before dinner. He's getting better."

Better than what? I wondered.

"And do not call him Nipper. He does not like it, and it gives him a complex. His name is Napoleon."

"And naming him after the little emperor doesn't give him a complex?"

"A small dog needs a big name to give him confidence. I think the shelter meant to name him for the dessert, anyway. Sweet, with layers."

Sweet was not a word I'd have used for a three-legged, six-pound, fluffy Cujo. "What about your other dogs?" Mom was always fostering a few shelter rescues until homes were found for them.

"Eve is taking in Dobbin and Shad. She'll feed them, and her new man Sean McBride agreed to put them out in our yard a couple of times a day, where they can't damage the plants. He is very helpful."

I wondered if he was trying to get on my mother's good side. After all, she was a good-looking divorcée, with a house and a business of her own. No one had said how old the new help was. Or why he needed a place to stay, or what he did besides odd jobs. Hey, if he'd take on Nip—Napoleon, I'd be maid of honor.

"No, Sean cannot keep the Pom. He is not ready."

Sean or Nappy? I wasn't ready, either. "Are you sure the dog can't go along with me to Rosehill?

"He digs. And marks. And gets jealous of other dogs. He does not like men, either."

"And he bites."

"Not hard."

The poodles started barking hysterically when we skidded around a corner and tore up a hill toward a long driveway. Halfway up, Rosehill loomed like a castle, or a fortress. The whole place was big enough for a day camp or a small convention center. Instead, one rich guy rented it, and hardly used it. The estate used to belong to the same multimillionaire who'd donated the money for the new arts center, to help the community and house his own collection after he died. Now a charitable trust owned Rosehill. The phenomenal rents it brought in financed its upkeep as well as the arts building's. From what my mother told me, Mr. Parker and his movie empire could afford it.

Mom told me the combination for the gate and how to open the garage. I could use Rosehill's Escalade. Mom was going to leave her Outback at MacArthur Airport in Islip, so no one had to drive her or pick her up. Meaning me.

We fed the dogs, then walked them on the property—with plastic bags in our hands lest they foul the perfect sod lawn or the specimen plantings. Gardeners came in three times a week, Mom told me, and the pool cleaner once a week.

The dogs were a lot calmer now that they were fed, and seemed easy enough to manage. So was Mom. That is, she was less hurried now that the boys had their chow and walkies.

Mom knelt down and stared at both of the poodles. Lord knew what she told them, or what they told her, but she seemed satisfied. "They'll listen to you. You could try to listen to them, you know."

It never worked for me. I heard them panting, that was all. Poor Mom, a dud for a daughter.

We made a tour of the house, which was mostly decorated in white emptiness, except for the screening room, the billiards room, and the orchid room, which was mostly glass. A specialist came every other week to tend to the plants.

The housekeeper's suite next to the kitchen pantry was bigger than my apartment. It even had a door out to a private deck and small fenced-in yard. According to my mother, the dogs were mostly kept here, with Cousin Lily, so they did not scratch the floors or dirty the white upholstery and rugs. Or shred the floor-length curtains, as they did once when they were left alone too long. They had crates in the pantry room, monogrammed beds in Aunt Lily's sitting room, and a basket of toys next to her bed. "Where the dogs do *not* sleep," Mom reminded all three of us.

I wondered why the hell Mr. Parker kept dogs if he left them with the housekeeper, away from his living space. No wonder the boys needed tranquilizers if they did not know who their pack leader was. I carried in my suitcases and laptop, then gave the dogs a treat before shutting them off from the rest of the house. I told them I'd be back right after dinner, but I couldn't tell if they believed me.

They liked the biscuits.

Back at Mom's, after a much less harrowing ride, I met the Pomeranian. He was definitely the cutest, nastiest little beast I'd ever seen. He attacked on three legs, faster than you could jump out of his range.

Of course he did not attack my mother. I swear he smiled at her, while I rubbed my ankle, looking for blood.

"He doesn't have enough teeth to do much damage,"

Mom said after she'd carried him back to his crate and told him to stay.

I thought he'd stay better with the crate door closed.

"No, he has to understand that I trust him. I know, I know. He's a hard case. But he's been battered. The x-rays show lots of broken bones, most of them mended by now. I cannot imagine the suffering, or the life he led before they threw him out of a car on Montauk Highway. He deserves a chance."

Okay, I'd try to get along with the little red-haired terror. I was a sucker for a hard luck story, which my mother well knew. And he was adorable, for a spawn of the devil dog, like a stuffed animal a little girl would keep on her pillow. Until he bit her nose.

I handed Ippy a treat while Mom changed her clothes. I decided on Ippy because Nappy had too many connotations, and I could not bring myself to call the furball after the megalomaniac who tried to conquer all of Europe.

He took the dried liver bit from my hand very gently, put it down, and growled at me to step back so he could eat it without fear of my stealing his treat.

See? I was already beginning to understand dogs. The rest of the family was still a mystery.

CHAPTER 17

BEFORE WE LEFT FOR GRANDMA'S, Mom handed me one of those tiny oriental embroidered pouches. "Right after the heart attack your father said I should give you this, for luck."

But he was the one facing life-threatening surgery or more heart attacks. He needed a rabbit's foot way more than I did.

"Take it. You know what crazy notions that man gets. If I didn't give it to you and you got a splinter or a bee bite, he'd blame it on me."

I unsnapped the pouch and poured a gold chain out onto my palm. At the end was a long narrow pendant, a thin gold strip with a deep incised knot design, maybe Celtic. A round diamond dangled from the bottom. Certainly not a rabbit's foot!

"But it's your wedding ring, isn't it, flattened out? I recognize the design. And the diamond must be from your engagement ring. How can you part with them?"

"Well, I parted with your father, didn't I? I loved the rings, though. I thought if I made both of them into a necklace I'd wear it, but it never felt right. I don't blame the jeweler, who did everything I asked her to."

"It's beautiful," I said, holding it toward the hall lamp so the diamond caught the light.

"But it felt wrong on me, as if I'd stolen something I wasn't entitled to. For once the old fool and I agreed on something, that you should have it. I was going to wait, but if it makes him feel better knowing you have it now ... "

She let her voice fade away, without saying what we were both thinking, that a man's last wishes carried extra weight. She cleared her throat lest I get the impression that she cared one way or the other about Dad's chances. I knew she did, or she wouldn't be rushing off to Florida. I felt the lump in my own throat, too, which I tried to hide by turning the pendant over to see the inscription.

"There's a lot of history in that piece, handed down from generation to generation in his family. There's writing on the back of what was the ring, but it's so worn with age no one can read what it says anymore. Sarah, my jeweler friend, took it to a science lab to hold it under their microscopes, but she couldn't decipher it, either."

I could barely make out some marks. I would have assumed they were from the artisan, or the carat weight. "I thought Dad had it inscribed."

"No, the writing was already there. He always said it was an ancient prayer, supposed to bring luck."

I didn't know how lucky a wedding ring was if the marriage didn't succeed, but an heirloom was an heirloom, and just holding it made me feel better about Dad's operation. I hugged my mother after she fastened it around my neck.

I liked how it felt against my skin, and how it made me feel, as if I were cradled in my father's love. I might be thirty-something, but he was still my dad, and he thought of me when he might be facing eternity.

Mom loved me, too. She touched the pendant, then kissed my cheek and said, "May it keep you safe and happy. Wear it in love and peace and luck, baby girl. And maybe someday you'll be blessed with a perfect daughter, just as I am."

"Perfect, Mom?"

She sniffed, this time maybe to hold back a tear. "She'll be my granddaughter, won't she?"

I'd pick strawberries until my back broke from bending over, just for this one moment. And I would eat hardly any of them, to keep Grandma happy. I was warm, loved, protected. Nothing could bother me now.

Until we went across the dirt road to dinner at the big house.

I'd expected a perfectly cooked and well-seasoned vegetarian meal, on Grandma's pottery dishes.

I'd expected to sit down with a destitute migrant worker, or a con man, one I might have to protect my silly relatives from.

I had not expected to see my grandmother all spiffed up. A beaded barrette held her long silver hair in a ponytail, instead of flying loose as usual. Her denim dress didn't have a single grass stain or compost smear, and her shoes were canvas slip-ons, not the high rubber galoshes she always wore to protect against ticks and chiggers and poison ivy. I thought I spotted a touch of blush on her sun-weathered cheeks, and a trace of liner over her blue eyes. I did not suppose for an instant that the old woman was doing the pretty for me.

So it wasn't Mom the new handyman was trying to impress, or vice versa, but Grandma Eve. Mom was still in her ragged dog-walking shorts, and all she'd done to get ready for dinner was wash her hands, while Grandma set out the porcelain plates and the stemmed goblets. So the old girl still had a spark. Good for her, I thought. But only if the hired man was good enough for her.

He was not.

He was not Sean McBride either.

His Irish accent was as fake as Grandma Eve's tofu meatballs.

His denim work shirt was brand new. His—

"It's right pleased I am to meet you, Miss Willow. Your granny's been singing your praises all day." He held his hand out. I did not take it.

No one called Eve Garland "granny."

She did not sing, and she did not like me.

His hand had a blister, from holding an unfamiliar rake.

"That's not your name," was the first thing that came out of my mouth, although I was thinking far worse. "And you are no farmer."

He turned to my grandmother and smiled. "And canny, just like you said the wee lass is. Looks out for her kin, too, just as she ought." He turned back to me. "Tcha, but that is my name, lass. Sean Louis Johnson McBride. You can call me Lou if a touch of the auld sod offends you." My mother and grandmother both gasped at my discourtesy to a guest. I did not care. The auld sod was fine. The old fraud could go to hell.

Lou the Lout stayed right where he was, smiling. I wanted to leave, to curse, to hide. The man still scared me, no matter what anyone said. I should have known he'd show up at Paumanok Harbor—he said he would—but at my family's table?

He was going on: "And born on a farm in the old country, I was. My da was an artist, the starving kind when he couldn't find a bit of work painting houses, so

we lived with my granfer. Sheep and chickens and potatoes, just like I saw growing in the fields on my way out
here. Who'd of thought of potatoes in the Hamptons?
Vineyards for sure, money trees, maybe, but potatoes?
Anyway, I helped tend my granny's kitchen garden,
a'course. It wasn't nearly the size of Miss Eve's, naturally, just a few rows fenced in against the goats, but I've
picked many a bean and pulled a lot of carrots. Dirt is
dirt, no matter which side of the pond it sits."

Dirt? He wanted dirt? I reached behind me for one
of Grandma's African violet plants. Before I could toss
it at his head, my mother said, "Why don't you go fetch
the salad, Willy?"

Grandma tried to cover the obvious awkwardness by
naming the fifteen kinds of lettuce she'd gathered this afternoon. "I am sorry the tomatoes aren't fresh or local,"
she said, but I knew she was apologizing for what she considered my outrageous conduct, if not my very existence.

I did not say anything else during the meal. The last
thing I wanted to do was get my mother worried before
she left for Florida, or get Grandma involved in *Troll
Gate*, which was what I was calling my new book so far.

We had strawberry shortcake for dessert. Lou acted
like it was ambrosia from the gods, only this time I didn't
think he was acting. Grandma's fresh-picked strawberries were the sweetest anywhere; she made the shortcake from scratch; the cream for whipping came from
the dairy near Sag Harbor. I had two helpings. Lou had
three. Grandma smiled.

My grandmother loved to feed people, and who
wouldn't be pleased to see her cooking so appreciated?
But I didn't trust the old bird. I'd always suspected her of
putting extra stuff in her cooking, stuff that could change
the mood of a gathering. She kept an old-fashioned still

room that was always locked, but I knew it was filled with weird ingredients, dried plants and bottled liquids that were most likely illegal in forty-nine states, if anyone ever heard of them. How else had she kept my parents from killing each other all those years?

Right now, Mom wasn't checking her watch every few minutes, or fretting about what time she should leave for the airport in the morning. And I wasn't so angry anymore that Lou had invaded my private circle, or ruined my earlier contentment. In fact, I appreciated what a good guest he was, telling stories of his family or listening to Grandma's plans for her summer crops, and carrying plates back to the kitchen. He even volunteered to drive Mom to the airport.

She refused the offer, but asked if he'd drive me back to Rosehill tonight, so she could finish her packing and explain to Napoleon that he was not being abandoned.

"I'll remind him he's in charge of guarding the house. It's a big responsibility, but I'll tell him I have confidence he can do it."

No one commented on my mother's plans for the dog conversation. My grandmother and I were too used to the insanity, and Lou must have heard worse at his job at the Department of Unexplained Events. He just nodded and said he'd bring the car around whenever I was ready to leave.

I told Mom to tell Ippy I'd be over in the morning to give him a run and change his papers. "Tell him I'll bring a treat if he promises not to do his kamikaze routine."

I didn't have a lot of hope of saving my ankles, but Mom said she'd remind him I was his family now. Then while Grandma packed up the last of the shortcake for me to take to Rosehill—she did have an ounce of affection for me, after all—Mom pulled me aside.

She gave one of her censorious sniffs and told me to behave myself with Sean.

"You mean Lou."

"I mean your grandmother's friend."

"He's her employee."

"She likes him. Don't scare him away. I don't want to think of her in that big old house by herself. I've tried to get her to hire a live-in, but she refuses to have anyone else touch her collections or work in her kitchen."

"She's not feeble," I protested, feeling guilty I hadn't done much to help recently, leaving it all to my mother.

"Of course she's not feeble. I swear she has more energy than I do. But she's not a youngster anymore, either. Neither is Sean, so they can help each other."

My mother was a devoted, maybe fanatic, match-maker, but Grandma with a thug like Lou? "I don't like him."

Mom wrinkled her nose this time. "You don't like any man. That's why—"

"Bye, Mom. Give my love to Dad. Safe trip. Call when you land. Remember not to eat anything on the plane."

She sniffed again.

"And you might consider seeing a specialist about that nasal drip while you're busy with all his doctors."

"Nasal drip? I don't have any such thing," she said. "You always were one for letting your imagination run wild."

Yeah, I guess I did.

Like wondering if Lou was going to kill me once I got in the car and we drove away from Garland Drive.

CHAPTER 18

LOU DID NOT ASK DIRECTIONS, which meant
he knew the way because he'd been to Rosehill before, which meant the place was bugged, wiretapped,
and surveilled by cameras from every angle.

Which was pretty much what I expected, though none
of it was going to make me feel any safer.

He was a decent driver, better than my mother.
Fafhrd would have been a better driver than my mother,
but Lou kept checking the grass verges on the roads for
deer—or an ambush.

I couldn't let myself forget he was a secret agent, a
man trained in weapons, prepared for violence. In the
dark, with no streetlights and little traffic on these deso-
late back roads, anything could happen. Including losing
a passenger.

"If you're going to murder me, I think you should do
it after my mother gets back, so the dogs and Grandma
won't be alone. And my father's heart will be stronger,
to handle the news."

The car almost swerved off the narrow road when he
spun around to stare at me. He looked angry enough,
almost demonic in the glow from the dashboard light,

to shoot me right now. "You really are crazy, aren't you?"

"Maybe, but I am being logical."

"Logical? Willy, I am trying to keep you safe. That's my job."

"No, you are trying to keep the world safe. *That* is your mission. Preserving my life is only incidental. And you know what an impossibility it is if you checked out Rosehill. Gardeners, pool service men, and house cleaners are in and out of there every day. Then there are these dark, deserted roads I'll be using to travel back and forth to check on the dogs and my grandmother."

He got the car in the right lane again, but slower, with the brights on. "So we'll send for more men. You have a panic button in the Escalade. I installed it myself. And a GPS, if anyone tries to highjack you. The entry gates are wired, and we changed the passcode so you have to check the camera to let anyone in. If we're going to all that trouble, why the hell do you think we'd, uh, get rid of you?"

"You must have heard by now that I am not cooperating. So you cannot use me to get to . . . whoever you think is behind all this. Agent Grant explained the threat to the whole fabric of reality as we know it, a threat supposedly only possible if the missing boy and I are near to each other. You cannot find the child. But if you get rid of me, you wouldn't have to worry about our meeting or communicating or me being kidnapped and forced to help your saboteur take over the world."

His fingers drummed on the steering wheel for a minute while he thought, then he nodded. "You have a point. A crazy one, but a point. Except Grant has a lead on the boy in the city, so we're close."

"Nicky Ryland is not in the city."

"How do you know?"

"Because Fafhrd wouldn't leave him behind. He's looking for Nicky, too."

"The troll? How do you know that? Does he talk to you?"

I answered the last question first: "No, I've never heard him speak, but he smiles and waves at me, so I know he's aware of my presence. How do I know he's searching for Nicky? Because that's what I wrote and it feels right, if that makes any more sense than the rest of this insanity. I am certain Fafhrd left the city, though."

"You saw him?"

"There was an accident on the LIE. That's why our bus was late. I hope to heaven Fafhrd didn't cause the crash, but he was playing in the water from the fire trucks."

"Damn. What does Grant say?"

"I have not told him."

"Double damn. That's what you mean by not cooperating? You had a lovers' quarrel with the field agent, and now you won't help us find the kid? When you know what's at stake?"

"We are not lovers; we did not quarrel; I am still not certain I believe in the ultimate danger. Besides, it is a matter of principle."

"Your granny is right: you think too much. What happened to using your intuition instead of your daft logic?"

I ignored the mention of my grandmother and the insult to my intelligence, or my sanity. "I am not one of your pet empaths, if they exist. Furthermore, I am not so sure the child will be any better off with your group. Ruthless, that's what you people seem to be. You want the boy to stop him from opening the gate or whatever it's called between worlds. Killing him might be your best chance. What's one life—maybe two if you count mine—against saving the universe from leprechauns?"

"I saw one once, you know. In Ireland, naturally, when I was a lad. No one else could see the wee sprite, but he was there all right. They shipped me off to Royce before I could ask where his pot of gold was. Seems there'd been some kind of disturbance in the atmosphere, sunspots maybe."

I couldn't tell if he was serious, or feeding me more blarney. "Would you kill the child?"

"Me? If the world depended on it? Hell, I hope I never have to face that choice. But I won't have to. If we find the boy, we can keep him safe, teach him how to close those gates. Or maybe communicate with the other side, so they can add more shields or guardians."

I shifted around to face Lou better. "You can't even talk to him."

"I can't, but maybe the people at Royce can. They've been working on all the tapes they made before the boy was stolen and I hear they're close. They have telepaths using some of the words he used as a toddler, with mental imagery. A lot is possible at Royce."

When we arrived at the gate to Rosehill, Lou punched in the code and drove up to the covered colonnade at the front door. I suppose I should be using the rear service entrance, but since I was doing a favor for Mr. Parker, I considered myself entitled to go in like a guest.

I made no move to get out of the car, or to invite Lou in. Our conversation was not finished.

He knew it. He turned the car off and stared at the house, which was well lighted by automatic timers. Instead of talking about the fate of the world—which still sounds like a bad movie to me—he said, "Nice to see how the other half lives, huh?"

I couldn't even remember how many rooms my mother thought the place had. "That's not the other half. It's the top ten percent, the filthy rich who hold ninety percent of the country's wealth."

"That doesn't sound like a good little capitalist to me."

"Oh, I'm all for making money. I just think this amount of it is obscene. The really well off should spread the good fortune around better, so no one goes hungry or lives in the street. Life is unfair, but this is ridiculous."

"From what I saw of this little town, your local nabobs do a fair job of opening their purses. Your granny told me the whole community center was built with a legacy and private money. And a camp for needy kids."

"The former owner of Rosehill bequeathed the land and a lot of the money. He was a famous art critic. Dante Rivera put up the rest. Dante made his fortune in technology, then added to it with real estate. He was the local bad boy, so I guess what he's done is even more admirable. I knew his wife Louisa when we were younger. She was another summer kid, and used to keep me company some afternoons at the farm stand. They are nice people, with social consciences everyone should emulate." I added, with emphasis, "And they are entirely normal. No second sight, no ghosts in the attic." I would have noticed, from my time with Louisa. Of course neither of us had realized how strange the locals were. With our city-kid arrogance, we figured they were just odd or inbred. Fixing the weather, finding lost keys, lie-detecting? Coincidences, we decided, lucky guesses. We were kids. Anything else was impossible. It still was. "Louisa is ordinary."

"Did I say otherwise? They're not on our list of gifted families. Mrs. Rivera wasn't even born here. Her husband never went to Royce, either."

"I should call Louisa while I'm here. See how she's doing. See how many kids she has by now."

He looked over, as if he wanted to say something more, but I unfastened my seat belt, not wanting to talk about babies and marriage.

He was looking up at the house. "Are you sure you are going to be all right here alone?"

"I still fear you more than I fear anyone else."

He shook his head, frustrated. "What can I say?"

"Nothing. Besides, the dogs will protect me."

"They're not your dogs."

I shrugged. "They'll defend their house."

"Maybe. Are you going to call Grant? I'll have to tell him you spotted the interloper, you know. And your theory that it's looking for the boy."

"Fafhrd is a he, not an it. And I haven't decided about calling your partner." I sure as hell didn't want to, after throwing him out yesterday.

"He'll be here by the weekend anyway. You'll have to talk to him then."

"I'll think about it."

"Do. And think with your gut, lass, not just your brains." He opened his door and got out. "I'll wait here until you go in."

"No, go back to Grandma's. You'll need your rest to keep up with her."

"Grand woman, your granny. You're lucky. I'm lucky to meet her."

That sounded serious. "How old are you, anyway?" In the city Lou seemed like an ancient derelict. The night he drove Grant and me to dinner, he was a much younger debonair sophisticate. Now in this casual reincarnation, I had no idea of his age. The man was a chameleon, as changeable as his disappearing Irish accent.

Then his words registered. "Luck had nothing to do with you staying at Grandma's, did it? You came with references from the Institute, I bet."

"A few phone calls was all it took. Eve is a firm supporter of the work we do."

"So she knows about me?"

"She's always known about you. That's why she pushed so hard to get you on the right track."

Right now the path I was on was a railroad track. I felt like the train ran over me while I was waiting at the station.

Lou continued: "But she does not know about the breach in the barriers. No one does. We don't need a bunch of espers trying their hand—or talents—at communications or evocations. Or exorcisms."

"Is Grandma a witch?" I always wondered, since I was old enough to see her mix her brews.

Lou smiled, there in the bright outdoor lights. "I don't know as she dances skyclad at the full moon, but I wouldn't mind peeking to see."

I almost gave one of my mother's sniffs, but it came out as a snort. Grandma Eve, prancing in the altogether?

Lou turned serious. "From what I know, she's a wise woman with a huge warehouse of knowledge, some of it unknown to modern science. We send students to study with her whenever we can."

"The foreign college kids who help at the farm in the summer. I always wondered why they worked so cheap."

"For room and board and a place at the beach, plus a mentor like Eve Garland? They'd do it for free. Two more are coming in July. We tried to get them here sooner, but there's a holdup on student visas. We didn't want to draw attention to the crisis, so made no push to nudge the State Department."

"But you could have?"

"As part of Homeland Security we could bring in an army of overseas psychics, or send out a call for every paranormal in America. The boss doesn't see the need yet. Too much chance for publicity and exposure of the organization. I'm hoping we can handle it without calling up the reserves."

Me, too. And soon. Then I mentioned how Mr. Parker had been looking for a young boy the last time he was out here, supposedly for a new movie. "How does that coincidence feel to your intuition?"

"Only a shade suspicious. I'll have our people look into it tomorrow."

"What about the VanWetherings, who are expecting their grandson to arrive from France any day? Mother asked Susan if she knew anyone looking for a summer nanny job."

"I'll add them to the list, too."

After that, I told Lou he could leave, that I could get into the house by myself. My mother had told me how to disengage the alarm system, then reset it when I was in for the night. Lou said he'd wait outside until I flashed a light.

I went in, looked and listened, then hit the light switch. The poodles never barked. So much for my watchdogs. I guess they were trained not to cause a commotion in a city apartment, or wherever else they lived. They were happy enough to see me, doing a prance and a pirouette. Or maybe they just needed to go out.

There was no way in hell I was going to walk them around the perimeter of the property in the dark, and the little fenced-in area around the back door looked too small for such big dogs. Besides, I had a better idea.

I took the dogs through the house and out to the

pool. That area had a fence of its own too, most likely for safety regulations. This fence was more decorative than the high perimeter chain link or the plastic mesh around the rear dog run. As I recalled, the pool had a surrounding garden, lounge groupings, and floodlights. I was thrilled to see the floodlights and how much ground they covered. I'd clean up after the boys in the morning.

Ben and Jerry seemed ecstatic, running, playing, wrestling with each other, and barking at the shadows. I guess they weren't allowed in this area, but I didn't care.

Despite the clouds that hid the stars, the temperature was comfortable and I decided to sit outdoors awhile and think while the big dogs frolicked. I figured they'd been kept penned up too long. I'd hate it, no matter what my mother said about dogs liking their crates as a secure environment. Besides, I shouldn't go inside without them, in case one fell into the pool, and I didn't think they were done playing or taking care of business for the night. They must know how to swim—didn't all dogs?—but might have trouble finding the stairs to get out of the water.

I brought my cell with me, in case of trouble, or in case I could bring myself to call Grant. I knew Lou was most likely on the phone before he left the Rosehill driveway, so what else could I report? Nothing. Grant was still a rat and I was still feeling used. On the other hand, no matter what I said to Lou, I wasn't real happy about being alone at this isolated estate in the middle of the night.

I made myself sit on one of the lounge chairs, without fetching a cushion from the bathhouse at the other end of the pool. I sat and listened to the dogs, spring peeper toads, and the pool machinery, inhaling the scent of roses and chlorine. I touched the pendant on my neck and tried to relax. I told myself how silly I was, to be afraid of the dark. I'd spent twenty-something summers in the Harbor, and never heard of a single crime worse than kids breaking into vacant houses, bar fights and a couple of domestic quarrels. After a while the peace of the night and the sheer joy of the dogs acted like a massage for my spirits. I leaned back on the chaise, at ease.

Soon enough the dogs came to lie beside my chair, panting from their exertion but content to stay out in the night air. I thought they'd go toward the house when they wanted to go in. One of them—I had no idea which—got up to sniff around a blooming azalea. I rubbed the other dog's curly head, and he rested it on my thigh. Nice.

The clouds parted a little, and I admired the moonlight on the clear pool water for a minute or two. Then I picked up the cell phone and called Grant.

He answered right away. "I'm glad you called. I want to apologize again. And I really hate you being at that place by yourself."

Nice, too. "I'm okay. I'm sitting out by the pool, watching the moonbeams on the water. The dogs are great company."

"Good. I'm glad to hear that. And that you have your phone with you outside. Lou called. He said you spotted our friend on the highway."

"Yeah. Do you want to speak with him?"

Grant's voice took on a rougher edge, one I willfully interpreted as jealousy. "Lou is there?"

"No, but Fafhrd just broke the high diving board in half."

Chapter 19

THE DOGS WERE BARKING SO loudly and frantically that I could barely hear Grant shouting, loudly and frantically, "Take his picture! Take his picture!"

My phone was wet. So were the dogs and I, from a ton of stone gargoyle falling into the pool. More water flowed outside on the decking and chairs and potted plants than in the pool itself. Fafhrd looked surprised, then he started hopping up and down, delighted to see more tidal waves sloshing over the sides.

I wondered how long before the pool collapsed, but I yelled, "Stop jumping," to Fafhrd, "Shut up," to the dogs, and "Sorry, I didn't mean you," to Grant. "Hang up and I'll get back to you."

I dried off the phone on the back of my shirt, yelled at the dogs again, with no results, switched modes, and snapped Fafhrd's picture. He waved, as if he understood what I was doing. I half expected him to mouth, "Hi Mom," but he went back to playing in the water. He'd throw himself backward as if he were making snow angels. Or seeing if he could float. Oh, boy.

I pushed the right buttons, sending the picture out to the ether, then I pushed redial and got Grant.

"Did you get it? What did you see?"

"I see a big red . . . "

"Yes?"

"Tree. A big red maple tree that fell into the pool."

Then he said a word that did not usually have two o's in it, but I guess that was the British pronunciation. He sounded so disappointed that I couldn't help feeling sorry for him. This was what he lived for, what his whole raison d'être wrapped itself around. I wanted him to see Fafhrd, too, to validate my own experience.

On the other hand, I was the only one. Agent High and Mighty, due-consideration Grant could breach every civil liberty a liberal lawyer could name, but he couldn't see a single swimming troll.

He cursed again. "It's part of the ancient covenant. No images."

"No matter, he's gone now." I got up to make sure he hadn't just sunk to the bottom of the pool, but he was gone. The dogs were racing around, bewildered and bedraggled. I wonder if they could see Fafhrd, besides hearing his commotion. Did he have a scent only dogs could recognize? Would they chase him—or would he harm them? I kind of wished my mother was here so she could ask the dogs, but she'd have a fit at the damage from my first hour at Rosehill. I wasn't thinking about the pool, either. If Ben and Jerry were nervous before, I'd hate to see what a disappearing Goliath did to them.

"Are you still there?"

Somehow I'd forgotten about Grant.

"Yes, but neither the pool nor the dogs will ever be the same."

"Me, neither. What now?"

"I don't think he'll come back tonight."

"No, I meant about us."

"Us?"

"I want to be part of this. Your troll is the most important event of the century, any recent century. His appearance is amazing, astonishing, and dangerous."

"You sound like a geek hacking into the Defense Department."

"We made sure no one could. But this is not just research and study and speculation; Fafhrd is real, and the threat is real. To you, to every single person alive today."

"Yeah, I already got that. Look what he did to the pool."

"That's not what I mean. One troll is nothing compared to what else could be unleashed on unsuspecting humanity. They won't even see it coming, no more than I could see your friend. I know I can help stop the threat. That's what I was trained to do, Willy. You have to let me. I can do it; I know I can, but only with your help. I need you to trust me."

The dogs had given up. They came to sit beside my chair, their tongues lolling out. I knew I ought to hang up and get them fresh water and towels, but this was too important. My life, my future, my happiness—to hell with the rest of the universe—might depend on what we said now. "How can I trust you when you don't tell me anything? Not just about the wiretaps, but you don't tell people about Fafhrd, about Unity, about DUE or what the Royce Institute really does. Heaven only knows what else you aren't telling them, or me. So how do I know I'm not hearing only what you want me to know? You have too many secrets to be trustworthy."

"Damn, Willy, I don't make all the rules and decisions about who knows what. The choices were made centuries ago to protect those who were different, who did not fit the common mold. Haven't we seen enough so-called ethnic cleansing to know what evils men can commit on anyone who worships another god, speaks another language, has a different color skin? You say you do not trust me. Picture the fear and loathing if people suspected enclaves of their fellow citizens could read their minds, could predict their deaths, could distinguish lies from truth?"

"I suppose."

"Further, what good would it do to tell people about Fafhrd, when they cannot see him? They'd consider such a warning proof that we were all insane."

"Not just me, for once."

"You are not crazy. You're special. I've never met anyone like you."

I sure as hell had never met anyone like Grant, but I lived in small circles, despite living in Manhattan. "You expect me to believe that you've never known another woman who claims to see the supernatural, when you work with weirdos all day?"

"That's not what I meant, and you know it. And I don't lie."

We were back to the big issue. "But you do withhold truths."

"Sometimes. So do you."

Like not admitting how much I wanted to trust him? How he was the hottest, sexiest man I'd ever known? How his voice sent shivers up my spine? I considered that self-protection. "Listen, I don't live my life on the edge like you do. I am not used to it. I don't want to get used to it. You live for it. You are part of it. I can't be."

"But you kissed me back."

I felt heat in my cheeks and was happy he couldn't see the blush. "I thought we were talking business."

"As you said, this is a crazy business. We operate more on feelings than cold logic. We have to, because we cannot ignore the talents of our associates. We listen, not just to the words, the evidence, but also to the belief in our peoples' strengths. We learn to trust our own feelings, too."

"I thought you Brits didn't put much stock in emotional stuff. Stiff upper lip and all that."

"That's for public show. Inside? You can't be part of this without trusting what others know, with other senses. I believe you see the troll, even though I will most likely never see him. I believe you don't intentionally call him forth, or encourage him to break the treaty rules, because I believe in you. There's no logic I could demonstrate, no rationality. Just feeling."

I could go with that, since not a whole lot of Troll Gate made any sense.

He lowered his voice. "And I felt something else with you. Something I will not deny."

I was feeling it now. His deep, mellow tones, with the clipped British accent, were sending tingles to places that never heard of reason.

"I felt it the second I saw you. The instant your hand brushed mine. As soon as I caught your scent and saw your eyes sparkle. Something is there between us. I know you felt it too, like a jolt of electricity, or a spark from a bonfire. Call it magnetic attraction, call it hormones or lust or magic, but don't deny its existence."

I couldn't, not when his words made me shiver. No, that was the cool night air on my damp clothes . . . and thoughts of taking them off, with him.

"I'd like to see where that feeling leads," he continued. "I'd like to finish what we started at your apartment."

"Finish? I'm no one-night affair."

"What if it takes fifty years to finish? We'll never know if we don't start."

"Pretty words. Is that what you tell every female you want to sleep with? What's the British word for it? Shag? Swive?"

"Screw, same as here, with other expressions, depending on the company. But there's also 'making love.'"

"I don't want to be one of your girls in every port."

"I don't have a girl in every port. Or in any port, for that matter. I date—I'm no monk—but I don't sleep around, and I've never had a relationship with a woman lasting more than a few months."

"Commitment problems, huh?"

"I never found a woman I wanted to stay with longer. That's better, I'd say, than settling for an Alvin."

"That's Arlen. That was, anyway. He was nice."

"But no electricity?"

"Only when I tried to unplug the toaster at his apartment."

"We can do better."

I could hear the smile in his voice and I was tempted. Oh, so tempted. Like a moth by the candle flame, I suppose. "How do I know you're not feeding me a line of bull, just to get my cooperation? Or get in my bed?"

"Because I don't lie. And I can prove it to you by sticking around after we fix the troll problem. You'll see, with time. That's the only way you'll learn to trust me if you cannot take my word on it. I could get character references from my boss, I suppose, or the PM."

"You know the Prime Minister?"

"What, you'd rather have a note from the Queen?

That might take a bit more time than we have right now. Come on, Willy, say I can come out to Paumanok Harbor and act the lovesick swain so I can be with you day and night."

"Here? You want to stay here?" Sharing Cousin Lily's bed? "No, that's impossible. I know half the people in this town, and I know how they talk. Good grief, my mother would hear about it in twenty minutes, in Florida."

"Your mother knew about Alvin, didn't she? Or does she think you're a thirty-five-year-old virgin?"

"I am thirty-four, and my mother and I do not discuss those things."

"Your birthday is next month. And how can I protect you, and watch out for dangers, if I am not with you?"

I knew I'd feel better about being out here at Rosehill if he were near.

"Besides, how can we find out how far attraction can take us if we don't get to know each other better? And how can we add kindling to that spark if I stay at your mother's house or a motel in Montauk?"

"I suppose you could stay in the apartment over the garage. I could tell people you are a writer friend of Mr. Parker's, working on a screenplay."

"Parker wouldn't put his friend up in the chauffeur's quarters."

"Is that what it is?"

"That's what it was. Now it's housing a battery of security devices that feed right to the men I have staying at the guesthouse. And no, I am not staying there, either."

"I didn't know there was a guesthouse."

"It's that cottage beyond the tennis courts."

"I thought it belonged to the next-door neighbor." I thought about it. "So I already have bodyguards?"

"I told you, Lou told you. You are not expendable. We don't want anything to happen to you. We would love to nab anyone who threatened you, then follow their trail back to Nicky's kidnapper."

I wasn't crazy about being set out as bait, but I liked the idea of bodyguards. Except I'd waved at the people at that cottage when Mom and I walked the dogs. "Your men are disguised as two gay guys?"

"It's no disguise, which is another reason I don't want to stay there. Not that I have anything against them, but no one would believe I'm your lover if I hang out with Colin and Kenneth."

I ignored the lover part. "Are they good at their jobs?"

"The best. Colin's eyesight is twice as sharp as the average person's, and Kenneth is a precog. Together they are tech wizards, weapons experts, and kickboxing champs."

"So I don't need you here to protect me."

"You need me, sweetheart."

"Not too sure of yourself, are you?"

"They can't follow you around. They can't go to the beach with you or out to dinner." He paused. "They can't help you sleep better at night."

He didn't mean warm milk or herbal tea. Oh, my. And oh, my aching, needy body. My nipples hardened, just at the thought of sex with the secret service.

"Quit stalling, Willy. Can I come?"

Fast and hard, or slow and long, if there is a god. And unselfish, if there is a goddess. I took a deep breath. "How soon can you get here?"

Now he paused. "Um, not for a couple of days. There's been a development here concerning the boy's location."

"A development?" I echoed. "And when were you going to tell me about it?"

"When I uncovered more information."

Lust died aborning. "You see? You don't trust me, either."

"Bloody hell, Willy. A woman's been killed a block away from your apartment. I don't want to frighten you until we know who she was."

"But you think she might be connected to Nicky?"

"We know she was an undocumented immigrant, nanny to a handicapped child, a boy no one ever saw or heard."

"So now you know where Nicky is? If that boy is Nicky, of course."

"We know where a handicapped child was. He and his supposed uncle are gone. The only thing they left was the dead nanny for the cleaning lady to find."

"So you can trace phone calls, credit cards, Interpol IDs, that kind of cloak and dagger stuff."

"We could, if all the information we had wasn't false: the uncle's name, his bank accounts, his social security number. That person does not exist. Which leads us to believe someone has something big to hide, and money and connections to get it done. Even if Nicky is not the boy, your FBI wants to find out what secrets were worth killing a Polish nanny to keep. She did not speak English, according to the neighbors, which means nothing in the city. She would have drawn a great deal of curious attention, though, in a small village like Paumanok Harbor."

"She would have received three job offers and a marriage proposal. Or she could have gone to Riverhead, where there are still people who speak Polish. They even hold a Polish Festival every summer. She could have fit in there, but I see what you mean."

"We have no proof. It might have been a domestic quarrel, a crime of passion, or the uncle caught her mistreating the child, then fled before he could be charged with the murder. Or the nephew could have been a psychotic killer who already did in his own parents."

"Have you ever thought about writing detective stories? You'd be good at it."

"I'll leave that to you creative types. Meanwhile, I have psychic locators going to the apartment tomorrow. One of those last-thought espers is going to the morgue. And we are contacting all the Polish employment agencies, social networks, and churches to see if anyone recognizes her picture. Maybe a friend heard about a change of address, or knows something about the boy."

"And you need to be there to coordinate the investigation?"

"To get my people into the apartment and the coroner's office, yes. To get the local police to cough up the info we need, yes. It's my case, and I have the authority to pursue any leads."

"But you think it sounds like Nicky? Like he and his captor are headed here?"

"That's what we thought they would do all along. So you see how important your involvement is, and why I need to be close?"

I saw how dangerous this situation was becoming. I could see the headlines now, one dead au pair, one dead pet sitter. "You're right. I wish you hadn't told me."

"Do you want me to send my agents up to the big house tonight? Or you could call them if you get frightened. Just speed-dial ICE on Parker's phone line."

"Ice?"

"In Case of Emergency. Don't you have that on your cell phone?"

"No. Whose number would I ring?"

"Program mine in tomorrow. I'll try to get there as soon as I can. The suspect will have to find lodgings, get the child settled, and reconnoiter your position, so I do not expect any trouble soon. Or maybe the uncle is just a killer and he's fleeing the country altogether."

Just a killer? Instead of a maniac trying to take over the world, after he ran my brain through a cosmic Cuisinart. I very carefully did not inquire exactly how the nanny died.

"Hurry," was all I said. In a panic, I herded the dogs inside, through the house. Sorry, Mr. Parker. I locked every door and window and found a fireplace poker, like a heroine from a historical romance, to keep under my pillow. I didn't bother with a shower. Psycho, anyone? But I washed, threw my damp clothes on the bathroom floor—sorry, Aunt Lily—and huddled in bed with the phone and two wet poodles. Sorry, Mom. But instead of having nightmares, or staying awake all night in a raging anxiety attack, I fell asleep dreaming of having my body's every wish granted. Sorry, scruples.

CHAPTER 20

I WAS GOING TO HAVE AN AFFAIR. A mind-numbing, soul-shattering affair. I was most likely going to be killed, too, but, hey, I might as well enjoy great sex first, right? I knew, without the slightest dash of extrasensory anything, that sex with Grant would be like nothing I'd ever experienced. The anticipation alone was enough to dampen my drawers and make me forget, for a while, at least, that death, doubt, and doom loomed. Like the old song said, anticipation was making me crazy. Okay, I didn't have far to go, but this was a good crazy, not the "I'm alone in the world and everyone hates me" kind of crazy. This was "the hottest man on two continents wants me, and my skin is too tight" kind of crazy.

I took the dogs for a run around the property, with Baggies but no leashes. When I waved to the guys at the guesthouse, one of them started jogging behind us, keeping pace with us. Sometimes he got ahead, because Ben and Jerry stopped at every interesting bush and tree trunk and I stayed with them. I still wasn't sure they'd come when called, to say nothing of needing to catch my breath now and again. They were nice dogs, well trained.

My mother had been working on their high-strung nerves, but she couldn't run some of their excess energy out of them. I could, so we did another lap of the estate.

Then I went in, made sure the dogs had their morning kibble rations and pills, and took a shower. I reveled in the strong water pressure and the constant temperature—so unlike the finicky pipes in the old brownstone where I live. Maybe, when Grant got here, we'd try out Mr. Parker's sauna. And the hot tub. Or the pool, if it's not wrecked. Hell, maybe the pool table.

I was going to have an affair, a torrid, tongue-hanging-out-like-the-dogs' affair, right here in Paumanok Harbor. I didn't care who knew.

Except for Grandma Eve. Damn, I could hear her saying Grant wasn't the man for me; he wasn't in my tea leaves; he wasn't the steady sort; I should consult with the Institute for the proper bloodlines. She always swore that my future lay with a man who could do magic so our children were exceptional. Not a super-cop.

I bet there was magic in Grant's touch. Besides, this was a love affair, not a lifetime. I knew it, no matter what Grant said. He was so out of my league, so alien to the world I knew, so far from my comfort zone. Half the time with him I felt like Alice at the Mad Hatter's Tea Party. The other half I felt like a schoolgirl with a crush on the captain of the football team. So nothing could come from this except glorious sex, and I was okay with that. I resolved to keep my expectations low and avoid disappointment later. Why start a relationship waiting for the dream to die?

Nope, I'd think positively. He'd give me great protection, and greater pleasure. I would not think about him giving me beautiful blue-eyed babies and a lifetime of excitement. Not when there was no chance in hell. Who needed excitement anyway? I had enough in the plots of my books.

The morning was too gorgeous to worry about having my heart broken or my head being messed with. Kidnapped? Here, in this sleepy little town, with the sun out? By daylight, everything looked better. My father would be fine, my mother would take care of him, Susan's parents would be home tomorrow at the latest, and Lou was looking after Grandma Eve. I had days of luxury ahead, Rosehill and the beach, waiting for Grant.

The way I rationalized myself into a sunny mood was that the scum who threatened me and the world couldn't call up the troll. I could. So I wouldn't. Simple. Then the bad guy couldn't use Fafhrd, or me, or Nicky. And Grant would find the bastard before he hurt anyone else.

Meantime, I'd avoid children. And work. Don would be upset, but less than he would be if the new cleaning people found me on Mr. Parker's white carpet, as stiff as the poor Polish nanny.

I had plenty of other stuff to do to fill up my time. Like calling the pool people about the diving board, brushing twigs and leaves out of the poodles, and unpacking my suitcases. I also had to see what the refrigerator held, so I could make a list for the grocery store when I went out to feed the Pomeranian.

The poodles were being so well behaved—and were so tired from our morning run—that I didn't have the heart to lock them in their crates. Instead, I left the doors open in case they wanted to go into the cages, but gave them the freedom of the housekeeper's apartment and the kitchen and pantry rooms. I gave them each a biscuit, rubbed their ears, and promised to be back soon.

The Escalade was twice the size of any car I'd ever driven. It seemed to take up way more than its half of the roadway, but I didn't hit anything or scrape its sides on the gateposts going out, so I considered that another success. I passed Colin on his bike—those guys must do nothing but keep fit all day—and noticed the Bluetooth in his ear. They were looking out for me, most likely calling ahead to unseen watchers to take up the vigil. Good.

Ippy the three-legged Pomeranian? Not so good. I called out before I unlocked the door of my mother's house, so he would know I was a friend. Despite my advance warning, the wretched red-coated runt launched himself off the bottom step and snapped at my leg. He got the hem of my capris in his mouth, thank goodness, not my calf muscle, but he wouldn't let go. I raised my leg and the Pom did an imitation of a furry pit bull, hanging on with all three legs off the ground, growling.

"You are being ridiculous, and I don't have time for this," I told him, trying to shake all six pounds of him loose. "I have to go save the world." And buy frozen waffles for company breakfast.

He held on. Finally I bent down, grabbed him around his middle, tight enough that he opened his jaw to bite, or breathe. Free, I lifted him to my eye level—but far enough away from my nose. "Listen, half-pint, you are the dog. I am the master. You *will* behave." I didn't shake him, but the dog was terrified enough that he was quaking. "I know people hurt you. Then, when you finally got rescued, the first thing they did was cut off your mangled leg and your balls. I'm sorry for the past, but I didn't do it! I am not one of the bad guys."

At least he'd stopped growling and scrabbling his legs in the air. The quivering was pitiful enough. I lowered my voice and told him, "If you don't like the power structure, you should talk to the troll about setting up your own society, but be careful. The King Charles spaniels might want to rule all of dogdom, or the big herders might round all you little dudes up. Ever hear of a dog-eat-dog world? Till then, you live in my world. You need me to open your cans and shovel out the Kibbles 'n Bits. I'm willing to do it, yeah, and change your piddle papers, too, but I will not take any more shit from you. Do you understand?"

He went limp in my arms and for a second I thought I'd given him heart failure. But no, he was just relaxed finally, happy enough in my arms that I brought him closer, against my body so I could pet him. "See? We can be friends."

He ate, he did his business, and he hopped right along with me on the way to Grandma's house. I decided to change his name to Little Red. No one knew what he'd been called before, so what I called him didn't matter. He seemed to follow the sound of my voice anyway, and a "Come on, good boy," worked as well as "Napoleon, avaunt."

I picked him up before he could raise a leg—how the hell he managed that when he walked on three was another mystery—against the impatiens lining Grandma Eve's front walk. I'd been warned he tried to kick up dirt behind him like the stud he wasn't anymore, so I wasn't taking any chances with Grandma's precious flowers. The dog didn't protest, just hung out in my arms. "Don't get too comfortable, Red," I warned him. "No dogs are allowed in my apartment."

Grandma and Lou were having tea in the kitchen, making lists. I learned years ago not to drink tea at my grandmother's, but I poured myself a glass of orange juice, put a muffin on a napkin, and sat with them. I pretended not to see Grandma's glare or Lou's knowing grin while I tried to put the Pomeranian down. He growled and tried to grab my wrist, but his silly mouth wasn't wide enough. I got the idea anyway. So now I had a Velcro dog. At least he ate the crumbs that fell in my lap.

I smiled at the two tacticians. "What can I do to help today?"

Grandma looked at Lou and he looked at her. Uh-oh. I wondered what they were plotting, and just how friendly they'd become overnight. Then they both nodded and held out a stack of posters with Nicky's pictures.

"You can go into town and hand these around," my grandmother said. "You'll do better than Lou, who is a stranger. And it's a good way to reintroduce yourself to folks, so they know you're home."

I did not interrupt to say this was not my home.

"Good to be in the public eye," Lou added. "Instead of off by yourself."

The old safety in numbers ploy. I didn't mind, now that I wasn't trying to work on my book.

"And you can remind people about the poor Ryland girl and her son. Tell everyone the police think he's back in this country, but they need help finding him. Make sure you say that he won't be going back to that nasty drunk of a grandmother, or no one will bother to call if they spot him."

I picked up the flyers and decided to add my mother's phone to the 800 number listed. I knew this close-knit community. They'd talk endlessly among themselves, not so openly to newcomers. I'd check the messages whenever I came to feed Little Red. "Sure. I can do that. I need to get some milk and bread anyway."

I took another muffin and the list they'd compiled of places to leave posters, glad to have a job and a plan.

I stopped by Susan's house on the way back to get

the car. I carried Red like a furry fox stole. Every once in awhile I'd pet his back or rub his ears and he'd sigh. "I suppose you'll want to come to town, huh? Maybe someone will see how cute you are and offer to adopt you. How's that sound?"

Susan was just starting her day, still in a nightshirt with Snoopy on it. She liked dogs? I had the perfect one for her—until Red snapped at her fingers when she reached out to pet him. I guess my plan needed a little more work.

Susan sipped at her coffee. "It was a late night at the Breakaway. Two carloads of East Hamptonites came just before the kitchens closed. Trolls."

I almost dropped the dog. "Did you say trolls?"

"You know the kind, rich enough to think they own the world, with no manners. They criticized the wine list, made the waitress cry, threw fits when we ran out of lobster tails, sent two perfectly cooked meals back to the kitchens, then left a puny tip."

That's not what trolls did, but I wasn't supposed to think of Fafhrd. "What did Uncle Bernie do?"

"He told them to get out and never come back. We had enough assholes of our own without importing any from East Hampton."

"He didn't use those words, did he?"

She smiled over her coffee cup. "He did, and the wait staff applauded, but now I worry that we'll lose a lot of business. They say the economy is so far down, we'll have fewer diners this summer anyway."

I tried to put Red down again. This time he latched onto my watch, so I gave up. "You don't need that kind of customer."

"We do if we want to stay in business. The winter was

really slow. I feel bad Uncle Bernie had to pay for my health insurance."

That was the problem with being a summer resort; you had two or three good months to make a year's worth of income. So you had to put up with the demanding, over-bearing ogres. I would not insult Fafhrd by calling them trolls. Quickly, before I could think about Fafhrd at all, I asked, "What do you hear from your mother?"

"I just got off the phone with her. The hotel smelled of cigarettes, even though she ordered a nonsmoking room, and Daddy can come home if we get the visit-ing nurses to come administer the IV antibiotic drip. I'm making calls this morning."

"Great." Then I asked her to take one of my flyers to the Breakaway when she went in to work. "You know the story, so tell people to keep an eye out for a little boy with a speech defect who's with someone that may be pretending to be his uncle."

"So that's what Grant is working on?"

"Yes, it's an international case." Not the whole truth, but enough of it to satisfy her, I thought.

"And a personal mission?" she asked, prying, smiling.

She'd find out soon enough anyway, so I admitted he was coming to the Harbor, to stay at Rosehill with me.

"Good. I'm glad you two made up. I liked him."

So did I. I wondered if he liked dogs.

Chapter 21

YOU KNOW HOW, when you buy new sunglasses that have a different color lens, or cheap ones that aren't quite in focus, you see things differently? Or when some realtor's trying to sell an expensive piece of land and they build a wooden tower to show buyers the water view they'd have if they blocked the neighbor's? You get a different perspective, a look from another angle.

That's how I felt walking down the main street of Paumanok Harbor, all three blocks of it, with the Pom in my arms. Red suddenly seemed to have lost the use of his three good legs, and much preferred being carried around like a pocketbook. At first I thought he was a great conversation starter with people on the sidewalk, but he stopped the chatter just as fast. "How cute" turned into: "How could you bring a vicious beast like that out in public." He never drew blood, at least, and I quickly learned not to let anyone pet him. But then I realized everyone recognized me, whether I remembered them or not. Maybe they recognized Red as one of my mother's rescue dogs, but total strangers called me by name, asked about my books, my dad, and did I know if Mr. Parker was coming out to Rosehill soon.

Was Paumanok Harbor just a small town, or did it have a big dose of the supernatural, as Grant believed? I decided to put Red back in the car, in the shade, with the windows open. God knew, no one was going to steal him.

I went into the library and sure enough, there was old Mrs. Terwilliger still behind the desk, smiling over her half glasses, and holding out a book for me. *Know Your Pomeranian*.

My throat went dry. "How ...? Are you really psychic?"

She laughed. "No, dear. Your mother ordered the book through interlibrary loan. As soon as I saw you come through the door, I knew you were here to pick it up."

I hadn't known anything about a book, but I took it and said thank you. Then I showed her the picture of Nicky as the authorities thought he might look now at age eight.

"Such a sad story," Mrs. Terwilliger said. "I remember the poor little boy's mother." She shook her silver-haired head. "Tiffany read steamy romance novels, and look where that got her. At least she read. Her mother Alma never stepped foot in the library."

That seemed to be a greater sin than abandoning one's pregnant daughter and calling one's grandson a freak and a bastard.

"I always assumed the child's father came to get him in England, whoever he was. Maybe he loved Tiffany Ryland with all his heart, but was already married. Then, when Tiffany died in that accident, he took the boy to have a piece of her with him forever. He'd make a good father, and Nicholas was such a pretty baby the man's wife would accept him and love him. And teach him to speak, of course."

Of course. I guessed old Mrs. Terwilliger read romance novels, too. I saw no reason to remind her that Tiffany always claimed she'd been drugged and raped and never knew the father's identity.

"He still shouldn't have stolen the child away, I suppose, even if he was the rightful parent. And you say the authorities in England have been looking ever since the accident?"

"Yes, with the help of the Royce Institute." I watched for a reaction, but she just nodded.

"That was the best place for him and his mother. I helped write the letters to get them accepted there."

I wanted to ask why Royce was such a good choice, when Tiffany'd been killed there and her baby abducted, but Mrs. Terwilliger was going on: "So now the people at Royce think young Nicholas Ryland might be in our vicinity?"

"That's what they say. I'm not sure how they came to that conclusion."

"Oh, because so many people can help him here. A lot of Harborites offered to adopt him, you know, after the accident. Not his own grandmother, I'm sorry to say, and the grandfather died years before." She looked around to make sure no one else could hear. No one else was in the library at all, but she still whispered. "His liver, you know. Drinking. At least Tiffany never did that."

Except for the night she was out partying and ended up pregnant.

Mrs. Terwilliger went on: "Scores of families in England wanted him, too, I recall. But they never found him, poor child. You say the man he's with is claiming to be an uncle? Impossible. Tiffany was an only child."

"We—that is, they, think the man is lying. He could be anyone, with bad intentions."

"Oh, the Evil Genius you use in your books."

I was touched that she knew my stories so well. Not so touched to think she simply accepted a villain in real life.

She didn't. "Well, the people at Royce know how to take care of any scoundrels. Don't worry, dear, you can trust them."

I figured she was just reciting the standard litany of praise for the school that paid college tuition for the local kids.

"And that nice man who is coming. You can trust him, too."

I swear she winked at me. The woman had to be Grandma's age, and she winked! And how the hell did she know about Grant, or my involvement with him, anyway? Susan was the only one I'd told.

Except Grandma and Lou knew, and the guys at the guesthouse and everyone else they'd spoken to. I told myself the gossip was nothing out of the ordinary, just the small-town grapevine. Until the perennial librarian handed me another book.

Principles of Etymology of Ancient Languages by T. Grant.

My Grant? I swore I did not say it aloud, but Mrs. Terwilliger answered anyway.

"Oh, no. That's his father." She handed me another book to add to my pile. *Metzger's Dog* by Thomas Perry. "Your Grant likes mysteries."

Janie at the beauty parlor in the back of her house stuck Nicky's picture in the mirror. She worried no one could spot an unknown eight year old once school was over and all the tourists and second-home owners came out for the summer with their kids and grandkids. And no telling what story the "uncle" would use. But she'd keep an eye out, and show the picture to all her customers. Oh, and didn't I want to add some highlights to my hair before my gentleman arrived?

The pharmacist at the drugstore was new, but he'd heard the story about Nicky and hung up the poster near the cash register. He closed his eyes and declared the child's eyes might be green, not the blue mentioned. I checked his diploma on the wall. Yup, the Royce Institute. Turned out he'd studied under Grandma Eve one summer, too, and was going to her place for dinner on the weekend. He slipped some sample condoms into my bag of toothpaste and deodorant.

The post office already had a stack of flyers, and so did Town Hall—all three offices of it—and the one-room, one-cell police station around back. Uncle Henry, who wasn't really my uncle, was the police chief. He gave me a hug, asked about my father, and told me I'd left my car keys at the drugstore.

Sure enough, there they were. I thanked the pharmacist for calling Uncle Henry.

"I never called anyone. I didn't know whose keys they were, but figured whoever lost them would be back soon. Can't get far without the keys, can you?"

I needed cash, and the bank was on my list, so I went around the corner. I used the ATM, but went inside to hand Mr. Whitside the poster. He stared at Nicky, handed the picture back. "I've got it here," he said, pointing at his head. Then he told me my father's heart attack was the best thing that could have happened.

I gave a half nod. "Now maybe he'll take better care of himself."

"No, now your mother will take care of him. They are meant for each other. It's in the stars, you know. Don't ignore yours, either."

At the deli, Joanne handed me a turkey on rye.

"How did you know that's what I wanted?"

"Seems half the town knows what you want, Willy. We're just waiting for you to figure it out."

That was Paumanok Harbor for you. Weird. I guess I just accepted it as a kid. If it's all you know, it's nothing exceptional. Except maybe it was.

And not always in a friendly way. My last stop was the market. You couldn't call it a supermarket because of how small it was, but it stocked the necessities. A lot of folks drove to Amagansett for better variety, and a lot went out of town altogether, to the big King Kullen in Bridgehampton or all the huge new stores in River-head, where they had a warehouse club, Home Depot, and Wal-Mart. My family always tried to support the local economy by shopping in town. Besides, Mr. Findel bought fresh herbs and greens from Grandma Eve, and some of her preserves when the farm stand was closed for the winter.

Mr. Findel's wife was at the cash register, as always, with the same sour disappointment on her face from when I was a kid. Maybe she always dreamed of marrying a prince, not standing on her feet all day making change and listening to complaints about the prices, the lack of choices, the narrow aisles and poor lighting.

"That kid? Who cares? Been gone five years, hasn't he? Likely found his feet somewhere, or dead like his tramp of a mother. A retard, wasn't he?"

If I hadn't unloaded my rickety cart onto the counter I'd have left. "No. He was possibly autistic, but under-going therapy. He might be a genius by now for all we know."

She stopped chewing her gum long enough to say, "No foal out of that stable could be a winner. And I've got too much to do to ask everyone who comes in with an eight year old if he's really theirs."

"Just call my mother's number if you suspect anything not right."

"Like knocking bottles off the shelves, switching price tags, eating the fruit before they pay for it? That's what the little trolls do, and that ain't right either."

"Did you say trolls?"

"Monsters, the way people raise kids these days. And when are you going to have some of your own anyway, like your ma wants? Not setting any great example for the town, are you, shacking up with a foreigner you barely know."

I decided I'd shop elsewhere in the future, no matter how far I had to drive.

Which reminded me to get gas.

Red was so ecstatic to see me, or the liver snaps from the grocery and the turkey sandwich from the deli, that he didn't try to bite my fingers until I tried to put him in the backseat. We compromised. He got the passenger seat. I got most of the sandwich.

Bud at the gas station took a poster and my credit card. I fully intended to keep a tally for my mother because I sure as hell wasn't paying for this trip. Then he told me to hurry home, a storm was coming. I couldn't see a cloud in the sky. So much for espers.

I checked my list. The community center was all that was left. I brought Red in with me because I couldn't find a shady enough parking space.

I hadn't been into the art part of the building since it opened, and I vowed to come back without Red to admire the incredible artwork on the walls. Having such treasures this far from Manhattan made it even more impressive. I sighed.

"Yes, we were lucky to get Mr. Bradford's collection when he passed away," a voice said.

I turned to see a beautiful, very pregnant woman. "Louisa, it's me, Willow Tate."

We hugged, Red made a lunge for her ear, but she laughed. Then she walked me to the other side of the building, where they held art classes, after-school activities, lectures, and programs. They had a gym and a senior center, too. Quite an accomplishment for such a small town.

Louisa told me she'd had to resign as manager of the whole community center because of her own rapidly growing family. She showed me pictures of laughing, happy children, and I could tell by her own smile that those pictures were more priceless than anything on the gallery walls. She invited me for dinner, but I didn't know when my company was arriving, so we left it that I'd call. She promised to tell all the kids who came to the center to keep a watch out for a newcomer.

What a relief, talking to Louisa, who made no sly innuendoes or nasty comments. She made me feel normal, too.

I still wasn't sure about the rest of Paumanok Harbor.

Then I had to drive home in a pouring rainstorm, with thunder and lightning. Bud must listen to the Weather Channel, I told myself. I told Red that sitting in my lap while I drove wasn't safe for either of us, but I didn't move him. I was afraid of electric storms, too.

Back at home—my mother's house—I dried off the dog, made sure he had fresh water and pee-pee pads, then checked the phone messages. There were five already.

The first was from Aunt Ellen, who was older than dirt, and no one's aunt that I knew of, but everyone called her that. Her raspy voice croaked, "Vern says a boy in trouble is coming next week. But he's not sure if it's the right boy."

Vern was Aunt Ellen's husband, who'd been dead for twenty years.

The second message was from a woman whose dog was humping the drapes. She insisted my mother had to help her. She left the third message, too, indignant that she'd called twice with no reply. I wanted to tell her to shorten the drapes and get the dog neutered, but that was my mother's business, not mine. I made a note of her number, so I could call back to tell her Mom was out of town.

The fourth message was from Kelvin at the auto body shop at the edge of town. He'd seen the kid's picture at the deli, he said, and his left big toe started to ache. That meant the boy was Nicky Ryland. If his right big toe had itched, it wasn't.

The last caller hadn't left his name, just some real bad vibes. "Stop poking into the devil's doings. That boy is the spawn of Satan who should have died with his mother. We don't want him here. We don't want any of your kind here."

I wasn't sure what kind I was, but I was pretty sure I knew why no one ever called our world Unity.

CHAPTER 22

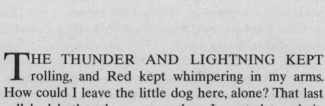

THE THUNDER AND LIGHTNING KEPT rolling, and Red kept whimpering in my arms. How could I leave the little dog here, alone? That last call had bothered me more than I wanted to admit. Someone thought Nicky should have died because his parents weren't married? Or because he was different, imperfect by that moron's standards? Poor Little Red was imperfect, too, with too few working legs and too many hang-ups. My mother hadn't let anyone kill him, and look what a love he was turning into. My new best friend was a comfort to me in the storm. I don't know who was more afraid of the noise and the flashes, but we had each other.

And a lot of older people's bones ached before a storm, didn't they? So Kelvin's throbbing toe didn't mean anything. I'd mention it to Grant, anyway. He liked that kind of nonsense.

The rain bothered me another way, too. What if Fafhrd came out to play? No, I wouldn't think of the you-know-what. I mentally pictured the poodles romping in the puddles instead. Damn, the poodles. The high-strung, nervous poodles. I had to get back to Rosehill. I had groceries to put away, too.

On the other hand, the rain cooled the temperature, so nothing was going to go bad so soon. Maybe the storm would pass. Thunderstorms seldom lasted too long. That's what I told Red, anyway.

I decided to call Grant in the meantime, to tell him about the locals and the phone messages. And to hear his voice.

He answered right away. "How are you?"

"Fine. I'm over at my mother's, with the Pomeranian."

"You don't sound fine."

I did not want to admit I was terrified of electric storms. "There's a lot of static on the line. We're having a thunderstorm pass overhead." Before he could ask more questions, I told him about the VanWetherings' grandson and Mr. Parker's search for a boy actor. He just went "Hmm," so I described the phone calls next. "Aunt Ellen? That would be Ellen Grissom? If Vern says nothing will happen for a week, that's a relief. We need more time from here."

"You believe Aunt Ellen? Vern is dead."

"So?"

I couldn't tell if he was kidding or not. "What about Bud's forecast or Kelvin's big toe?"

"Maybe the gout. Maybe a guess. Maybe Bud listens to NOAA. Or he could be a weather dowser. I'll check his file."

"And the nasty phone call about Nicky?"

"We'll find him first, worry about his welcome later. But I can have a tap put on your mother's phone so that we can trace the calls back. Then we can keep an eye on any threats, if they come."

So he was taking crank calls as seriously as the real ones. As real as a ghost could be.

"If that's all right with you? I am asking this time, you understand."

I hoped I understood what he wasn't saying, that he cared about me and my safety. "Sure, what's one more intrusion into my privacy?"

He laughed, deep and rich. Then another clap of thunder came, louder and closer. Red yelped. Or maybe that was me.

"What's that?"

"Just the storm. I guess I better get off the phone." Only I didn't want to lose the connection. I liked his voice, his listening to everything I had to say, his caring. "When are you coming out?"

Not soon enough. They'd run a scan of computer records for crimes similar to the dead nanny's murder, and found another one: another live-in babysitter, another woman who did not speak English, another instance of the missing employer having a stolen identity. This murder took place a month ago in Florida, where the man was posing as a young boy's widowed father. The neighbors thought the child was severely handicapped, because he'd been carried into the house, limp, then never seen again.

"If it's Nicky, I bet the bastard keeps him drugged when they're on the move so he can't talk to anyone. If he can talk."

"That's what I'm thinking, too. But there are a lot of sick kids out there."

"Whose foreign-born caretakers have a habit of turning up dead, and whose guardians use aliases? That's too far-fetched."

"There is another nanny who proved dispensable. This one lived, barely. She's in a hospital in Georgia, but she's in a coma so no one can figure out what language she speaks. I have to go tomorrow."

"You?"

"I told you, I'm a linguistics expert."

"Like your father."

He didn't ask how I knew about his father. I suppose he assumed I'd done a Google search—which I intended to do as soon as I was back at my computer.

"And I am meeting a few people there, some who have helped people in comas, stroke victims, even autistic kids, that kind of thing. I'm hoping they have some ideas about Nicky, too."

"Royce people."

"Yes. Telepaths and Visualizers like you. Maybe we can get an image of the killer or a more current description of Nicky, even what car they were in. Anything that could help, if this woman is connected to them. If she is, we have the murderer's path to New York. Someone is bound to have seen him. So I cannot get to Rosehill as soon as I want, Willy."

"I understand." I was disappointed, but I knew how important his investigation was. Murder was a lot more immediate than Apocalypse by Aliens from another dimension. "Just how many languages do you speak, anyway?"

A clap of thunder interrupted his answer, if he was going to give one. I must have screamed. Red jumped down and ran under the sofa. I wished I could fit.

"Willy?" Panic was in his voice.

"Sorry. I just don't like all the noise."

"Damn. I wish I could be there, to hold you in my arms until it passes. Should I have one of the men at Rosehill come over to sit with you? *Not* to hold you."

"No. I am going back there as soon as the storm passes. I'll be fine, I promise."

"Be careful."

"You, too."

"I'll get there as soon as I can."

"I'll be waiting."

A lot more than static flowed through those telephone lines. It kept my mind off the wild elements outside, and on the wild wanting thundering through my body. I almost suggested a little phone sex, but not during an electric storm. "Hurry."

His breathing was as heavy as mine. "Count on it."

I coaxed Red out from under the sofa with a bag of Milano cookies I found in my mother's refrigerator. Desperate times called for desperate measures, didn't they? I made sure to eat all the chocolate parts and only give Red tiny crumbs of the wafer. We watched the water pour off the eaves together, and tried to convince each other that the storm was passing.

Grandma Eve called to tell me the rain was starting to flood the roads. I should get back to Rosehill before they became impassable. Did I want Lou to drive me?

What was I, a wimp? I'd bet Grandma didn't pull an afghan over her head when the windows rattled with the thunder. The tough old bird most likely used the lightning bolts to boil up her potions. Of course I didn't want anyone to drive me. I just didn't want to leave Little Red.

"Who? Oh, the snapper."

"Are you sure I can't bring him over to you? He'd like the company."

"He does not get along with the other dogs your mother foisted on me. And he's too small. I'm afraid of tripping on the little monster. Or mistaking him for my fuzzy slippers. But there's a calmative in the right cabinet next to the sink. You can put a couple of drops in water, then take the bottle back with you."

So add hopeless neurotic to my grandmother's opinion of me. Now I needed a home-brewed rescue remedy. "I'm fine. Not worried at all."

"I meant for the Pom and the poodles, Willow, not for you, although the mix won't hurt you."

"Oh. Well, I think the rain is tapering off, and the Escalade is like a tank, so a little water won't affect it."

"The dratted deluge is ruining my strawberries and flooding my lettuce. Seeds are bound to rot in the field, and the farm stand is closed, naturally."

Yeah, I was worried about the farm, too. Not. "I'm sure everything will be okay tomorrow. I'll see you in the morning when I come for Red."

His ears twitched. "Do you know your name already?" I asked, after hanging up the phone. No, he had to go use his papers in the back bathroom. Afterward, he took a sip of Grandma's doctored water, shook his head at the taste, and then curled up into the blanket in his crate. He turned his back to me, tucked his nose into his plumed red tail like a fox cub, and went to sleep.

There went my excuse to stay here, so I found a yellow slicker in the closet, made a mad dash for the car. Mud spattered my legs and squished through my sandals. Rain poured off the slicker and onto my pants. Then I had to spend time figuring out how to get the windshield wipers going, and the lights and defroster.

I crept down the roads, trying to avoid potholes that were so filled with water I had no idea how deep they were. Forks of lightning shot through the night-dark sky, illuminating branches swaying madly in the wind. Damn, if the lightning didn't strike me, I didn't drown in a sinkhole, or flip the car in a skid, I could get killed by a falling tree.

Except a troll was holding one up to let me get by. Then he let it drop across the road behind me, taking who knew how many wires with it. I couldn't see him in my rearview mirror, but I beeped the horn and hoped he wasn't electrocuted. I couldn't get back to check, not with the tree down.

Don't touch the wires, I thought, and yelled in my head. Maybe out loud, too, I was so petrified.

I managed to get to Rosehill, punch in the codes, drive through the gate. This time I drove around to the back entrance, which was nearer the kitchen and the house-keeper's apartment. I didn't want to drag the shopping bags or my muddy shoes and dripping raincoat through the house.

The dogs bounded through the door to greet me. "Good boys."

No, they weren't.

One—or both—had chewed my new sneakers and shredded my nightgown. The other—or both—had the runs. "Oh, shit." Literally. Throughout the kitchen, pantry, Cousin Lily's sitting room and bedroom and bathroom.

I couldn't blame the dogs. I'd left them out of their crates, alone too long, during a loud, scary storm. My own stomach was none too steady, getting worse from the stench and the sight of dog sick. And knowing I had to clean it.

First I let them out the back door, on their own. At that moment, I didn't much care whether they came back or not. They did, at the next clap of thunder, almost knocking me down in their rush past me.

I poured half the bottle of rescue remedy into their

water. I thought about drinking the other half myself, but had a diet Coke instead. I put away the groceries, threw out my nightgown but saved the sneakers as wearable in an emergency until I could buy another new pair. Then I gathered buckets and paper towels and seven kinds of cleaning supplies, three of which specifically claimed to work on pet stains. This led me to believe today was not the first repugnant, revolting incident. Someone could have warned me. Of course I would have refused the dog-sitting job then, which might explain why no one told me.

I found rubber gloves, thank God, but what I really wanted was a HAZMAT suit and an oxygen mask, if not my mother's head on a platter.

I took a deep breath and started in. The dogs that were so stupid they lost their lunches at a little thunderstorm were smart enough to keep out of my way. I rubbed and scrubbed and sprayed and blotted and vacuumed for what seemed like hours. For sure I spent more time than I'd put in cleaning my apartment in the past five months. At least the storm had passed enough that I could put the plastic bags of garbage outside, and leave the door open to air the place out. Somewhere between my second and third trips to the shed with the trash cans, the phone rang.

The caller ID gave my father's Florida phone number. "You could have told me the dogs have nervous stomachs, you know. High-strung, my ass. How's Dad?"

"Feed them boiled beef and white rice. He's cranky. Wants his own robe and slippers, so he's recovering. The doctor says he'll be fine, so I came here to get his stuff. His condo is a regular pigsty. Disgusting."

"You want to know about disgusting? Let me tell you—"

"You used to have projectile vomiting."

That shut me up. "So how was your flight?"

"The flight was fine, only half an hour late, which is good by today's standards. At least we got out before the storm they said was coming or we'd be sitting on the tarmac still. But listen to this: when they handed out those little bags of pretzels, I gave mine to the woman in the next seat. From Staten Island she was, going to see her first grandchild. A girl. She had pictures."

"And I have chewed-up sneakers. I'm never getting a dog."

"Yes, well, I gave her my pretzels because of what your father said about not eating anything on the plane. The old fool's never been anything but a bag of wind, but why take chances? So the woman opens *my* bag and a cockroach falls out. She starts screaming, jumps up and hits her head on the luggage rack, starts bleeding. The software salesman in the seat across the row sees the blood and passes out."

And I thought my day was eventful. "Wow, I guess Dad was right."

"Right? They gave the woman and the fainting guy free tickets for another flight. That could have been me, except for your jackass of a doomsayer father. Do you know what they offered me? Another bag of pretzels!"

"What did Dad say?"

Mom gave a big sniff. "Do you think I'd tell him? Oh, but he did mumble something about your paying the toll. Or saving the stole. I couldn't make it out. He was still woozy from the anesthesia, so don't worry about it. But, baby girl, don't go on any boats, just to be on the safe side, okay?"

"Sure, Mom. You know how seasick I get. Give Dad my love, and call me when you can. Love you."

"Me, too. Boil the chop meat until it's brown and pour off the fat. Ben and Jerry'll be fine."

They'd be fine with dog food. I wasn't cooking, or looking at food, not after cleaning shit all afternoon. In fact, I didn't want to touch anything until I'd sterilized my hands, despite the rubber gloves. I decided to settle for a long bath in Mr. Parker's guest Jacuzzi. Lord knew, I deserved it. I've never taken so much as a shower during an electric storm, figuring the lightning could come through the pipes and fry me, but everything seemed quiet outside except for a lot of wind. Even the rain had stopped.

The guest bathroom was gorgeous, white like everything else in the house, but with delicate flowers painted on the tiles. The same flowers were embroidered on the hand towels, and hand-painted on a porcelain pitcher that was filled with matching silk flowers. I found bath salts, a pile of fluffy towels, soap that must cost more than my apartment rent, and candles.

Why not? I convinced myself I was practicing for when Grant came, although I doubted either one of us needed any seduction scenery. Besides, the cleaning crew was coming in the morning, so I wasn't permanently desecrating Rosehill's perfection with my dirty feet and detergent-scented skin. I was no thief or trespasser, either. I wouldn't use the thick terry robe hanging on the back of the door, although I did touch it, to check for softness. Yup, it was.

I went back to my rooms—this time I'd shut the dogs in their crates—and grabbed a clean T-shirt and workout pants, and my iPod.

If this was heaven, I couldn't understand why Aunt Ellen's Vern didn't stay there. I might even have to reconsider my definitions of opulent, over-the-top luxury. Everyone ought to be so indulged.

I had music in my ears, the scent of roses in my nose, an inflatable pillow cushioning my neck, bubbles tickling my skin, and swirling hot water doing a message on the rest of my body. The only thing missing was a man to share the pleasure with. Hell, who needed a man? I was so relaxed my limbs were limp.

For now, I had no thoughts of men or monsters or murderers. I let my mind float on a rainbow-colored soap bubble and drifted with the current.

That's when the lights went out.

CHAPTER 23

S HIT.

I'd forgotten how often the power went out at this end of the island. Heavy rain saturated the ground, high winds uprooted the trees, and trees took down wires. And here I was, in the bathtub, with nothing but two puny votive candles, half burned through. No phone to call my grandmother to see if she lost electricity, no cell phone I could have used as a light, no idea where to find a flashlight in this house, or more candles. So I waited a minute or two to see if the lights would come back on. A place like Rosehill might have a generator of its own.

That was my first thought. My second thought was that a place like Rosehill had buried electric lines. The main could be out for the entire neighborhood, which happened sometimes. Or else someone could have cut Rosehill's power lines at the street to shut down the security system.

My third thought was to get the hell out of the tub. I dropped the iPod, grabbed that plushy robe and one of the candles, which instantly went out. I picked up the other one, far more carefully. That's when I heard the poodles barking. The big dogs could scare away an intruder . . . if I hadn't locked them in their crates.

I almost called out to them, to tell them I was coming, but I thought I heard a man's voice through the excited yelps. The only man who had any business here was Mr. Parker, and he was in California. Besides, he didn't know the new passcodes.

That left a housebreaker. A thief? A kidnapper? A murderer? I didn't want to meet up with any of them, not in the daylight, not in a big, empty, pitch-black house. Okay, I'd hide. Where? Under a bed? In a closet? Too obvious. I hardly knew the layout of Rosehill, or my way around the upper stories. All I knew was it was sparsely furnished, with sharp angles. No nooks, no heavy drapes. Double shit.

Then I heard more voices, one from the front of the house; the other, I thought, came from the sliders to the pool. One guy I might have been able to avoid. Two or three, in different directions? All they had to do was release the dogs and follow them right to me. I was a dead woman dripping. But I was not going to go down without a fight, not me. I knew all about heroes from my books. I knew karate. I picked up that pretty porcelain ewer and dumped out the silk flowers. Then I blew out my last candle.

I heard footsteps pounding up the stairs, shouts from below. Through the crack in the door, I could see a beam of light. The bastards came prepared. I waited until someone neared the bathroom where I'd been so relaxed and content. I opened the door, closed my eyes, and threw the vase.

If the last sound I ever heard was the thunk of the porcelain hitting the killer's head, I'd take that satisfaction to my grave.

The pitcher cracked, and the guy's head must have, too, because he went down, heavily. The noise had the other two housebreakers charging to the stairs from the front and back of the house.

"Man down," one shouted.

The first one to the second floor had a flashlight in one hand, a gun in the other. I wished I could remember a prayer. All I could think was: Dad, it's not a boat.

"Boss?"

Boss?

The man on the floor grunted. "Put your weapons away. Miss Tate is fine. For now. As soon as I can get up off this carpet . . . "

"Grant?"

"Do not say one word. Not yet."

Colin from the gatehouse gave him a hand up. His partner holstered his weapon and brought out another flashlight. I could see his grin as Grant rubbed his head and groaned.

I leaned back against the wall. It was either that or fall forward on my nose. "Grant?"

In the shifting beams of light, he looked as if he was struggling to control the pain—or his temper. I guess he lost both fights. He staggered two steps toward me, then put his hands on his hips, maybe so he wouldn't put them around my neck. He started to curse, in heaven knew what language that had a lot of *cht*'s. Unfortunately for me, he switched to English. "Who the devil were you expecting? And why didn't you answer the phone? I called your cell, the house phone, and the housekeeper's number. My agents said you came in, alone, and never left. Then you didn't pick up, not even on the phone you were supposed to have next to you every minute, the one with the panic button. Then the lights went off. What the hell was I to think?"

"I . . . I was in the bath. Listening to music. And the Jacuzzi made noise."

"Yeah, I got that idea." His gaze drifted down the long terry robe to the puddles under my feet.

My heart was beginning to sink from my throat back to my chest. "What are you doing here? I thought you were going to Georgia or Florida or wherever?"

"The airports shut down because of the surprise storm. And you sounded so anxious I decided to spend the night here and fly out in the morning. I rented a car and drove through a bloody near hurricane to get here." His voice rose. "For you, lady. For you! What do I get for it? Two years off my life and a freaking concussion!"

Colin handed him a wet towel from the sink in the bathroom I was using. Grant held it to the side of his head.

"I'm sorry?"

"Yeah. Me, too. I shouldn't have bothered."

"No, you shouldn't have." I turned to Colin and Kenneth. "Thank you for coming to my rescue."

"The sight was worth it, ma'am," the redheaded Colin said.

"Of Grant on the floor?"

"That, too."

Colin winked, and I realized I'd never belted the robe. Oh, my God. At least it was dark and he was gentleman enough to keep his flashlight directed on Grant, where Kenneth was checking him for damage. I started to say, "Aren't you supposed to be gay?" But changed it in time to "Aren't you supposed to be clairvoyant or something? Couldn't you have predicted I was all right?"

"That's Kenneth's specialty."

The younger man said, "And I did tell the boss he wasn't using his head, rushing in here like that." He smiled. "I guess he took my warning to heart and used his head after all."

I pulled the robe tighter and put a knot in the belt.

Grant noticed and dragged his own eyes away from what I'd belatedly covered and growled at his men. "Are you done laughing, or are you going to reset the alarm system today, or wait until someone does manage to break in? Who knows, maybe Miss Tate will do the moke a favor and leave the door open next time."

Kenneth and Colin left, leaving one flashlight behind.

I was almost breathing normally again, or as normally as I ever did, near Grant. He smelled of wet clothes, spicy cologne, and a little sweat, which is to say, virile male animal.

An angry male animal, wounded and unpredictable. I kept my distance. "Are you badly hurt?"

"My pride or my skull?"

I guess he was okay if he could curse in three more languages when he saw blood on the towel. It wasn't a *lot* of blood.

He didn't seem to want my help. He glared at me when I took a step in his direction, as if he figured I'd hit him again, so I picked up the pieces of pitcher before I stepped on them in the dark. Maybe I could glue it together. I sure as hell couldn't afford to commission another one. Who needed a vase to match their towels, anyway?

The lights came back on, thank goodness. I was still seeing spooks in the shadows. "The poor dogs must be frantic." Even if I couldn't hear them barking anymore, they were still a good excuse to get out of Grant's way.

"You go. I'll wash up in the bathroom here."

"Are you trying to make me feel guilty?"

"A little pity wouldn't hurt."

"I said I was sorry."

"And I suppose I am sorry I yelled. Not that I wouldn't yell again if you pull another harebrained trick like disappearing off the radar."

Since he was already shouting, I went downstairs, barefoot, in the borrowed robe. The dogs were fine. One of the agents had tossed them rawhide chews, and they were busy gnawing. I filled the coffeemaker and started it.

Grant came down, his black hair wet and smoothed down.

"Are you okay?"

"No permanent damage," he said, that steely look gone from his blue eyes. "Everyone always said I was a hardheaded s.o.b. I guess I should be glad."

"I'm glad, too." I couldn't help myself. I ran right into his arms. "I was so scared."

"I know, sweetheart. I'm so sorry. That's why I was angry. I wanted to make you feel safe; instead I terrorized you."

Suddenly I was crying, like I hardly ever cried, great sobbing gulps and runny-eyed tears. It was all too much. The fear, the aloneness, the incomprehensible situation, the guilt. "I am not a crybaby," I cried, wetting his blue shirt worse.

"I know, Willy. You are the bravest woman I ever met."

"Me? I thought I was going to have heart failure in the dark. Even before I heard voices. The storm already had me frazzled, and the driving and the lightning and—"

"Shush," he soothed, pulling me closer. "You fought back. With good aim, too. That took real courage."

I had to admit that my eyes were closed when I threw the pitcher.

"Then maybe you have telekinetic powers, too."

Maybe I did. I could feel something stirring at the front of his jeans, where he was pressed against me. I did that! I moved my hips forward, and he moaned. I definitely had a stirring effect on him, and I liked it, too. Oh, boy, did I. My own temperature was rising—or was that from the steam he was giving off?

Meanwhile he was stroking my back, smoothing my hair, rubbing my neck. "You smell like roses."

"And fear."

"No, just roses. Lovely."

I sniffled. He put his hand down, almost between us, and I thought— He found a handkerchief instead.

I blew my nose and turned my back, knowing I must look horrible, all red and swollen. Grant kissed the back of my neck, under my hair.

"You always look beautiful to me."

"Are you sure you can't read my mind?"

"Would I have raced in here if I knew you were lolling about in a bubble bath, naked and warm and sweet smelling? Hmm. Damn right I would have. But you'll have to tell me what you want. Should I go to the guest-house? Sleep on the sofa?"

He kissed me instead of waiting for an answer. Swaying the vote? I was swaying, leaning into him, rocking with the tempo of his tongue dancing with mine. Was I dreaming? Hell, was I breathing?

When he pulled back, he was breathing heavily, too. He raised one expressive eyebrow in question.

I took his hand. "Here. Now."

I led him toward the bedroom of the housekeeper's apartment, shutting the door behind us so the dogs couldn't see. I turned on the reading lamp next to the bed, but then I hesitated. "I'm not easy, you know."

"That's all right," he said. "I'm hard, too."

CHAPTER 24

HIS HANDS WERE ON THE belt of the borrowed robe, untying it. He swallowed audibly, then smiled when his view rose from the unwieldy knot that now let the robe fall open. I didn't have time to be embarrassed or modest or insecure. Not when his hands followed his line of sight. I swear he could hear my heart beating when he raised one finger to the tip of one nipple. "Yup, you're hard, sweetheart. Hard as nails, and soft as silk." Now his whole hand cupped my breast. "You are perfect."

After that, I stopped thinking. For once, I was there, in the moment, mind and body working together. I didn't have to wonder if my partner was happy, if my reactions were encouraging enough, if I'd come, or if he'd care. That was not an issue.

Grant cared, and I almost climaxed the minute he carefully unfolded the robe off my shoulders and touched his lips to my breasts, each in turn.

Maybe he was a mind reader, no matter what he said, because he knew just what I liked, and when. He definitely had magic in his strong, capable hands, hands that touched me everywhere, as if he was learning me, playing me, worshiping me. And he liked what I was doing with my tongue, my teeth, my exploring hands. He urged me on with murmurs of appreciation, sweet words I'd think about later.

No thinking was allowed here, only feeling. I felt . . . I felt like I was soaring, rising on a wind of passion aiming for the roof of the world. Rising, rising, his fingers gently inside me, his thumb stroking, his mouth on my breasts, his erection hot on my thigh— When had he taken off his clothes?

Rising, his mouth moving to my lips, his hands still busy. Rising, until there was no place to go, but going anyway. Rising until I was desperate to reach . . . to reach . . .

Yes! Oh, yes. I touched the top of the sky, and it was beautiful.

Grant thanked me.

"You are grateful to me? You . . . " I had no words to describe what I felt, no energy to give him back what he'd given me. I'd used all my adrenaline and emotions during the afternoon, and all my hormones just now. I was limp, wrung out, empty. But then Grant started to trail kisses from my eyelids to my mouth to my neck, tiny kisses and a lick here or there, a nibble, a taste, on my breasts, my nipples, that ticklish spot over the side of my ribs.

I could see where this was going—where I hoped it was going anyway—and dredged up enough resources to show signs of life, like grabbing his shoulders with my fingers and calling his name.

"I am right here, sweetheart. I'm not going anywhere."

But I was, flying again, when his tongue touched my navel, my thighs. I thought, *Hey, you missed somewhere!* But he was teasing, playing with the curls there, and touching and spreading those inner lips. And breathing warmth on me before touching with the tip of his tongue.

Oh, God.

That's what he was, a god from another time, another place, with wondrous powers. I tried to tell him, with what was left of my ensorcelled mind.

He laughed. "I'm just a linguist."

I found another language his tongue was fluent in.

Then I claimed my turn. I tried to touch him, but Grant pulled away.

"No, I couldn't last a minute that way. Hell, it's all I can do not to embarrass myself now like a schoolboy. I want to feel you, all of you, and have you feel me completely."

He was off the bed and searching for his jeans and cursing. We must have kicked them under the bed or something. I still wasn't certain the whole thing wasn't a disjointed dream or a trance because I couldn't remember getting to the bed at all, that's how moonstruck I'd been.

I told him to stop looking, that I had protection. I'd put the sample packet from the drugstore in the night table drawer.

"Two?" He laughed. "Baby, that won't last long. I've been waiting since the minute I saw you. No, since I knew you existed."

While he was discreetly turned, I admired his broad back and sculpted muscles that tapered to a firm ass with the tiniest shadow of dark fuzz on it. Then I admired his impressive erection when he faced me again. "Definitely a super power. Or a magician's wand."

"You're the Enhancer here, Willy, only you hold the magic to do this to me."

I didn't care if he said the same thing to all his women. Or how many women he said it to. He was mine today, tonight, and until he had to leave tomorrow. All mine, all of him. All of me.

I doubted I could be ready again, but it didn't matter. I decided this was for him, but he refused to travel solo, waiting for me to catch up. His strokes were long and smooth, with no chance of hitting my head on the bed frame, not when my legs were locked around his waist. Every internal muscle was working, too, to hold him, to keep him, to rock with him.

He reached between us to touch my most sensitive spot. So I reached behind him to cup his sac.

"Ah, and I was trying to last."

Sure, like a race car can go slow. That's not what it's built for. I flexed those inside muscles again and he went deeper, no words now, no gentle, tender, teasing strokes, only power and friction, at just the right tempo. I could feel the pressure building again—had it ever subsided?—and knew I was close to coming again.

This time I wanted him with me. I bit his shoulder.

He ended in a rush, a spasm, a pounding frenzy that sent us both over the edge and nearly off the bed. This was what sex was really about? Why hadn't anyone told me it could be this good, this fulfilling, this absolutely rapturous? I'd never have settled for less if I'd known what I was missing.

Then I developed a new fear, not that I needed another. What if the great sex wasn't because the man had great technique, a well-practiced talent, and a lot of patience? What if it wasn't the sex but the sexual partner? I worried I'd never find this grand passion again. I missed it already, and Grant was still inside me.

"A tear, macushla? Are you sorry for what we did?"

"I am sorry we cannot do it forever."

"Who says?" And he started to stir again. Again? I didn't think I had the strength. He rolled onto his side, facing me, touching me, still filling me. His caress was like a gossamer touch on my sensitized skin; as if he knew more pressure would be more pain than pleasure. This was lovely. He was lovely. I told him and he laughed, which was loveliest of all. I raised my leg over his, bringing us closer. And we kissed until I was filled with his breath, his strength, his passion, his heat and rapture, too.

Did people die of too much lovemaking? If so, okay. I'd lived a full life, after this. When he got up to use the bathroom, I rolled onto my stomach, arms and legs spread across the mattress. Every cell in my body had declared surrender and refused to fight another second to stay alive, or awake. I could smother in the pillow for all I cared, without the energy to lift my head. My brain wasn't talking to me anymore, my blood had surely boiled over, and my bones had turned to mush. Maybe I was dead already. I hoped someone threw a sheet over me before calling 911.

Grant came back with a towel for me. "Go away," I think I mumbled.

His deep laugh sounded next to my ear. "Never, sweetheart." Then he started to pet my rear end and the back of my thighs, molding the planes, firming the skin in his hands. "The most perfect butt in the universe."

My ass was too big; the muscles not toned enough no matter how much I jogged. I huffed.

"True. I don't lie, remember. You are exquisite, from the tips of your toes"—somehow he had one of my toes in his mouth; I never felt him shift—"to the top of your gorgeous curls." His hand fingered through my hair, combing it smooth.

"Flattery won't get you anywhere, buddy," I said into the pillow. "I am brain-dead at the least. Kiss me good-bye when you leave in the morning."

He laughed again. "The morning is hours away. You don't really want to waste them in sleep, do you?"

His hand was following the curve of my spine, up my neck, down my tailbone, then reaching lower, between my spread legs.

"Go away," I repeated, trying to put some conviction into my voice.

"I'll let you be on top."

"I'd fall off and land on the floor."

"I'd hold you tight."

"Not good enough."

Now he bent over me, nipping love bites on my tush, then my thighs. I moaned.

"How about if you stayed just like this and I did all the work?" His fingers were reaching beneath me.

"That's necrophilia. Are you into kinky?"

"I am into you."

With my last ounce of life, I drew my legs together and pulled the pillow over my head. "If you have so much energy, go take the dogs out. They can use the exercise."

"You are a hard woman to please, Willow Tate."

"No, I was too easy to please. You obviously didn't expend enough effort on it if you have this much in reserve."

God, I loved his laughter. Even in my comatose state, my heart warmed at the sound.

"Are you complaining?" he asked. "I thought I'd done a fine job. Those groans and whimpers sounded authentic, but maybe you were pretending. I could try harder next time."

"Don't beg, Agent Grant. It's beneath your image."

"Damn, all I want is you beneath me again. I'd beg on my knees if I thought it would work. Watching you come has to be the most satisfying, most stimulating sexual experience of my life. You think I could just roll over and go to sleep?"

"Alvin always did."

"I thought his name was Arlen."

"Him, too."

"I know what you need, and that's food. I do, too. I can't remember when I ate last. I think I grabbed a croissant at the airport while I waited for the rental car."

I had a sandwich for lunch, but I had no idea how long ago that was. Two days, at least. I needed sleep more. "I stopped at the grocery store. There's a box of macaroni and cheese next to the stove."

"That's what you were going to have for dinner? No wonder you have no stamina. As soon as I get back we'll start you on a proper regimen. Healthy food and good aerobic exercise like sex."

I rolled over to look up at him. "You are coming back, aren't you? I mean, what if someone identifies your bad guy and you go arrest him?"

"I'm hoping it's that easy, but I doubt it will be. But, sweetheart, I'd come back if there was no missing boy, no misplaced troll. I waited my whole life for you, it feels like. Do you think I'd just walk away?"

Everyone knew a man said anything before, during, or after sex. Or when he hoped for more of it. I let his almost-promise pass. I tried to memorize it, though, for tomorrow. "He saved my life, you know."

He was bent over, fishing his jeans out from under the bed. He bumped his head on the mattress frame and winced. I'd forgotten completely about his injured skull.

I know I had my hands wrapped around his head at one point. "Does your head hurt?"

"Who saved your life?"

I don't know how Grant managed to look and sound like a man in black when he was naked, but he did.

"And when?"

"Fafhrd did, this afternoon, in the storm."

"You saw the troll again? And didn't tell me?"

"You didn't exactly give me a chance to say anything, did you?"

Grant zipped his jeans—no boxers or jockeys beneath them. I made a mental note to check under the bed later, before the cleaning crew came in tomorrow, just in case. Then I watched as he smoothed out his blue chambray shirt and put it on. He left it unbuttoned, which gave me a great view of his flat abdomen and the dark line of chest hair that arrowed toward the low waist of his pants. Maybe I had a smidge of stamina left after all.

Grant was all business. "What did he do? Did he communicate with you?"

So I told him how Fafhrd held up a falling tree so my car could get by safely. And how he nodded to me before dropping it afterward. "He had to have been waiting there, looking out for me. I wasn't thinking about him at all, only about getting back here in one piece. I never drew him with an oak tree in his hands, so I didn't call him up. He came on his own, to protect me."

"I don't like it."

I repeated, slowly: "He saved my life."

"He's not human. Who knows what he's thinking, what he wants from you. Bloody hell, he could be a deranged stalker for all we know."

"I know he would never hurt me. Don't ask how I know, but I do. He's young and playful, and sweet."

"Sweet? He's got to be stronger than an elephant and stupider than a stone if half the stories are true. And mean."

"Fafhrd is not mean. Maybe some trolls are, or maybe they just got a bad rap. He held up a tree for me, for crying out loud. How could that be mean?" I didn't mention the electric wires Fafhrd ignored. That might have been stupid, but how was a troll to know?

"He's never stopped to introduce himself, to explain what he's doing here, why he picked you, has he? You cannot trust him. And do not go getting attached to him like you're getting attached to your mother's dogs. You cannot keep a troll, Willy, no matter if no one else can see him."

"I don't want to 'keep' him like a lost puppy. I want to help him get home. The old ET bit. I owe him that help." I pushed hair out of my eyes to get a better look at Grant, who was scowling and stomping his feet into his shoes. His socks had to be somewhere else, too. The cleaning ladies would have a field day.

"And I don't see what has you so pissed off about it, other than you're jealous I can see him and you can't."

"It's not that."

"Then what?"

"I'm jealous, all right, damn it. Jealous that some vanishing myth got to save you. That's my job."

"That's dumb."

"So is being jealous of an invisible troll that you like better than me."

So then I had to show him that I didn't really like Fafhrd better. Grant's blue jeans landed on the ceiling fan this time.

CHAPTER 25

I THINK I FINALLY EXHAUSTED HIM. He was all spread-eagled and limp on the bed beneath me, with a big grin on his handsome face. Yippee-ki-ay.

He was right about pleasure begetting pleasure, too, because bringing him to the peak, then sending him over, was just about the best aphrodisiac I'd ever known. And the most reinvigorating. I kissed him on the lips, just to see what he would do, but my stomach growled. I was starving. We both needed sustenance if this evening was any indication of the long night ahead.

Before I could get up, though, he reached for the necklace that was dangling almost in front of his eyes. He studied the intricate design on the front, and the diamond pendant, then asked where I got it.

"It was my mother's wedding ring, from my father. The diamond was from her engagement ring."

"It's a lot older than that."

"That's what Mom said, too. An antique or something."

"The design is ancient, not just antique." Grant was trying to read the inscription on the other side, pulling

the chain, and me, toward the bedside lamp. "Do you
have a magnifying lens?"

"That won't help," I told him. "My mother had it to
a jeweler who couldn't decipher the words, either. We
think it's been handed down from bride to bride for so
many generations that the engraving has worn off. I'm
surprised the gold didn't get so thin that the ring broke."

"If I'm right, there's more than gold holding it together. We need to show it to Colin. He can see things
no one else can."

"Like elves and fairies?"

"No, like words that have been erased, or parchments
so faded no one else can read them."

"Can he translate them?"

"No, but he can copy them out, and I or another agent
can see if we can interpret the writing."

"There are more of you?"

He smiled, showing a dimple. "None as good. Remember that."

"What about your father? The library had one of his
books."

"I learned from him, but he had to quit his studies
early because of other responsibilities. I kept on, and
keep up with every new advance. New technologies my
father never had make it easier."

He did not question how I knew about the book, as if
he accepted that I'd gone snooping. I wish I had. I never
did get a chance to check the Internet for Grant's background and, now, the idea of putting Grant's name in a
Google search felt somehow disloyal. We were lovers,
not adversaries.

I knew that was just naive. Everyone checked out
everyone else, usually before they became intimate, not
after. Then again, I doubted the Department of Unex-

plained Events let their agents' real bios show up for public viewing. DUE was so secretive, so private, I'd bet they blocked access to most of their records. I'd look tomorrow. I knew enough for tonight. And macaroni and cheese was sounding better.

"There's ice cream, too."

"Ah, another food group." He set the necklace back against my breastbone, then let his fingers rove lower. One of his eyebrows raised in silent query.

I shook my head. My stomach was growling, I needed to pee, and I wanted to check the dogs. I rolled off him and headed to the bathroom, without bothering with the terry robe, on purpose. Teasing felt good, now that I had no reason to feel self-conscious. The man had looked at, touched, and licked every inch of my body already. He seemed to like it, very well, so what was the point of modesty?

He wasn't looking. With his hands behind his head, he was staring at the ceiling. "You know, you could make a drawing of the front design, then enlarge it. Maybe your rocky pal could recognize it and start to communicate back. We need to know what he's doing, and why."

I'd already thought of that, but without the words, I couldn't see where it would make much difference. "I've been trying not to think of him, not draw him. I haven't worked on my book at all. I figured he'd stay away if my mind didn't somehow reach for him, but that's not working. Fafhrd's way more independent from my thoughts than I feared at first. That's good, isn't it? I mean, now I can go back to work, without worrying I'm conjuring up a monster."

He thought about that. "I think it means he's more comfortable here, used to coming and going so he can do it by himself. Or maybe Nicky is calling him too, getting closer. I'd still like you to try establishing a way to communicate. So you do what feels right to you. Trust your instincts, but be careful."

"I know, no elves or fairies."

"And no fauns."

I came back and sat on the bed next to him, playing with the dark curls on his chest. "What have you got against baby deer?"

"No, f-a-u-n-s. Hairy interbreeds, you know, cloven hooves, horns on their heads, and horny as hell."

"And you're not?" I looked, but he had the sheets and blankets in his lap.

"Not right now, thanks to you. Later? Only for you. I don't want anyone else sniffing around you."

"So you're not worried about Fafhrd in my story?"

"I don't like your being involved at all because of the danger, but my contacts say that things are coming closer to a climax. Not this week, but after that. I'll be back in time."

"How did they reach that conclusion? Grandma's tea leaves?"

"Crystal balls are just as effective. Checking sunspots for energy fluxes, watching which way butterflies migrate, how many infants are born left-handed. Lots of ways."

I couldn't tell if he was kidding or not. I still didn't believe half of what he said, except the parts I wanted to, like how he'd come back.

The phone rang before I could ask any more questions.

Grant waited until I said it was Susan, then headed for the shower while I talked. Or listened.

It seemed Uncle Bernie had decided to close the restaurant with the power flickering and the streets so treacherous. He'd leave two waiters to serve coffee and sandwiches to the road crews by the low light of the auxiliary generator as long as they could, but no paying customers were getting past the roadblocks. Uncle Bernie didn't want to serve anyone stupid enough to try.

Unfortunately, they had a lot of half-cooked food Susan refused to save and serve tomorrow, especially with the power so uncertain and the freezer full. Besides, Uncle Bernie and Grandma Eve and Lou were worried about me alone out at Rosehill. They'd gone to the Breakaway for dinner, before the lights went out, she and Lou.

"I'm not alone. Grant is here."

"Oh." I heard her speak to someone in the background. "Grandma wants to come anyway."

Of course she did. With Grant here, Grandma was more certain than ever that I needed a decent meal. And Rosehill had a generator; Garland Farms did not. They could get here in half an hour. "Okay?"

No. But I said, "Sure. I'll invite the guys at the guest-house, too. I don't know if they have any power back to cook by. But how are you going to get here if the roads are closed? I missed a falling tree by inches on my way back this afternoon."

"We'll go around them. Grandma still has that old Jeep that can manage anything. I have a lobster dish and stuffed flounder. And a vegetable gratin for Grandma."

"Perfect."

"She says she really wants to talk to Grant."

Maybe not so perfect. I lowered my voice, even though I could hear water running in the bathroom. "You keep her away from him. I don't want her interfering."

"In what?"

"In it's none of your business either."

"That good, huh?"
"Better."

Grant took the dogs out while I had a quick shower. I should have told Susan to wait an hour. We could have shared that Jacuzzi. Now I had to scramble just to tie my wet hair back, find clean clothes the dogs hadn't played with or slept on, and set the table.

I didn't feel comfortable seating my guests in the huge chrome-and-glass dining room with the crystal stemware on display in lighted cabinets, and porcelain plates with pedigrees longer than mine.

I did find nice, everyday dishes in the pantry along with tablecloths, paper napkins and glasses I wouldn't be afraid of dropping. The kitchen table was large enough, if I moved my laptop and the portable printer I'd brought with me.

The guys from the guest cottage brought a bottle of wine and extra flashlights for me, just in case.

The restaurant group arrived, along with Uncle Bernie's much younger second wife, Ginnie, who acted as hostess for the restaurant. She wanted to meet Grant, too, once Susan described him. I gave her a dirty look, to stop her drooling.

It seemed half the people there knew his father, or each other, or had mutual acquaintances. Susan, who had spent one summer at the Royce Institute, asked about some of her instructors and advisers. Even Ginnie had gone to college in England for one year. Gossip was she'd flunked out for partying, but she and Kenneth thought they attended one or two of the same courses.

I was the only outsider, and I spent more time talking to the dogs than to my company.

While Susan heated up her leftovers in Rosehill's huge commercial ovens, Grant asked about the roads.

According to Grandma and Uncle Bernie, the damage was terrible. Everyone with a chain saw would be out tomorrow gathering firewood for the winter. They saw a few deep puddles, but no washouts. There would be beach erosion, and heaven knew how long power would be out on some of the private streets or to individual houses.

No one mentioned a fried figment of my imagination. They went back to asking about former friends. Grant kept giving me smiles of reassurance that did not do the job while he answered questions. I kept the poodles by my chair, feeding them crumbs so they'd stay with me.

Susan's cooking was extraordinary, of course, making my offer of macaroni and cheese—from a box, no less—look slapdash, lazy, and incompetent. The lobster was mixed with asparagus and peas, and the flounder was stuffed with crabmeat. Everything had been caught, cleaned, or harvested within twenty-four hours. I'd forgotten how different real food tasted and almost started to enjoy myself until Grandma noticed the razor burn on my cheek.

"I bumped into the door when the lights went out. It's an unfamiliar house, you know."

"You should have had the candles and flashlights ready once you knew how bad the storm was. You'd been warned. In fact, you should have left your mother's house much sooner."

I should have been in New York City, where I felt like a capable, intelligent adult most times. I'd been warned by a guy who pumped gas. And how could I have left

Little Red any sooner? I felt horrible about leaving him alone now. "No one said anything about such a major storm. Not even on the radio."

"It was localized."

I asked Uncle Bernie about business, trying to be part of my own party. Ginnie didn't want to discuss the restaurant; she wanted to hear all about Grant's work, as much as he could tell her.

He talked about linguistics. I doubt she understood one word, but I think she got the message when Grant turned to Susan and asked about her parents.

They'd stayed in Stony Brook, rather than drive out in the storm. Her father was better, although not entirely cured. Grandma added that Cousin Lily had called to report that her pregnant daughter was doing fine, that Lily was enjoying her spoiled grandchild more than Parker's spoiled dogs.

For dessert, I pulled out my ice cream. Grandma had made incredible strawberry topping from blemished fruit. Lou looked orgasmic, and Kenneth and Colin swore they'd never go back to their cottage until it was all gone. Ginnie declared herself on too much of a diet to eat any. Good. That left more for the rest of us.

Grandma finished her bowl and said, "Speaking of spoiled, your mother would not approve of feeding dogs at the table."

Or the wink Grant gave me. Or my wishing everyone would leave so I could take him back to bed. Maybe with some of the strawberry topping if the DUE men left any.

Over coffee and tea—Grandma brought her own; I had coffee—talk turned to Nicky Ryland. Again, no one mentioned Fafhrd, but everyone was concerned about the boy. He was one of theirs, almost kin, and an important prodigy. They speculated on why he was kidnapped five years ago, but not how the people at Royce suspected he was back in the country.

While they tossed implausible theories around, I wondered how I could have lived my entire life without realizing these people were so extraordinarily different. I always thought it was the small-town atmosphere that made them odd. Boy, was I wrong.

They all promised to work harder spreading the word and gathering information about the missing child.

Grant asked me to take off the necklace, and everyone passed it around. When it got to Colin, I watched carefully to see what he was doing. He pulled a lamp closer, then got his high-power flashlight and studied the back of the pendant. Then he closed his eyes, as if seeing in his head what his eyes had seen, or magnifying it like some psychic Photoshop.

I put paper and pencil beside him. He squeezed his eyes tight, then opened them and started writing, but not in any alphabet I'd ever seen. He told us he could not get the last section at all.

We looked at the page on its way toward Grant. He turned it upside down. "Ah."

"Ah, what?"

"Ah, it's a love message."

"Of course it is," my grandmother snapped. "That is a wedding ring."

"In what language?" I wanted to know.

Grant wasn't committing himself. "An old one."

Grandma shared a look with Lou, who nodded.

"Can you read it?" Ginnie asked, gazing far too adoringly at Grant for a married woman.

Uncle Bernie patted her hand. "Of course he can. He's a pro."

Grant shook his head. "I can only guess. The symbol for one is repeated. Twice, maybe three times. One—"

"Love, it has to be," Susan said. She looked over at Kenneth. I'd have to set her straight about that later.

Meantime I asked Grant, "Are they all symbols, or can you say the words?"

"They are not really meant to be spoken out loud, I think."

Grandma thought that was for the best. "You never know what else is embedded in an oath like that."

Lou agreed. They both understood it was the language of Unity, filled with magic and meant to be received telepathically. "Yeah, boss. You might end up in love with the dog."

Damn, I never imagined half the stuff everyone else took for granted.

CHAPTER 26

A FTER THE RELATIVES LEFT, we walked the dogs back to the gatehouse with Colin and Kenneth. Grant walked ahead with Colin, with a flashlight in case the lights went out. The men spoke too quietly for me to hear, but I knew Grant was giving instructions.

When we got back, he helped me clean up. How could you help liking a guy like that, a great lover who loaded the dishwasher? Now that's my idea of a real hero.

I thought he'd be in a hurry to go back to bed, but he went toward the brightest light in the housekeeper's living room with Colin's drawing of the necklace inscription. I spent the time playing with the dogs, explaining that they could not share my bed, not tonight.

I was really tired, and I knew Grant must be, too, but I was looking forward to a little cuddling, a little nestling, and sleeping wrapped in those strong arms. No bad storms or bad dreams could touch me there, I thought. After a little rest, maybe neither of us would mind another serving of dessert. I did not mean ice cream, either.

Before then, I wanted to know what my grandmother said when she took him aside as she was leaving. I'd done my best to keep them apart during dinner, but I'd been busy packing up Susan's pots and platters to go back to the restaurant. The old woman pounced, like a spider waiting near its web, and dragged Grant off to the little outside deck. She wasn't reading his tea leaves, I'd bet, and he was so damned closemouthed, I'd have to pry the information out of him with a crowbar. Or with a sexy negligee.

Unfortunately, I hadn't brought many clothes with me, not when I had to carry my laptop, camera, portable printer, and notebooks. I packed a couple of pairs of slacks, shorts, a bunch of T-shirts and jeans, one dressy dress just in case, a hoodie for cool days, and some comfortable exercise pants to sleep in. There wasn't a fuck-me outfit in the bunch.

At home I usually slept in sweats, or cotton shorts and a tee, stuff that was comfortable, wouldn't strangle me during a restless night, and I could answer the door in when Mrs. Abbottini knocked. My friend Sherrie once gave me a sheer black slip thingy, trimmed with black feathers. To spice up my love life, she said, while she was between husbands. Arlen got a feather up his nose and started wheezing. I think the nightie was in with my craft supplies, for if I ever needed the feathers.

I thought of looking in Cousin Lily's closet, but she was about three inches shorter than me, at least fifty pounds heavier, and thirty years older. Whatever she considered sexy wasn't going to work for Grant. Besides poking in her drawers being immoral, I really had no desire to see what my mother's widowed cousin slept in.

So I washed my face, brushed my hair out, and turned off all but one lamp in the bedroom. I called out a good night, then climbed under the covers in the best suit I had. Who knew how long he'd be gone? I wanted this night to last, in time, in memory.

I guess Grant had enough memories already, because I'd almost fallen asleep when he finally came into the bedroom.

He sat down beside me, but on top of the covers, with everything except his shoes still on. Maybe I'd been too impetuous, too hasty. Maybe he needed longer to recoup. Maybe I could keep the sheet wrapped around me so he wouldn't know I had hot expectations. Sex wasn't the only thing I was interested in, after all.

He was not thinking of sex. Before I could ask what my grandmother said, and how embarrassing it was, he told me, "I think I have the beginning of the ring's inscription."

He seemed pleased, so I asked, "Can you say it without becoming trapped by some old witch's love spell?"

He kissed my nose, then my eyes and my forehead. "You are bewitching enough without any extra enchantments."

I felt so warm I almost tossed the covers aside. "Tell me."

"I am fairly certain it starts: 'One life. One heart.'"

"That's beautiful. Especially if it's a marriage vow. What else do you think it says?"

"Maybe another symbol for One, and something else Colin could not pick up. I've spent the last half hour trying to decipher what Colin drew."

"Maybe Susan was right and it's 'One Love.' 'One Life, One Heart, One Love.' That makes sense, doesn't it? It would be perfect."

"That would be my guess, too, but there's no knowing if the words together mean something else. We know so little about the eldritch tongue, except that what's written does not show the whole meaning."

"Maybe the words really do have a binding spell to

go with them, because look at my mother. She flew to
Florida to be with the man she divorced years ago."

"Perhaps she's just a good woman."

I thought about that. "Nope. She's still so mad at him
for his supposed infidelities that only powerful magic
could get her to leave her own life to go take care of
him. And there's nothing one-ish about them. Different
personalities, different lifestyles, different ideas about
everything, right down to their politics."

He laughed and reached for the pendant around my
neck. "I doubt either of them knew what the ring means,
or how to say the words. If they never said them, I doubt
the vow could be binding. It's not as if the ring was made
for your mother. It must have been handed down for
centuries. In England, according to your grandmother."

So maybe that's what they discussed, not my single
state.

"Either way, Mom said, 'I do,' and that was enough
for her. And she never lets a creature in need go without
attention."

"I'd bet she still loves him, too. In some small, hidden
away niche at the back of her mind. Maybe she doesn't
realize it."

"I was wondering about that myself, but I made myself stop thinking about it. I gave up hoping they'd get
back together when Dad moved to another state altogether. What about your family? Are your parents happily married?"

"As content as two clams, after over forty years. Of
course they are both so busy with committees and foun-
dations and such that half the time they lead almost separate lives, but they have a lot to speak about when they
are together, which is as often as possible."

That sounded even better to me than the ring's pretty,

poetic message. Two people who could still retain their identities and interests. Two hearts, two lives, without losing themselves. Of course, I've never been in love, not like that, wanting to crawl into the other person's soul and take up residence there. Maybe . . .

Nah. I pulled the pendant back and took Grant's hand in mine. That was close enough, for now. "Can you say the words for me? If some of the inscription is missing, you cannot cause any rift in the cosmic flow. Or get trapped into marriage, with a bearded wizard holding the shotgun."

He brought my hand to his lips and kissed the knuckles, then each finger. "The words are not meant to be spoken aloud. In fact, they are not actually words, but intricate symbols. Their meaning varies by context, according to my research and my father's before me. It's possible Unity has different semantic systems for written and spoken languages. Like the Egyptians, who did not speak in hieroglyphics, but had another language for talking. Our distant ancestors had far more ways to communicate, through their minds."

"Then think it. Maybe Fafhrd can understand if I try to project my thoughts. He'll know that I am trying to communicate, and he'll see that I mean him no harm by such a tender expression. I doubt he'll take it as a proposal of marriage, just an offer of friendship."

Grant lay down next to me, still on top of the covers, but pulled me close, so my head rested on his shoulder. His other arm touched the necklace at my throat. "Close your eyes, stop thinking of anything else, and see if you can hear what I don't say aloud."

A minute went by while I tried to clear my head and open my mind. I heard his breathing. I heard him . . . snoring.

Maybe he wasn't such a hero after all.

*   *   *

He got up while it was still dark and we made love before he left. Or maybe I just dreamed the last part. Either way, he was gone when I woke up and I felt good. A little sore and stretched, but totally satiated. I rolled over and went back to sleep until I heard the dogs barking.

The dogs! Damn, how could I have forgotten my responsibilities? My mother'd kill me! I scrambled out of bed, found some clothes, and ran to free them from their crates and put them out. I followed with a scoop, in my chewed-up sneakers, lest my feet find what they left before my bleary eyes did.

Back inside, I put the coffeemaker on before I went to brush my teeth. More alert, I noticed the fancy LED flashlight Grant had left for me on his pillow. More useful than a rose, I suppose.

In the kitchen, I found that he'd twisted one of the dish towels into a crane shape, like origami, and put it next to my usual seat at the table. Who needed a rose? My guy had talent and imagination. Of course now I'd have to buy a new towel for the house; I'd never part with this one.

Also, of course, I had to stop thinking of Grant as my anything except my last night's lover. By the time he got back, he could have a new woman, a new case, a new doohickey to translate. If he came back. A flashlight and a bird towel were fine. Where was the note promising he'd miss me, he'd count the hours until he returned, he'd be thinking of me night and day? In a romance novel, that's where. That love note sure as hell wasn't anywhere in the kitchen or the housekeeper's apartment, because I spent a half hour looking.

The day was too nice for such depressing, self-defeating, and downright stupid thoughts. I was a mature woman, not an empty-headed adolescent with a crush, for Pete's sake. I never believed I could try to emulate my cousin Susan, so casual about sex and men, but I swore to put Grant and tomorrow out of my mind and enjoy today.

It was a perfect June day, clear with blue skies and a tiny breeze. Baseball weather, kite-flying weather, a walk on the beach weather. No one should have to work inside on a glorious day like this, especially me. So I declared a well day.

I felt guilty about leaving Ben and Jerry alone again, but I had to spend some time with Little Red at my mother's house, and I wanted to pump my grandmother about last night, too.

Not that Eve Garland ever told me anything I wanted to hear. Maybe I should let her read my tea leaves again. I hadn't in years, but now the future had so many questions I might get better answers. At least she couldn't say I was destined to go to Roycc Institute, not when I was this many years past college age.

Which reminded me that I ought to offer to help at the farm until those college kids got here. Maybe she'd part with some of those fresh asparagus spears in return.

Grandma's old Jeep was gone, though, and I didn't see anyone I knew in the closest fields, so I drove on toward Mom's house. Red was yipping when he heard the car pull up in front.

I guess the little dog's chickpea-sized brain wasn't big enough to remember we were friends, because he tried to snap at my feet when I got inside. Or maybe that was his odd way of showing affection. I mean, Grant had nibbled on my toes, too

I picked Red up and had yesterday's conversation about who was top dog, and I guess something registered. He gave me a lick and a tail wag, and I fed him his morning munchies, then put him on a leash to go see if Grandma'd come home.

We went past the dog run where Mom's two latest rescues were napping in the sun. Red's ruff stood up when he saw the fat old shepherd mix and the older, arthritic retriever. His legs went stiff and his bark grew deeper and louder. The old dogs barely looked his way. One gave a thump of his tail on the ground and went back to sleep; the other watched me to see if I had a treat—dammit, I should have remembered to bring them biscuits—then rolled over.

Red kept yapping. I picked him up before he exhausted himself, and had another conversation with the fleabrain.

"Okay, you don't like them. You've made that clear. How come? They're too common for such a thorough-bred like you? They get more food at chow time? Mom loves them better? Hell, she loves them better than me, too."

Red settled down the farther we got from the dog run, so I put him on the ground again and kept talking. No one was watching, so I didn't feel as crazy as I must have looked, talking to a belligerent ball of fluff. "What do you think about poodles? I bet their pedigrees are longer than yours, and they're so rich, there's plenty of food to go around, I swear. If you could get along with the boys, I'd try taking you back with me."

The more I thought about it, the better I liked the idea. That way I wouldn't have to leave any of them alone too long. Nor would I have to pass my grandmother's house two or three times a day.

"Will you try?" I asked the Pomeranian as we walked back to Mom's house without seeing the Jeep or Lou.

"Everyone should try to get along. Think about it: no wars, no fights, no gangs. What do you say?"

He grabbed the hem of my pants when I tried to shut him back in the house. "You don't want to be left, huh? I can't blame you. But one accident in the house, one bite out of the gardener or the cleaning lady, and you're back here before the screaming stops. And if you mess with the poodles, I'll let them eat you for breakfast."

Not that I'd let that happen. I introduced everyone from opposite sides of the fence, letting Red do his Rottweiler routine, letting Ben and Jerry sniff the little guy. They nosed each other through the fence, lifted their legs and kicked grass, then the poodles went back to chasing each other.

"See? They're nice dogs. What do you think? Want to join their pack?"

No, he wanted to rule it, strutting into the house like he owned the place. The poodles ignored him, but stayed out of his way. They let him growl and show his teeth, and jumped right over him. He had no interest in their toys, and they could care less about his pee-pee pads. We were golden. I set up separate bowls, distant feeding areas, and Red's crate in the bedroom. That way, when I went out, there'd be no accidents, no fur flying when the alpha dog was away.

Success! Red seemed content, and my life was easier, with a lot less guilt.

Speaking of guilt, I called my mother.

CHAPTER 27

MOM HADN'T LEFT FOR THE hospital yet. Dad was doing fine, he wanted bagels and nova for breakfast. He wasn't getting it. "I did not come here to kill him. How are the dogs? Have you brushed them out and checked for ticks? Remember to look in their ears, too. Wear gloves when you do the Pom."

Jeesh, I'd only been here a day and a half. An eventful day and a half, if anyone cared. "The dogs are fine. We're all fine, thanks. When are you coming home?"

"When your father can take care of himself. Lord knows when that will be. And don't tell me you have to write. Use my office if you have to. I got that fancy new scanner for putting lost dogs' pictures up on posters."

"Thanks, I will." I brought my sketch of the front design on the necklace over with me, to enlarge on her equipment. "Mom, do the words 'One life, one heart' mean anything to you?"

"Yes, they mean what the surgeon came in to tell your father. If he doesn't take care of the heart he's got, he should start giving away his possessions. Not that the old fart's got anything of value left. I bet he gave the gold cuff links I bought for him away to some bimbo with blonde hair."

"He wore them the last time he came to New York. If you can't find them, he most likely hid them for safe-keeping when he went to the hospital."

"He went from the golf course. Without a toothbrush, even. There are grass stains on his shirt."

"Stains come out. The cuff links are safe. You could ask him where they are, you know."

"What, and have him think I am stealing his belongings while he's sick? Or picking out clothes for his casket? What kind of vote of confidence do you think that will be?"

"Right, Mom. Anyway, those words and some others we can't read are what's on the back of the necklace you gave me. The one made out of your wedding ring."

She sniffed. "And the old coot told me it said 'I love you.' No one could read it well enough to prove any-thing else. Your father never told the truth about any-thing. That's why—"

I was not going to listen to her rant about his affairs. I'd heard them a zillion times, and his denials, too. "That government agent I told you about, the guy from Eng-land? He brought over another expert. They figured it out, most of it anyway. It's really old."

"Your father swears it's lucky."

Well, I certainly got lucky last night. "I haven't taken it off."

"Good. But you don't need to wear it to the book party. It won't match."

"What book party, Mom? That's the first I heard about it."

"Nonsense. I told you on the phone."

I would remember a book signing.

"And it's written on my calendar."

Why would I read my mother's calendar?

"My friend Dawn wrote a book and they're throwing her a pub party in a tent behind the East Hampton Library tonight."

"Tonight? Saturday?"

"I do know the days of the week, dear. It will be good for your career to be seen with the literary crowd. Maybe they'll throw you a party for your next book."

Trolls in the Hamptons? That was its new name. I didn't think so. "My career is doing just fine, Mom. You know how I hate those things."

Are all mothers selectively deaf or is it just mine? I wonder if anyone's ever done a survey.

She went on as if I hadn't spoken. As if she didn't know I hated crowds, literary snobs, and most of East Hampton. "You're supposed to dress up as your favorite literary character, but don't worry. I have a Dr. Doolittle costume in my closet."

"What?"

"You heard me. I need you to go in my place. I thought you could carry Napoleon."

"His name is Little Red, and he bites, in case you don't remember. He's sure to be a big hit at some tent gathering. If he doesn't lift his leg on everyone's feet."

"Sarcasm is unbecoming, especially in one's daughter. I have a tiny muzzle for him. You'll carry him. He'll make the costume."

"You never told me about a muzzle or I mightn't have been bitten ten times. And I am not going. Red is not going."

"I already told Dawn you'd be there."

"Well, you are just going to have to tell her differently. And stop managing my life. I am doing enough, aren't I, staying with the poodles, toting a feral fou-fou dog around with me?"

She snorted this time. "If I managed your life, I would have shipped you off to high school in England. I would have made sure you went to Royce Institute, as my mother insisted, and met the men they hoped to match you with. If I were managing your life, I'd have grand-children by now. I'd have—"

"I am not going. I am not dressing as any character, but if I did it would be Lizzie Borden. You know, who gave her mother forty whacks?"

I could see the pursed lips, the narrowed eyes, right through the telephone line. "The party is for charity, for all the animal shelters on the North and South Forks of Long Island. Dawn's book is called *Rescue Me*, and not only has she taken in a dozen of the dogs I've re-habbed, but she's donated thousands of dollars to ARF and other local nonprofit, no-kill shelters."

"Great. She's rich, likes dogs, and found someone to publish her book. Congratulate her for me on her success. She doesn't need one more moron in a stupid outfit."

"The book is dedicated to me."

Oh, boy. "What time tonight?"

How could I sit down to write after that? Where was the open, uncluttered mind that I needed to be creative? Wearing a Dr. Doolittle costume in hell, I suppose. Sitting at the computer was no help. I had nothing in my head but a headache. The glow of after-sex, of Grant's tenderness, was long gone. One of the dogs shredded his towel crane anyway. Fafhrd didn't scare me anymore. Cocktails with the glitterati did.

I'd wear my black dress, I decided, and I'd drag Susan with me. No, she was cooking at the restaurant every night. Grant wouldn't be back. That left Kenneth and Colin. They were here to protect me, weren't they? They could protect me from making an ass of myself under a tent.

They said no when I walked down to ask. The word was not much could happen for another week, until the full moon when psi connections were stronger. So they were going back to Manhattan this morning to help locate the nanny's murderer and see if any of the ghost whisperers had arrived to talk to her at the morgue.

Maybe they wouldn't be such great escorts anyway, looking for lost souls at a library book signing.

I decided getting my hair done might make me feel better about being the stand-in Tate. Janie had an open appointment at the salon in her house. She also had stars in her eyes about Mom having a book dedicated to her.

"Of course you did one. But you're her daughter. That doesn't count."

A nasty part of me wanted to know if her friend Dawn had to pay to get her book published. There was a lot of that going around these days. Or her publisher might be one of those new small presses that sold two thousand copies, if that. My books counted. They won awards, got great reviews, and paid royalties. My dedicatees were proud to be named in the front of them. And I hated having to sit and listen to the small-town gossip while I waited for Janie to wind my hair in silver foil. I didn't remember half the people they mentioned, or care about how the Patchens' third daughter was finally getting married at the church Sunday morning, with the reception up at a converted estate. I certainly did not want to hear about how a native Harborite badass had returned to the neighborhood, on a yacht, no less, docked in Montauk.

Janie and Mrs. Chemlecki, the judge's wife who was getting a smelly perm, were fascinated about Turley Borsack's resurrection as a rich guy, not that the one-time bay fisherman/suspected drug runner'd made good, but that he had enough nerve to show up back in town after umpteen years. Word had it, I was forced to hear, that his wife ended up dying in a mental hospital some-where in Europe, where she had family.

Too much sampling the wares, a woman under the dryer shouted to be heard. But he had loved his wife and daughter, so maybe he wasn't all bad. Money covered a lot of crimes. And bought a lot of luxuries, no matter where it came from. No one knew what happened to the pretty, dark-haired daughter.

I decided to get my nails done while I waited for my streaky blonde hair to get a life, in Janie's words. By moving to the other end of the room, I hoped to avoid hearing more about the wages of sin and the pharmaceu-ticals business than I wanted to know. Pauline the mani-curist chewed gum, had sunset-pink hair, and wanted to know all about Grant, Nicky, and my supposed boss, Mr. Parker. The movie mogul was still the most exciting resident of Paumanok Harbor, to Pauline, at least, who knew the exact age of the starlet Parker was currently dating. Young enough to be his daughter by a midlife marriage. Yuck.

I didn't know any of the answers to the million ques-tions Pauline threw at me between blowing bubbles and scraping my cuticles raw.

Agent Grant was chasing a murderer, Nicholas Ry-land was still missing, I never heard from the Rosehill renter.

"You will," Pauline said, turning my hands over to look at my palms. "Next week. But don't get excited. He's not the one."

"The one who? The one who has Nicky? The one who's my soul mate?" I snatched my hands back. Thank goodness the timer went off and I could get the crap washed out of my hair. Now I didn't have to listen to Marie Somebody's trip to Ireland, suffer Mrs. Noyes's knee replacement, or coo over pictures of Janie's new grandchild.

"There!" the small-town stylist announced, swiveling my chair so I could see the finished product in the mirror.

"There" was an over-the-hill Las Vegas hooker on a bad hair day. Oh, God, it wasn't me. Bright, big, my head looked like a dandelion that got chewed up by the weed whacker.

I exceeded the speed limit back to Rosehill by about three times, praying no one saw me before I could wash my hair. The color wouldn't come out, but at least I got the blonde spikes to lie flat, if not curl. Well, I'd be in disguise at the book party, if not in costume.

There was no way I could settle at the computer, so I gathered the dogs into the Escalade, all of them. The poodles took the backseat, each claiming a window to stick his head out. Red sat in the front, clipped to the seat belt so he couldn't get under my feet, into my lap, or jump out the window.

We went to the beach, which was illegal, according to local rules, after Memorial Day. The sand and salt was bad for the dogs' skin, according to my mother. Tough. I had Baggies, a towel, a bottle of water to share, and a desperate craving for open space.

Sun, sky, sea. Prozac for free, with no side effects.

My jaws unclenched, my shoulders unhunched, the line between my eyebrows unpuckered, without the Botox Mrs. Chemlecki recommended.

I spread my towel and sat down, facing the water so I didn't have to see the few other beachgoers. This was the bay, not the ocean that was just fifteen minutes away across Montauk Highway, so there was no surf, no crowds, and not the smoothest sand, either. But the waves lapped in natural order, the sun glistened off the water, and I couldn't see land across the Sound today, so the world was big, endless, eternal. My life was small; my problems were insignificant. Except that Red was missing.

Shit. He must have taken off when I threw sticks for Ben and Jerry. They were panting on the blanket next to me, but the Pom was not in sight. Then I heard his sharp yips and spotted him, down the beach, barking at the waves, stupid little creature that he was, nearly giving me a heart attack.

Maybe Red wasn't so stupid. There was Fafhrd waving back from fifty feet out, his reddish head and chest above water. Maybe Red thought he was a relative. Or were dogs color blind? No matter.

I grabbed Red, told the poodles to stay, and raced back to the car. I pulled out the enlarged design of the back of the ring pendant, and ran back to the beach, at the edge of the water. I held it up.

Fafhrd lowered his prominent brow and squinted. I turned the page upside down. He smiled, showing blunt teeth with wide spaces between them.

"It's from your home," I shouted, and tried to project mentally, too, whatever that entailed. "You need to be there. Home."

He shook his head, creating a miniature waterspout.

I tried my other possibility. "One life. One heart."

Fafhrd patted his chest, where his heart might be. The noise resounded like a rockslide with big boulders.

"Love? Is that why you are here? You love the boy, Nicky?"

He pounded his chest again.

"Do you know where he is?"

Now he slapped at the water angrily, sending waves big enough to surf on. I scurried back to dry sand.

"He's in the water?"

If a troll could shrug, he did. He shook his head in sorrow.

"He's not dead, is he?" I must have shrieked, because all three of the dogs started barking. Fafhrd shook his whole body in vehement denial, making another small tsunami. "Okay. We're looking. We'll help."

Two kids with boogie boards came running toward the waves. Fafhrd patted his heart again, boom-boom, and disappeared.

Well, at least I could talk to him. I hadn't learned much that would help. But I figured our conversation was more enlightening than any I'd have with the library crowd. And Grant would be happy.

I knew he'd be too busy to take a phone call, so I emailed him: *Loved the crane. Talked to F, N lives. Check with FBI, DUE, local police re. Turley Borsack. Drugs. Yacht. Miss you.*

That said it all.

CHAPTER 28

I KEPT CHECKING MY MESSAGES. At my mother's number, I got three reminders about the coming full moon. Was I supposed to join a coven or dig up Grandma Eve's garlic to ward off werewolves? I also got another of those unwelcome-wagon calls.

"Why don't you go back to where you belong and stop poking into other people's business?"

I wanted to call the guy—it sounded like a man or a woman trying to disguise her voice—and tell him to join the twenty-first century and learn about caller ID. The calls were being monitored. Someone would pay the crank a visit soon.

Another message came from someone desperate for a dog handler, then an automated reminder that the hydrants would be flushed next week—I guess I knew where Fafhrd would be—and a call from someone suspicious about the Patchen girl's coming wedding. The groom's nephew was going to be ring bearer; the groom was an only child. If we were looking for a little boy, we should check it out.

I made a note to stop by the church on Sunday to see the ceremony.

I also got a call from Officer Donovan Gregory. Van was coming to Montauk, after all. One of his buddy's wives had to cancel and so he agreed to share the reserved motel room. I should call him back on his cell if I was interested in dinner or something. We wouldn't discuss the case, of course.

Jackpot! An escort to the library thing. I called back, he said he was glad I did, which was gratifying, but he wasn't leaving Manhattan until after his shift tonight. He'd never get here in time. He was really looking forward to seeing me, though, in addition to three days of fishing, golfing, and drinking. So I was right up there with a striped bass and a bottle of beer. Great. I couldn't complain, though, not when I'd wanted a friend beside me in the gathering of snobby strangers.

We agreed on Monday afternoon, when the cops were planning time at the beach with their families. I couldn't stay late because of the dogs. I didn't invite him out to Rosehill because of my scruples about not sleeping with more than one guy at a time. Besides, I wanted to look over the yachts in Montauk, maybe hand flyers out at the marinas. "See you then."

"I'm looking forward to it."

So was I, actually. Van was a genuinely nice man, with no threats, no questions. Best of all, he was normal. I really, really needed normal.

I called Cousin Lily next, to ask about progress with her daughter. There was no baby yet, but Cousin Lily felt the full moon ought to do it.

Connie was giving birth to a werebaby?

"Gravity, Willow. Don't you know anything?"

About babies? No.

Louisa called and asked me to lunch at her house next Tuesday, so I guess I'd learn more then. I couldn't remember if she said she had two or three kids already, with another one imminent. Gads, what if she went into labor while I was there? I'd push the panic button on my cell phone, that's what I'd do. If the Department of Unexplained Events couldn't handle a baby, what good were they?

So now I had a full social calendar. If I lived through the book party.

I wrestled with my hair for another hour. Then with Red. He didn't want to wear the tuxedo-bow collar my mother had for him. Or the muzzle. What was he, a sissy pit bull? The poodles would laugh at him. He didn't want to stay home, either, latching onto the hem of my one good dress. We compromised. I tied the bow collar to my pocketbook, and put the muzzle inside it.

I couldn't believe it, but I had to pay just to get into the tent behind the library. My mother never mentioned that.

"It's all for charity, dear," a white-haired lady at the gate told me. "To help the poor doggies find good homes."

So I offered her Red. I'd even toss in another fifty.

"Oh no, dear. I have cats."

So? Red got along with cats as badly as he got along with everyone else. I paid and carried him in. For the fifty bucks I got either a glass of Perrier or wine, and some brown pasty stuff on a cracker. Red liked it.

Then I got to stand around on a long line waiting for Mom's friend to sign her name, after I paid another forty-five dollars for the big coffee-table, full-color, photography book. Mom never mentioned that, either. According to the jacket cover, Dawn, the friend, had done the writing. An arty type in a white linen suit with a braided queue down his back and a pound of pretension on his narrow shoulders had taken the pictures. He stood behind the author, shaking hands, making small talk, greeting everyone, it seemed, by name.

Not quite half the crowd was in costume. I saw two Sherlocks, a Great Gatsby, maybe Scarlett O'Hara, Captain Ahab, Elizabeth Bennett or some other Regency belle, and Darth Vader. I guess a bunch of people emptied their Halloween boxes, because there were a couple of Draculas and one Frankenstein monster mixed in with the Lily Pulitzer ladies and the yellow cardigan gents. Oops. They weren't in costume. Everyone was juggling their glasses and plates of paté while kissing the air around each other.

Dawn Elliot turned out to be a heavyset woman with poor eyesight and a lot of bling. Enough to pay to get the book published, I figured, since I'd never heard of the publisher. I knew gloating was unworthy of me, but I couldn't helping noticing that I had a lot more people waiting for me to sign my books at the last comic book convention I attended in Manhattan. Some even brought my old books, from their personal collections, for me to sign. God knows how many fans I'd have met at the big conference in California. Planes? Crowds? Dining alone? I stuck with Manhattan.

When I got near enough to have Dawn sign, she asked, "What character are you, dear?"

"Oh, I am pretending to be Rose Tate's daughter, but I'm not really."

Mrs. Elliot gave a yelp, jumped to her feet, and threw her fleshy arms around me. At which Red, also in my arms, along with the heavy book and the glass of water, panicked. He sank his teeth into the flesh of my biceps, and then either he peed on me or the frigging water spilled. I couldn't be sure, but there was still plenty of liquid in the glass. I was wet and in pain, probably bleeding on the forty-five-dollar book, and being smothered by sagging skin and sinus-clogging perfume.

"I looove your mother! She encouraged me to write the book. and it has changed my life. And I have heard so much about you. We must get together and discuss the publishing world."

Sure. Like we had anything in common. I collected my book, after the photographer signed it, too, unasked. He handed me his card. He did pet portraits if I wanted Little Red immortalized. I wanted Little Red stuffed at this moment, but I took the card, smiled, and tried to leave the crowded tent.

A woman with a microphone stopped me. She nodded toward a cameraman behind her and said they were from the local TV station. I thought she said "eh," but she must have meant East Hampton. "Isn't this a wonderful event?" she cooed, shoving the microphone in my direction. Red snapped at it.

"Terrific." I held up the book and smiled for the camera. "And the money goes to such worthwhile causes." I held up the Pomeranian, who growled for the camera.

"It does? That is, of course it does. I saw Dawn give you a big welcome. Are you anybody? That is, who are you supposed to be?"

"I'm actually not in costume. I'm Willow Tate from Paumanok Harbor and I write books myself, under the pseudonym Wi—"

"Oh, look, there's a troubadour. And a Tyrolean. Is that a famous trombone player? Quick, Larry, get a picture of that clever Trojan horse. No, the toreador."

I wonder what the camera would show, because I doubted anyone else could see Fafhrd juggling ice cubes from the buckets that cooled the wine and water bottles.

I blew him a kiss like a Hollywood star, and left.

I bought Red and myself an ice cream sundae on the way home.

The big dogs were glad to see me—and the melted ice cream I'd saved for them. I was happy to see them, too. They weren't half as snooty as they looked.

I was happier to hear Grant's message on my answering machine. "Good catch, Willy. You're brilliant, but we already knew that, didn't we? Your friend Borsack was near the Institute at the same time Nicky Ryland's mother brought him to Royce. Borsack was visiting his psychotic wife—I might have worked with her, although I don't recall—but who knows what he overheard about the boy. His boat has left Montauk, with no description available, which leads us to believe he's got some kind of mind control working, which marks him as our perp. The Coast Guard's been alerted. I am waiting for a sketch of Borsack, his police record, his psi standing if it's documented, and positive identification from the injured nanny in Georgia. With that kind of proof I can get an arrest warrant and an APB across the country. You did great. Want a job?"

I wanted him back.

I went to the wedding Sunday. The church part, anyway. I hadn't heard any connection to Borsack, but that story about the ring bearer did seem odd. Grandma was invited, so I drove with her.

The local church, which was whimsically nicknamed Our Lady of The Clamshell, was all festooned in that gauzy wedding material, with bows on every candle sconce, drapes of it swagged from pew to pew.

Grandma nodded to everyone she knew in the congregation, which was almost everyone, but she kept looking at the picture of Nicky I had in my lap. "What will we do if it looks like him?"

I noted the "we" and the quaver in her voice. For once Grandma Eve seemed uncertain of herself, maybe even fallible. I liked her better for that. "We don't do anything until later, when we try to talk to him. I'm hoping we'll know before then somehow."

The organ music grew louder. Everyone hushed. Ushers brought in the mothers. Grandma whispered that the Patchen sisters were matrons of honor. Then came the boy in a miniature tuxedo, his hair slicked over big protruding ears. He seemed very serious about his job, looking down at the pillow he carried with the rings tied to it.

"What do you think?"

I couldn't tell. Neither could Fafhrd. He scooped the boy up for a better look. The kid screamed and grabbed onto the nearest bow, taking down the streamers, the swags, the flowers, and more when Fafhrd put him back on the ground.

"Damn," someone behind me said, "the kid tripped on the tulle."

Now he was draped in an acre of it, crying. The groom raced down the aisle and picked him up, hugging him and kissing the top of his head and unwrapping him. The choirmaster came to help and carried the boy out, leaving the groom holding the ring pillow.

The young man, with his slicked-back hair and big, protuberant ears, looked around at the gaping crowd. "All right, he's my son. I never married his mother, but that doesn't mean I don't love him. If anyone has any objections to his being here—"

"Speak now or forever hold your peace," the best man shouted from the altar.

"No," the groom yelled back, bending over. "You can kiss my ass."

While the wedding guests laughed, or cried, he walked back up to the front of the church to wait for the bride.

"Nice wedding, wasn't it?"

"Lovely. I can't remember one I've enjoyed more. Have fun at the reception."

I went back to Rosehill to wait for Grant.

He sent me another email instead. This one had a picture of Borsack's boat, the *Painted Lady*, from its registration documents. He warned me that the yacht might look different or have another name; so might Borsack. The Feds were pretty sure he was guilty of something to come up with that much money. No one was certain he had Nicky, or if he'd killed the two babysitters. He was a known chemistry expert, which fit, too. Now they had specialists analyzing the surviving woman's blood for esoteric illegal drugs and her mind for paranormal interference. She'd talk more if they could counter Borsack's machinations and methods.

Grant closed his note by saying that he would be in the field, out of communication, until midweek, but the whole mess would be over soon. Then we could make plans.

For what? I wanted to know. Plans for what?

I had plans of my own. Van wasn't the same, but he was a good substitute. I'd forgotten how handsome he was, how buff in his NYPD T-shirt and denim shorts, and how easygoing. He'd sightsee, hike, rent bikes, sit at one of the outdoor bars listening to live music, or lie in the sun, as long as he could spend time with me.

Cool.

I chose sightseeing. With Borsack's yacht gone from Montauk, visiting the marinas was useless, and Van had gone fishing Sunday anyway. Now I drove Van out to the Point to see the Montauk Lighthouse, required of any visitor to the East End. Busloads of tourists waited to climb the steep steps, look at George Washington's signature on the original deed in the museum, and buy nautical tchotchkes in the gift shop. We passed on that, but drove slowly past the really impressive sight. Then I took him to Ditch Plains, Montauk's famous surfing beach. It was mobbed, but a truck had boards for rent.

"Do you know how?" I asked. "Want to try?"

He laughed. "A black dude from Brooklyn? No way. Besides, I put one toe in the water yesterday. It's still too cold. The surfers are all wearing wet suits."

We got smoothies from the snack wagon on the beach and sat on the rock jetty to watch.

Van watched me. "I like what you've done with your hair."

"What, the dumb blonde look?"

"Not dumb. Just not so studious now, not so intimidating."

Me? Intimidating? Hell, I was afraid of getting swept off the rocks, getting swept off my feet by his attention, and of everything else that could happen to my life.

He reached out to touch one of the ragged blonde edges I'd let curl this morning. "You look younger, happier. Like you belong at the beach in the sunshine."

"But I don't. I belong in the city, writing in my little apartment." Where I was safe.

The rest of the afternoon was nice. We went back to the beach in town, in front of the motel where his friends were staying. The other cops were friendly, the wives pleasant and patient about the jokes and horseplay. I didn't feel like such an outsider with them, until they started talking about kids, summer camps, and cooking.

Van and I went for a walk. He held my hand.

"I can see what the natives dislike about the tourists," he said. "Why they call them trolls." He gestured toward the blobs wearing too little fabric to cover what should stay behind closed doors, much less get sunburned; the slobs who came to one of the most beautiful places in the world, then left their garbage; loudmouthed jerks who needed blasting radios and raucous volleyball games that drowned out the sound of the surf.

"Oh, they're not so bad. Most are just ordinary, decent people having a good time. And we need them to keep the local economy running."

"'We'? You've changed your attitude, along with your hair."

"That just slipped out."

He squeezed my hand and smiled. "Any luck finding the boy?"

"I thought we weren't going to talk about that?"

"No, what we aren't going to talk about is the mayhem in Manhattan that you seemed to gravitate toward, or vice versa."

He must mean like that log rolling toward shore and all the swimmers, the one Fafhrd was standing on, arms outstretched, riding the waves.

"Oh, my God, people will get killed."

Van looked. "It's nothing but a big roller. And see,

there's a shoal that'll keep the wave offshore. The kids are having a grand time scooping up crabs and shells."

"I've had too much sun, I suppose. I better get back. The dogs, you know."

I left him with his friends, who yelled out, "Stay out of trouble, you hear?"

If they only knew. I told them to enjoy their vacation, and headed back toward the car.

"Call when you get back to the city?" Van asked.

"Yes, I will. Thanks for a nice afternoon." Where I'd almost forgotten about Fafhrd and Nicky. And Grant.

CHAPTER 29

GRANT CALLED FROM THE AIRPORT in Georgia late that afternoon. I told him about the book signing and the wedding and the surfing beach— without mentioning Van Gregory. He laughed at Fafhrd's antics, that warm, deep laugh that I felt down to my toes. "Man, I wish I could have seen all that through your eyes."

"I'm still not used to no one else seeing what I do."

"I guess you never do get accustomed to it." Then he turned serious. "Your friend seems to be sticking closer to you. Appearing more, whether you are drawing or not."

"I noticed that, too. He thinks I am going to help find Nicky for him."

"That's what I'm thinking. He has no idea where?"

"Near water, that's all I've been able to get from him. I think he might act differently if the boy was close, though. He seems really attached, however that happened."

"That's a plus for our side. All the projections are for late this week for a showdown."

"That's what the messages say." I told him about

the calls, including new ones about the weather—good through the weekend. And the crank ones.

"Lou's got that covered. A kid who wasn't accepted to the Institute. He had no talent, and bad attitude. He's joining the Navy as soon as the papers get processed, like tomorrow."

"Voluntarily?"

"Let's just say he had a choice. You've met Lou. The other options weren't half as appealing. Were there any other messages that might be a help?"

"Susan's mother told me to carry a safety pin with me."

He thought about that for a minute. "She's the one good with kids, isn't she? It's not much of a weapon, but it can't hurt, I suppose."

"I already pinned one to my bra."

He thought about that, too, judging from the silence at the other end of the line. "It's pink."

"The safety pin?"

"No, the bra."

"Are you trying to drive me crazy? This is business, serious business . . . Uh, what color are your panties?"

"Pink, too. With lace."

"Shite."

I assumed that was British for I want you too, babe. "So when are you coming in?"

"As soon as this bloody plane takes off. Until then, the entire department is on alert; we'll be ready for anything. You're not worried, are you?"

Who, me? Just because a madman was out there killing people to further his plans to conquer the world? "Nah, not much. I'll sleep better tonight when you're here, though."

I heard that sexy smile in his voice. "Sweetheart, you won't sleep at all when I get there."

My toes curled. He could do that, with just his voice. "I'm counting on it."

"You know I won't let anything happen to you, don't you?"

I didn't know if he could stop all the gathering forces. He was good, but this was big, as big as Fafhrd. "I know you'll try."

"Bet on it. Will you wait up for me tonight?"

Why else did I buy that expensive lingerie on my way out of Montauk Saturday? "I'll leave the lights on."

"And your clothes off?"

There went the pricy negligee. And my pulse rate, and my intentions to play it cool tonight instead of jumping on him the second he walked through the door.

Cool was all I got, because he called later. A plane was waiting for him at Kennedy Airport, to whisk him to Washington, DC.

"US One?"

"No, but close." He had to brief the Secretary of Homeland Security, the Joint Chiefs of Staff, the British ambassador, and the Vice President.

How could I lo— No, change that. How could I dream about someone who chatted with world leaders? Hell, he likely had lunch with the Queen on a regular basis. I had lunch with three dogs

The only thing I could do was make light of it. "You mean the welfare of the universe comes ahead of me?"

"Only if I want to keep my job. I thought about it, Willy, if that matters."

Not really. We were still worlds apart. And I was on my own. As usual.

*   *   *

Early Tuesday morning I took the dogs for a long walk. Colin came with us, back from wherever he went over the weekend. He wasn't talking, so I stopped asking.

Afterward, I checked in with my mother. Dad was getting released from the hospital in a day or two, if he had no complications.

"Great. Then you'll be flying home soon?"

"He'll need me more once he's at the condo. He's not supposed to drive for weeks. You know the jerk. He'll drive anyway and open up his sutures. Likely bleed to death on these ten-lane roads. I've never seen so many lights and turning lanes and—"

"I can't stay here forever, you know."

"Why not? Your family is there, people who love you. I'm trying to convince your father to come north when he's recovered more."

"That's nice, Mom. I'd like it if he were nearer. But my publisher is in New York, and my apartment. My friends."

"What friends? The ones too busy with their own lives to call you?"

I didn't know how she knew that none of my city friends had phoned since I got to Paumanok Harbor; I thought the guesthouse agents were the only ones monitoring my calls. "They're busy, Mom."

"And all the neighbors aren't? I hear they keep leaving messages. They care about you."

"Safety pins and weather forecasts, Mom. Listen, I think I saw a sign at the post office for a dog-sitting service. Maybe I'll call them about the poodles."

The only sound was my mother inhaling.

"I got your book signed."

"I hope you didn't pay for it. Dawn promised me a free one for all the work I did on it."

I got shafted again, by that charitable female, a friend of the family, no less. You couldn't trust anyone, could you? "I've got to go, Mom. The dogs are scratching their ears."

"You didn't take them to the beach, did you, Willy? I told you—"

"Bye, Mom. Love you. Love Dad. Talk to you later."

Kenneth followed me to Louisa's house, but he drove off afterward, knowing I'd be safe there.

The house was spectacular, the views awesome, her young son well behaved, her little girl adorable. Her gorgeous husband was charming, her job exciting, her face luminous with happiness, despite the swollen ankles of late pregnancy. Even the lunch she served was delicious and healthy. Damn.

Why couldn't my life be so ... so tidy? Everything in its place, a place for everything, not like my being up-rooted, my family scattered, my career on hiatus, and a troll depending on me to find another missing soul.

I left Louisa's house before I turned green with envy.

I went back and fetched the dogs, told Colin that I was driving to Paumanok Harbor's actual harbor. I didn't need to tell him, I suppose, because they had a GPS locator in my car, and another on my cell phone, but I felt better knowing someone knew my plans.

The village had private docks tucked here and there along the shoreline, but the more protected bay basin held two fancy marinas with ship's stores and amenities, one town dock for commercial lobstermen, draggers, and charter boats, and a rowboat and kayak rental service. A few sailboats were anchored in deeper water, along with a bunch of small craft bobbing at their moorings. Not many pleasure boats were out on a Tuesday afternoon, waiting for the weekend or after work. The price to fuel up a boat was so high, ordinary people thought twice about cruising around Gardiner's Island, or sailing to Shelter Island for lunch.

One fancy yacht was tied at the end of Rick Stamfield's Boat Basin, where Rick kept boats too big to turn into the narrow slips along the dock. I took the dogs down there and waved to Rick, whom I'd known since I was a kid when my father kept an outboard here for times he wanted to get away from my mother. I found a bench to sit on, one that cast shade for the dogs. I unfolded the printout of Borsack's boat, but nothing about this one looked like the *Painted Lady*. I saw no teak trim, no dinghy up on davits on the foredeck, no swivel fighting chairs in the stern where avid fishermen could be strapped in to wrestle with whatever poor fish was on their hooks.

Those were things someone could easily change, like dying your hair or shaving a mustache. Borsack couldn't alter the sharper point to the prow, though, or the wider windows for the cabin, not since leaving Montauk. Besides, this one had its canvas cover all zipped up, its windows closed tight, so no one was aboard. No other boat in the harbor was big enough, or luxurious enough.

I leaned back on the bench, Red next to me, the big dogs at my feet. The sun felt good on my face, even though I knew better, and the seagulls' cawing reminded me of past summers. Maybe I drowsed off, because I was startled by Red's barking, a loud thumping, the bench shaking under me. "What the . . . ?"

Fafhrd. I tried to hold up the picture of the *Painted Lady*, but his broad red back was to me as he clomped past and down the pier. I held my breath lest he crash through the old wood dock, but it held. The fancy yacht at the end didn't, not when a one-ton troll jumped onto it.

The boat seemed to fold in half, with the middle going down under Fafhrd's weight. Both bow and stern slowly canted upward.

Rick was running past me, then other dockhands and some fishermen, but they had nothing to do but watch the two halves gently sink into the shallow water. Both sides hit bottom and stayed up, pointing to the sky. The seagulls were gone.

"Where'd that effing trawler go?" Rick shouted.

"What trawler?"

"The red one that broadsided your boss' boat."

"My boss?"

I forgot about that when Fafhrd's head rose up behind the remnants. I'd been holding my breath, wondering if he was trapped beneath the debris. He shook his head, no. Not hurt. No, no Nicky, which I knew. "Fool."

Rick gave me a dirty look. "Parker may be a fool, but he's still going to blame me for whatever happened."

Then he got busy, ordering his crew to set up booms around the wreck to catch any oil spill and tow the other boats out of range in case of fire or explosion.

"No ignitions, no cigarettes. No frigging trawler."

He shouted for the ship's store manager to call the harbormaster, the Coast Guard, the Environmental Protection Agency, and the police.

I, he felt, should call Mr. Parker.

"Me?"

"I'll be too busy trying to explain to a hundred agencies how no rogue fishing boat is at the bottom of the harbor, only Parker's *Chorine*, in pieces. Did you see what happened?"

"No, I was napping. I only looked up at the noise."

"Maybe it was a blasted asteroid. Or a piece of a plane falling out of the sky. Does that make sense?"

Not when they didn't find anything like that in the wreck, either. "Maybe ice. A big chunk of space ice that melted when it hit the water."

Rick rubbed his ear. "You're not telling the truth, Willy. There's the old Royce blood in my family, too, that tells me the difference. But know what? I don't want to know the truth, not if half of what I hear is real. So you go on, do what you have to. But please, don't come back this way, okay?"

Fafhrd was long gone, but I heard sirens in the distance and decided I better go before I was in the way, or my car got blocked in. Or Rick started blaming me.

My bodyguard showed up when I was halfway back to Rosehill. I pulled over when I saw Lou's silver Lexus, with blue lights flashing.

"I heard an emergency call go out. You okay?"

"Fine. Nothing out of the ordinary." Not for me, anyway.

CHAPTER 30

I CALLED THE NUMBER FOR Mr. Parker and got a receptionist, a secretary, then a personal assistant, telling my story every time. I explained who I was, where I was, and why I was calling. No one seemed to care. Finally I got put on hold, listening to the theme from a movie I'd never seen. One of Mr. Parker's, I assumed.

After the third time through some really bad music, Curtis Parker himself got on the phone. Before I got in a word, he started cursing, shouting, acting as if I'd taken an ax to his expensive toy myself. In a way I suppose I had, but he couldn't know that. I tried to explain that Rick at the boatyard was certain the insurance would cover the loss.

"It's totaled? A total loss? I loved that boat!"

I said I was sorry, again.

"Yeah, yeah. That helps. Good thing I'm in New York this week. I'll be out as soon as I can hire a plane or a 'copter. Who the hell did you say you were?"

I could hear him giving orders to his underlings about canceling appointments, calling the airport service, and someone named Vonna. That must be the starlet du jour.

I raised my voice and said, "I am your replacement dog-
and house sitter. Lily Corwin's second cousin."

"Yeah, yeah. Well, I'll need a car at the airport in East
Hampton. See to it."

See to it? Now here was a moral dilemma. I wasn't
getting paid by the man, or anyone yet. So technically
I did not work for him, but for my mother's cousin, my
mother, or the Rosehill estate, unless I'd been drafted
as a volunteer. Either way, I felt no obligation to take
orders from any pompous ass. Granted his boat had
imploded for no reason that anyone could explain.
Granted he ought to come look at the damage himself
and sign papers so his insurance people could get to
work. Granted I'd been driving his car, taking baths in
his Jacuzzi, and swimming in his pool. But he was only
renting Rosehill; none of the stuff belonged to him.

And I did not take orders kindly. Writers seldom did.
That's why they worked at home, for themselves, at their
own speed, instead of in an office, listening to some Curtis Parker clone telling them what to do and when to do
it.

Being treated like a servant was worse. Not that there
was anything wrong with cleaning houses, chauffeuring
millionaires, serving them meals. Hell, I'd made lunch
for the cleaning people when they came. What rubbed
me wrong was the attitude that if you work for me, you
aren't as good as me, so I can treat you like shit because
there's always someone else to take my money. Kind of
like publishing, only less polite.

Maybe that was it. I appreciated good manners. Mr.
Parker had none.

On the other hand, I liked his dogs. I didn't want
to just walk away from them without knowing that he

was going to feed them on time, see that they had their nightly treats, or take them back with him when he left Paumanok Harbor. For all I knew, he intended to keep the chartered plane or helicopter—which the airport's neighbors despised because of the noise—waiting for him at the airport. That way he could play potentate for the marina masses and still get back to whatever big deal he had to make tomorrow.

In which case, was I still expected to be the dog sitter?

So I waited for the message to tell me what time to pick him up at the airport. It never came, only a furious call asking where the fuck his car was? The asswipes at the rental counter had no more cars available and were closing up for the night.

I said I'd be there in twenty minutes.

It was more like forty, because I had to pack up my stuff and Red's. I wasn't staying in the house with the foulmouthed movie mogul.

I called the guesthouse from my cell phone to notify my bodyguards and sped through the back roads to avoid Montauk Highway with its lights and traffic.

Parker was pacing outside the single terminal, swatting at flies with his cigarette. I guessed him to be nearing sixty, trying for forty, looking like a foolish fifty with his tanned skin and surgically smooth face. The paunch gave him away. His jacket was rumpled, his tie loose around his neck.

The dark-haired woman on a bench beside him was young and beautiful, if you liked that hard pouty look. She wore stiletto heels and a short, tight, black spandex dress—and diamonds. She might as well have "Bimbo" written across her impressive bosom. I wish I could remember what Pauline said her name was, or what movie she was in so I could avoid it.

No one introduced me. I was a better person than that, so I held up the Pomeranian and said, "This is Red. He bites."

"Yeah, yeah." Parker threw a suitcase in the backseat, but made to get in the driver's door, so I stepped out. The female got in the passenger side, clutching her tote bag.

He put the car in gear.

"Hey, what about me?"

"Lily always left the car here."

"Well, I am not Lily, and I need a ride home." That was a lie, but I hadn't found out how long he was staying, or if he knew how to tell which of his own dogs was Ben, which was Jerry. Besides, I wouldn't give puff-gut Parker the satisfaction of dismissing me so easily.

"But you promised me dinner at The Palm in East Hampton," the bimbo whined. "We never got to eat."

She was so skinny she most likely never ate anyway, so I didn't feel sorry for her. Besides, my macaroni and cheese was still in Rosehill's kitchen. Ha ha.

Parker looked undecided.

I held up Red again. "In case you didn't notice, I have my dog with me. I also have my suitcases and laptop in the trunk. It's getting dark, and this place is miles away from anywhere, and deserted at night. You cannot just leave me here."

Parker threw his cigarette—still lit—onto the pavement. "Get in." He lit another cigarette while I shoved his valise over to make room for Red and me, then he put his other hand on the starlet's knee. "We'll go to the new place in the Harbor, sugar."

I didn't bother to tell them that the new place was still closed on Tuesdays.

Red growled. He didn't like the backseat or the cigarette smoke or maybe the animosity in the car.

"This car stinks of dog," Sugar complained, with a snarky glance at Red.

I couldn't see how she could smell dog over tobacco, but I said, "I've been taking the poodles places with me. They don't get so lonely that way, or so anxious that they get destructive."

Parker turned the AC on high. "Some bitch was supposed to come straighten them out."

I held Red closer to me to keep him warm, and to keep me from throwing Parker's suitcase at his hairwoven head. "That bitch is my mother."

"Yeah, yeah. It's only an expression."

And Fafhrd was only a troll.

Snark-face complained some more. "There's sand on my seat."

What did they expect, when they had a beach house? "The cleaning ladies don't do cars."

He went through a red light at Newtown Lane in East Hampton. "So what happened to my boat?"

He didn't care about the pedestrians trying to cross the street, or the car trying to make a left turn, so I didn't care what I said. "A really big, heavy troll jumped on board."

He laughed. "I like you, honey. You've got balls, I'll say that for you."

The actress didn't say anything, but she did give me another look, then stared out the window, sulking.

"So what really happened?"

"I'm not certain. They're looking for whatever hit it, junk from space maybe."

"Come on, doll, that's the plot of one of my movies. Stuff like that doesn't happen in real life."

Now I remembered why I never saw his movies. "They have to wait to haul out the debris to see if the engines blew up, but there wasn't any fire. I know that."

"The insurance will cover it."

Not if it was declared an act of God, but I didn't say that. Maybe boats were insured differently.

With his sweet young thing turning sour on him, Parker looked in the rearview mirror, taking stock of me for the first time. I felt dirty.

"What did you say your name was?"

"Tate, Willy Tate. I write books."

"Everyone does, doll, everyone does. That's why there are so many house sitters and dog-walkers out there."

"Gee, I thought those were unemployed actresses."

That got me a glare from the skinny starlet, but another laugh from Parker, who tossed another burning butt out the window. Thank God we'd had so much rain the other night or he'd set the Hamptons on fire.

After a few minutes of silence, while I made sure my seat belt was tight, the female turned around. "Willy is short for Willow, isn't it? I've heard of you."

I doubted she could read, but I smiled graciously and said, "A lot of people have my books, mostly kids." I couldn't help bragging, after the insults. "I won a GRABYA award last year. That's Graphic Arts Books for Young Adults."

Parker laughed. "Grabya, heh?"

The arm candy wasn't amused. Or impressed. She waved a hand in the smoke, showing off long nails with red polish and rhinestones. "No, not that. Your mother is the one who's good with dogs, you said, and your grandmother is some kind of witch."

"She's a master gardener and an herbalist. Being good at what you do is not unusual for the residents of Paumanok Harbor."

Parker patted her knee again, and left his hand there. "I told you, sugar, lots of local color at the Harbor. Besides, you were the one who wanted me to rent a place out here. I would have gone somewhere with more . . . "

"Celebrities?" I offered. "Stars? Cachet?"

"Yeah, yeah. Cachet. That's it. Now you do sound like a writer, doesn't she, Vonna?

Ah, sugar had a name. Now I remembered, she was Vonna Ormand, who once dated Brad Pitt, according to Pauline the manicurist. I asked why she picked little Paumanok Harbor instead of the flossier Hamptons. I'd have thought a busty—that is, budding—actress would want the chance to meet influential people, get the publicity, be seen. "Have you been here before?"

"Oh, I always heard it was pretty." She went back to sulking out the window.

Parker wore smoke rings over his head, like a demonic angel. The image got worse when he said, "I'm thinking of making a documentary movie out here."

Just what we needed. Make Paumanok Harbor a tourist trap like Salem, Mass. Have every UFO-junkie, ghost-hunter, and cult-worshiper land on the beach.

Since we were already coming into Amagansett, the town before the turn for the Harbor, I quickly proceeded to tell them how to care for Ben and Jerry. She yawned; he took out his cell phone and barked into it at someone. He was driving with one hand again, the hand that held a cigarette.

"I'll be leaving town in a day or so," I told them, "if you don't need me anymore." I really, really hoped not. Sugar and her daddy were not my kind of people.

"Who'll cook, Curtis?"

Obviously that wasn't one of Vonna's talents. I recommended takeout from the deli, or dinner at Uncle Bernie's. Then I handed her one of my mother's cards, where I'd be staying, and told them to drop me off at the train station past the Amagansett Farmer's Market. I said I could call a friend from here.

I didn't want to listen to the bitching if I made them go down rutted Garland Drive, out of their way. Something about the way Vonna was staring at Mom's card made me not eager to show them where I lived, either. Not that everyone in town didn't know the way, but I was getting spooked by how angry she looked. Just because she'd have to turn on the coffeemaker herself? Or because Parker called me doll? Who wanted to be a rich old man's plaything?

The fresh air felt good, even if no one got out to help me unload my bags from the back. Parker revved the engine, in my face. Sugar did not say good-bye.

I slammed the trunk, walked in front of the Escalade so he couldn't drive off without running me down, and said, "By the way, the passcodes have been changed at Rosehill. Talk to the guys at the guesthouse."

I thought he'd explode, he turned so red under his fake tan. "I pay a fortune for that place, and what do I get? Uppity help and squatters? I'll call the cops if your friends aren't out of there when I turn the corner."

I wondered how he thought he'd get in if Colin and Kenneth didn't open the gates and the house for him. All I said was, "They're not my friends. That is, they are now, but they're also Federal agents, with warrants, and weapons. A lot of weapons. I'd be real careful how I spoke to them."

I stepped back and he peeled away, sending gravel

flying in my direction. I shouted after him, "Oh, and your dogs have worms."

I waited for the black sedan that followed us into the railroad station parking lot to pull up next to me.

"You let that twit drop you here, in a dark, empty parking lot? Are you crazy?"

"I'm happy to see you, too."

Grant got out of the car and folded me in his arms, after I put Little Red down. The man wasn't stupid. He felt good, too, solid, strong, safe.

"I saw the car at the airport, and I knew Colin or Kenneth wouldn't let me down. I was in more danger in the car with the turkey who thinks he owns the roads just because he's rich."

"I should have left you to walk home," Grant said when he let go of me to pick up my baggage. "By the way, which home are we going to?"

I opened the window so Red could clear his lungs of the smoke. "Mom's."

"Too bad. I was looking forward to that Jacuzzi."

The smoke must have reached my lungs, too, because suddenly I couldn't breathe. "Mom has a bathtub."

"Yes, but is it big enough for two of us?"

Who needed to breathe? "If we sit close."

"Oh, I think we can manage that. I missed you, Willy."

"Me, too. Did you really meet with all those important people?"

"No, the Vice President wasn't there. And none of them are as important as the big guy you talked to."

"Parker?"

He chuckled. "The really big guy."

"Did you tell the VIPs about Fafhrd?"

"Not exactly. I did not want to get you too involved.

Who knows how the big shots think? Politicians and military types are known for expediency."

"Like getting rid of me so no one can use me. I told you that in the beginning."

He kept his eyes on the road as we made the Devon turn to Paumanok Harbor over the railroad tracks, but I knew he was thinking about me. "No one is going to hurt you. I tried to keep your part minimum because I didn't want anyone thinking I was too involved person-ally. They might have tried to pull me off the case."

"Can they do that?"

"No, but it wouldn't have been pretty or polite, or good for foreign diplomacy. I'm staying, Willy. No mat-ter what. Do you believe me?"

I tried to show him how far my trust went by almost drowning in Mom's bathtub.

I was wrong. The tub really wasn't big enough for two people, especially when they were intent on wild, acro-batic, energetic, I-missed-you sex.

After we mopped up the bathroom floor before the kitchen ceiling beneath it started to leak, I led Grant to the bedroom I'd always used. It was pretty much the same as when I was a kid, with its jars of seashells and beach glass, a painting of a sandpiper on driftwood from the craft shows held every summer, a photograph of the beach from one of the art shows. Mom had left every-thing alone, except she'd changed the old bunk beds to a queen, so I forgave her a lot.

Red didn't like being locked out of the bedroom, but he knew this house and had his favorite chair in the liv-ing room. I'd forgotten his crate, damn it, so I'd have to go collect it tomorrow, along with a check, I hoped. I also hoped Parker didn't notice the broken pitcher in the bathroom or the bill for the diving board repairs that would go against his security deposit. He could afford it.

We talked in bed about Borsack for a while, letting the salty breeze from the open window cool us after the bath. Then we discussed plans and precautions for the upcoming time of the new moon.

I wondered how we could make love when the world might end in a couple of days. Grant wondered how we could not. What better way to spend the time than finding our bliss, making each other happy?

Oh, I was happy. Three more times, but who was counting?

CHAPTER 31

THIS TIME I FOUND A pink rose on the pillow next to me when I woke up. Okay, it was from my mother's heirloom bush outside the front door, and there was an ant crawling on it, but the man had class.

And company. I brushed my teeth, washed my face, threw on a pair of shorts and a tee, and went down to find Lou, Colin, Kenneth, and Grant all seated at the dining room table, all on computers and other machines that did God knew what that they must have brought over from the guesthouse. Grant handed me a cup of coffee, pointed to a box of pastries, and said he liked my hair. It reminded him of the hedgehogs back home; I'd have to go see them when this was over.

"I hate planes."

"We'll take a boat," was all he said, going back to work.

Since I was the one with the most need to know, they let me stay. By now they had pictures of Turley Borsack when he was young, when he was arrested a few times, when he had a passport as Boris Turlinskya, another as an African Tufu Borsa, one in a turban, one as a Hasidic Israeli. There might be more as the central computers searched for face recognition. He was always listed as a chemist. He was always suspected of dealing in designer drugs in high places that paid well and helped him hide his identity. He'd been on Interpol's list for decades, the wily bastard, and on Scotland Yard's since his wife died at the Royce Institute Hospital.

Her death had been declared a drug overdose, unknown compound, unknown source, but now the labs found the same traces in the blood of both of the dead nannies. The survivor had been shot. Unknown gun, unknown shooter.

"And he wants me?" My voice was none too steady. My knees, either.

"He will not hurt you," Grant swore.

"At least not until you get him what he wants," Lou added cheerfully.

They had no information whatsoever about Borsack's daughter, Vinnie, likely because he was already wealthy and connected enough to get her identity erased when she was young.

The day was going straight downhill. Especially when two phone messages made no sense, warning about colors and rainbows.

Kenneth looked up from his notes. "We're getting that from our own precogs, too. It's like static coming over a radio. Maybe a psi-blocker."

"Borsack can do that?"

Kenneth shrugged. "Who knows what he's picked up in his travels?"

My dad didn't help any, either. He called from the hospital to tell me not to drink coffee. It was bad for me.

I set my cup down. "I think I'll just go back to bed, pull the covers over my head, and let you guys work this out."

I would have, too, but the phone rang again. At Colin's headshake I let the answering machine pick up, to hear Vonna Ormand, from Rosehill. I answered out of curiosity, and because I really needed to get Red's crate back.

First, she apologized for any unintended—hah!—rudeness last night. She and Curtis had been tired and upset. Second, she asked if I'd come show her how to give the worm medicine to the poodles. And third, the clincher, she said that she and Curtis had looked up my books on Amazon last night, and one of them sounded like it might make a great animated movie. Could I bring a copy over?

Talk about offers too good to refuse.

Still pulling information out of the computer, Grant said I was good to go. The day was cloudy, with no rainbows likely. The full moon wasn't scheduled until Thursday night. And I should take the Lexus; it was safer.

"Safer, how?" I wanted to know.

So Lou walked me out to the car, showed me the reinforced panels, the bulletproof glass, the infrared sensors, and a hundred defensive tricks built into the car, besides its tracking system.

"I'll never remember all that."

"You don't need to. Just do not push the red eject button unless you absolutely must."

I grabbed one of my books from Mom's shelf, a baseball hat from the peg in the hall so I didn't have to hear any more comments about my hair, and Red. I took him before he got tempted by all the big feet in the house—or got stepped on—and so he could see his friends again.

I was glad I went. Mr. Parker was playing with the poodles on the front lawn, throwing tennis balls for them.

He couldn't be all bad, I figured, if he'd touch slobbery balls to keep his dogs happy. I waved and drove around back, not because I considered myself a servant, but so I wouldn't have to tote Red's crate through the house.

Maybe I was wrong about Vonna Ormond, too. She was still skinny, but a lot nicer. She tossed Red a biscuit from the paw print cookie jar on the counter, and offered me coffee.

I refused, remembering my father's warning.

Vonna seemed disappointed. Maybe she needed a friend. So I accepted an iced tea while I found the doggy med pockets for her. They were soft, sausage-smelling hollow treats that you could stick a pill in. Most dogs would gobble the thing whole, unaware of the trick stuffing.

Vonna smiled, well, not enough to cause wrinkles, but she looked happier. She brought out a plate of Oreo cookies—ones I'd forgotten to pack.

"No thanks," I said, "I already had a muffin for breakfast." And I already had love handles. Grant said he liked them, but a man in his condition—turned on and tuned in—was not about to tell a woman in my position—nestled between his thighs—that she was fat.

Vonna looked at the cookies longingly. "I'll have one if you do."

One cookie was most likely her fat content for the week, but I didn't need much convincing. I ate two, while she separated the halves, and ate the plain side, slowly, savoring every tiny bite. Then she licked the cream inside off the second chocolate wafer.

I never wanted to be so neurotic about my weight. So I had another cookie and washed them down with the iced tea. I was surprised she'd bothered to put a sprig of mint in it.

"Does it need more sugar? Curtis likes his sweet."

"No, I—" I couldn't finish the sentence. Or move my legs. "Wha—?"

"Don't worry," she said, all efficiency as she took my glass away to the sink. Her mouth had the hard lines of last night. "It'll wear off. Not that it matters where you're going."

I tried to say I wasn't going anywhere, but my mouth wasn't working. Maybe because my head had fallen forward into the plate of cookies. Drugged cookies, unless she'd doctored the iced tea with the minty taste to cover whatever she'd done. And here I'd been telling her how to hide a dog pill. Why not? You said coffee, Dad!

She yelled for Parker, saying she had to get me to a doctor. There was no time for the paramedics. "Help me get her into the car."

He really thought they should call 911, thank his flabby heart, but she took a gun out from under a dish towel on the counter.

I think I found Borsack's daughter. The dogs barked, Red snarled, I whimpered.

"What the fuck are you doing?" Parker shouted. "She needs an ambulance."

"What the fuck does it look like, old man? I am taking her with me. You are helping."

"I won't—"

So she shot him.

I must have gasped because she said, "Tranquilizer darts. He'll wake up eventually, but we'll be long gone by then. Don't make me use one on you."

I was limp, which I felt was marginally better than being unconscious, so I let her drag me by my armpits out the back door. She was stronger than she looked, so I really didn't have much choice anyway.

Vonna/Vinnie dropped me on the pavement and opened the car door, the Lexus, at least, with all its tracking devices. Grant would know where I was, wherever the bitch took me.

Panting, she hauled me up and shoved me facedown on the backseat. Red jumped in on top of me. I still couldn't feel my hands or feet, so at least I didn't feel the bruises I knew were forming.

She snatched the baseball cap off my head and put it on hers, to hide her dark hair. She took my sunglasses, too, and drove the Lexus down the long drive and out the gate, waving to the gardeners as she passed.

I wanted to tell Red to stop pawing at my head, trying to get me up, but my tongue still wouldn't cooperate. I tried calling Fafhrd in my mind, but he wasn't answering my calls, either.

I know we took some back roads, because of the bumpy ride, and went down a hill because I almost slid off the backseat. We drove over gravel, from the sound, then over a worse road, at slower speed. It didn't matter that I couldn't figure out the location. Grant could trace this car.

Except we stopped.

Vinnie Borsack got out of the car, slung my arm over her shoulder, and dragged my wilted body down a weedy path to an old rickety pier. I lost one sandal on the uneven boards. I almost lost my breakfast when I saw the sleek black-hulled speedboat tied to the dock.

Oh, no, not a boat!

She heaved me in, cursed when Little Red leaped after me, standing on my chest, growling and snapping his teeth. I shut my eyes—relieved they worked—so I didn't have to see her shoot the poor little dog for trying to defend me!

She didn't have time. She started the boat's engine and took off. Not fast enough to attract attention if any lobster men or paddlers were out in the bay, but fast enough to pound my back up and down on the deck as we skimmed over the water.

Oh, God. If I threw up, I'd choke to death. Which might be better than whatever the Borsacks had in store for me.

No, I told myself, Grant would save me. I had to believe that. I had to be brave.

Me?

But then I heard them, the voices in my head over the roar of the powerful engine. There was Mrs. Terwilliger from the library, and Joanne at the deli, Bud from the gas station, and everyone who'd called to leave messages.

"You are brave, Willow Tate. You can do anything."

"You could have done more, dear, if you'd listened to me in the past," came my grandmother's voice, but my mother told her to shut up, still in my head, although not as loudly. "You are tough, baby girl. I wouldn't have raised you any other way."

Yeah, I was tough. I could move my toes now. Good thing, because we bumped against the yacht. Vinnie yelled that if I didn't climb up the ladder she'd tie a rope around me, toss me overboard, and lift me with the anchor winch. So I climbed the metal rungs, all six of them that felt like six hundred. I mumbled a plea that she not leave Red alone in the speedboat. Or worse.

She thought about it, then said, "He might make you more cooperative." She threw him over the gunnel, onto the deck. I heard a thud, then a yelp. "Remember that. If you give me any trouble, he goes over the other side."

Now I really, really hated her.

I cuddled the shaking dog as best I could, checking

for broken bones. "Shh, Red. We'll be rescued," I whispered. "Or we'll save ourselves. I have a safety pin."

I raised myself up to look around. We were far out in the bay, past Gardiner's Island. Too far to swim, by a lot. Too far to call for help, and useless anyway since the island was private and seldom occupied. "We'll think of something."

Except Vinnie made me go down a short flight of steps to the inside cabin and shoved me onto a padded bench seat next to the dining table. I took a swipe at her, and she brought up the tranquilizer gun, aimed at Red. Whatever knocked Parker down would kill the tiny dog. I nodded and sat still while she tied my feet to the heavy table that was bolted to the floor, and put one of those plastic cable things around my wrists. She put the box of cookies on the table within my limited reach—as though I would ever eat anything she fed me again.

When she went back up on deck, I looked around. Another bench sat opposite me across the table. On most boats they flipped opened to form beds. I wasn't sure a yacht this size and luxury needed more beds, because I could see a vast stateroom ahead, several other doors to either side, another room under the stairs. Nearby I saw a galley that was more like a modern kitchen than anything I'd ever seen on a boat, or cooked in. It had a microwave, what looked like a dishwasher, two refrigerators, floor to ceiling storage units, and an overhead TV. All the amenities of home except it rocked.

"I get seasick," I warned when Vinnie came back, this time with a heavy suitcase and another bag.

So she plunked a bucket next to me.

I tried again. "The full moon is not until tomorrow night. Whatever you are planning won't work."

She didn't pretend to misunderstand. "Plans change."

"Uh, would you mind letting me in on those plans? Just so I can prepare myself, you know."

She sneered. "You'll find out when he gets here."

"Turley Borsack? Your father?"

"So you figured that out. And here I thought you were just another dumb blonde with a sappy attachment to dogs."

I wanted to tell her I wasn't really blonde, only sandy-haired, and the dogs weren't mine, but she went on: "It won't matter what you know, or think you know. Neither Turley nor I will hang around once we succeed. I'll be back with Turley before dark." Then she climbed the steps to the bridge and left. The boat rocked more when she jumped over the side onto the smaller boat.

"Wait," I shouted after her. "Where's Nicky?"

I heard her laugh as the engine on the speedboat kicked in. "You're sitting on him, pukehead."

CHAPTER 32

OH, HELL. They had him stuffed in a storage locker? Was he dead, and that's why I couldn't call Fafhrd? My troll knew his friend was gone so he went home? I tried to find the voices of Paumanok Harbor, to ask what to do, but they were silent also. Or maybe they'd just been in my head, brought on by the drugged iced tea.

I had a hard time standing up, with my ankles tied to the table pedestal, but I managed. I swiveled around as best I could to find a handle on the bench cushion. I pulled, my hands still tied together, and threw the seat back up against the cabin wall. "Nicky?"

He was still, and deathly pale, but he was definitely the child from the pictures we had. He was small and famine-thin. Had the bastards starved him, besides? I couldn't tell if he was breathing. My tether wouldn't let me bend over far enough to lay my head against his chest, and I couldn't tell if it was rising and falling with his inhalations or just the rocking of the boat. I tried not to think about that rocking. Or Nicky being dead, or no one hearing me.

"Nicky? Wake up, baby. It's me, Willy. I know I don't

look like much right now, but I'm a friend. I have other friends who can help. Wake up, Nicky, please."

He didn't. When I touched him with my joined hands, he didn't seem cold or stiff, so maybe he was just drugged. How long could it last? When had they done it? I tried shaking him, patting his cheek, tweaking his ear. Nothing. Miserable bastards, to do this to an innocent child.

"Come on, Nicky. Help me." I tried to think harder, if that's what it took. "I know I'm no telepath, but I need you to hear me, love, to wake up. We can't let them win. We just can't!"

I dashed my bound hands at my face, to wipe away the tears. Red was whining at my feet, so I yelled at him. "If you have a better idea, tell me. Otherwise, shut up so I can think."

I was too terrified to think. I sank down into a squat, half under the table, leaning against the wall of Nicky's container that looked all too much like a coffin. He had a cushion under him, a blanket on top, and airholes, now that I looked at the sides of the wooden banquette. So they hadn't been trying to kill him.

Of course not. They needed him. He was the Verbalizer. "So speak, damn it. Speak!"

Red barked.

"Not you."

I looked around for something that could help, some inspiration. I couldn't lift the boy out of the box, not being tied the way I was. He simply had to wake up and help me. I couldn't reach the galley sink for water to sprinkle on him, or the refrigerator for ice. All I had was some suspect Oreo cookies . . . and a safety pin.

I hated to do it. Maybe I couldn't do it with my wrists tied together. I had to try, and I had to keep from drop-

ping the damn pin out of my tethered reach. Using con-
tortions I didn't know my body could perform, I finally,
clumsily, slowly unclasped the pin from my bra strap.
The tiny bit of bent metal surely couldn't defend Nicky,
Red, and me from two maniacal murderers with guns
and drugs. I doubted it could pick a lock, either. It sure
as hell wasn't going to close up again, not after my gyra-
tions. So this must be what it was intended for, wasn't it?

I jabbed Nicky's finger with the pin.

"I'm sorry. So sorry. I didn't want to hurt you," I
sobbed when his eyes opened. He cringed back as far
as he could go. His eyes were blue-green, like forest and
sky together, and big, so big with fright that my heart
almost broke right then. I swallowed and stepped back,
showing my bound hands. "I'm not one of them, Nicky.
I'm a friend."

He just stared.

"I know you can understand me. I wish I could talk
to you mind to mind, but I just don't know how. I have
friends who maybe can, and they are coming. Yes, I know
they are. Meantime I need you to help me call Fafhrd."

His eyebrows rose. His mouth formed an f and made
a fuh sound.

"Yes, that's right, Fafhrd. You know, big, red, rock
solid?"

Then I felt it, inside my skull. Not like the voices from
Paumanok Harbor, not in words I could understand, but
I got the gist. "Yes, Fafhrd! Your friend. He's looking for
you, too." I didn't have any paper to draw the troll, but
I made a mental image and closed my eyes. "Do you see
him? Tell him we're on a boat in Gardiner's Bay and we
need help. I'll try, too."

I had no way of knowing if Nicky tried. Or if Fafhrd
heard, or if Borsack had somehow blocked any psi-

communication to or from the boat, which explained why I couldn't hear the voices from Paumanok Harbor anymore. I decided the poor kid—and I—needed encouragement, so I said, "I'm sure he'll come. Or Grant will. Can you get up? Maybe there's a knife in one of the drawers and you can free me?"

He understood, but was slow to rise. If I could direct my thoughts and put venom in them, the Borsacks would be dead. He was skin and bones, with an unhealthy pallor, as if they never let him out in the sun to play.

He stood up, then bent down to retrieve something in the box, a plastic figure, maybe one of those transforming monster things kids liked to collect. Maybe just a game piece. I didn't know. He held it out to me. I shook my head. But, hey, if this was show and tell, I had the prize. I pulled the ring necklace out from under my T-shirt and showed it to him.

He smiled, and I felt like I'd won the lottery. He touched it, so tentatively. "Yes, it is from Unity, I believe. Turn it over. That might be the language you speak."

He looked, then he touched his hand to his heart.

I touched my bound hands to my heart, too. "That's right. One life. One heart. There's supposed to be more, but I don't know it."

He climbed out and into my lap, there on the carpeted floor of the yacht. Red jumped in his lap and licked his face. Nicky laughed. So why couldn't I stop crying?

We couldn't waste too much time reassuring each other. "Go look for a knife, Nicky. We need to get me free, and find a way to get out of here."

The cabinets and drawers were all locked with electronic keypads. So was that big suitcase Vinnie had brought aboard. The safety pin wouldn't do any good. "It's all right, baby. Do you want a cookie?"

I remembered seeing Vinnie eat one, so I thought they'd be safe for Nicky. The minty iced tea had to contain the drug.

He chewed and smiled, then turned serious again. He patted my cheek, and spoke out loud. "I can't understand, Nicky. Maybe you can teach me when we're away from here. I can teach you how to play baseball, and swim, and pick strawberries."

His mouth formed an m. "Muh?"

"I'm sorry, pumpkin, your mother is gone. You know that. We can't bring her back. But we'll find you a family, friends, whatever you want. You don't have to be afraid anymore."

I was plenty afraid for both of us. Here I was promising the kid a future, when we might not live through the night.

Or our first confrontation with Turley Borsack, the dark-haired man of the most recent photos, smooth-shaven but swarthy.

"Well, I see you've introduced yourselves," he said, standing over us. "Excellent. The better rapport between you, the better results." He checked his watch. "We have a few hours to go until full darkness. Perfect."

The moon was not going to be full; no rainbow was visible in the night. Yet he was smiling in excitement, his dark eyes bright and gleaming and shifting from me to Nicky to the cabin windows to his watch. I decided he was insane, or else high on his own drugs.

"What do you want of us?" I asked.

He gave me a feral grin, full of teeth and gums. "Oh, nothing much, just great riches, infinite power, eternal life. And you two are going to get it for me. As soon as I have the third of my little triumvirate." He took the pocketbook Vinnie handed him, my pocketbook, and fished in it for my cell phone. He held it out to me. "Here. Call his lordship."

He must be crazier than I thought. "Who?"

"Lord Grantham. Your lover. The Translator. You thought I was looking for you the whole time, didn't you? You're all as stupid as I counted on. It's him I need. I knew they'd send him if you were in jeopardy."

Grant was a lordship?

"Dial! I know he'll find you by tracing the call. I'll even give him directions to a boat he can use. Do it now, or I'll drug the brat again. Or shoot the dog." He opened the suitcase, far away from me, to show vials and syringes and a gun. A real one, I suspected.

So I called the emergency number.

"Willy, is that you? Are you all right?" Grant sounded frantic.

"Why, yes, Lord Grantham, how nice of you to care."

He paused. "Willy, that has to wait. Where are you? We found the car. And Parker."

So I told him about the speedboat, the yacht, and Borsack's demand that he come by another boat they'd left for him. Vinnie told me to say that the proper coordinates for the yacht were already programmed into the outboard's steering system. And he had to come alone. If they saw one other boat, a plane, a swimmer, or a suspicious looking seagull, they'd kill me and take the boy away again.

"Your whore isn't half as important to my plans as you and the brat," Borsack said after he grabbed the phone away from me, "so don't think I won't get rid of her. And don't bother trying to get at me through the lines of power. I have them blocked, if your pet mentalists haven't figured that out yet." He tossed the phone aside and laughed. "He'll come. He has to."

"No," I told him, "Grant will sacrifice me to protect the world from evil monsters like you."

Borsack slapped me. Then he shoved a pad and pencil at me. "Draw. That's why you're here. All you're good for, except bait for his lordship."

My cheek burned, another black mark against this black-hearted fiend. I vowed to defeat him somehow.

I knew I could draw Fafhrd safely, because either he was already coming, or he couldn't be reached through the psi-blanket Borsack had cast.

Borsack preempted my plan. "Don't give me the fucking troll. I want the kid's father."

I was relieved. I'd worried that Borsack might be the man who raped Tiffany Ryland. Nicky was better off with an ogre as sire than this scumbag.

"I don't know who his father is."

"But you know what he is. The brat is a halfling, that's why he can't survive here, why he can't talk anything but elvish. The father will come get him. They don't procreate easily, the eldritch kind. He'll want his son before the brat dies. He'll come, I say."

Actually he shouted. The man was demented, horrifyingly so. Nicky made a sound, but I pulled him away before Borsack could strike him.

Borsack glared at both of us. "Lord Grantham can interpret for me, tell him my terms, what I want in exchange for the freak. I'll have it all, then." He pounded on the pad on the table in front of me. "Draw, Willow Tate, as if your life depended on it. It does."

"But . . . but I don't know what an elf looks like, much less Nicky's father."

"He does." He pointed to Nicky. "That's why I set the mind-block outside the boat. You draw until he tells you to stop."

"How can I draw with my hands tied together?"

"You really don't want to get on my nerves this way, bitch." Vinnie handed him a switchblade, which he snapped open without looking at it, showing me a long, curved, deadly knife. I shut my eyes, but all he did was slice through the plastic tie at my wrists. "Now draw. I want it done by the time the linguist gets here. If not, your dog is shark bait. Then you. Then the kid. Understand?"

They both left, loving family that they were, climbing up to the flying bridge, I thought, where they could check radar screens for incoming vessels.

I looked at the pad and the pencil, then at Nicky. "He'll destroy the world, this world, maybe your father's world, if he gets his way. But he'll kill us if I don't give him what he wants."

Nicky put his hand over mine and said something I couldn't possibly understand. But I did, in pictures in my head, like my imagination, only not mine. "Images of your father?"

He nodded. "D'ref."

"He's very handsome."

He nodded again.

"But he won't come for you, will he?"

Nicky smiled, a mischievous little grin I was thrilled to see. "How come?"

I had the image in my head of the incredibly good-looking figure being stripped of his power, of his magic, for the sins he had committed. I already knew he'd trespassed into the humans' world, breaking a millennia-long treaty. He'd likely bespelled a human girl and impregnated her. Who knew what evil he'd committed in Unity itself?

"And no one else will come?"

Nicky shook his head, and I saw another beautiful man, this one with a crown, looking sad but determined. "J'omree."

"It's your grandfather, isn't it? He's king, and he will not, cannot, disobey his own laws."

Nicky gave that little boy grin again.

"So Borsack's plan fails before he begins?"

Nicky managed a "Ys."

"Good boy." Red wagged his tail, so I gave him part of the last Oreo. Then I drew. Not the magnificent elven king, but the maggot that'd started this whole mess, D'ref, Nicky's father. I made him beautiful because he was, and I made him sinister, because he was that, too. I made him sneer, because he could not do any more harm.

I was satisfied. The problem was, what would Borsack do when he realized his grand scheme was foiled? He couldn't let us live, not knowing what we did. He couldn't return to his nefarious way of life now that he'd been so well identified. For that matter, I doubted he could escape the forces sure to be gathered in the bay or in the air above. As for Vinnie, shooting Parker, even with tranquilizer darts, put an end to her Hollywood career whether we lived or not. Neither of them seemed to have any great respect for human life.

I'd leave the endgame to Grant. He was the secret agent, the soldier, the blasted British aristocrat!

And he was coming now, walking into certain death.

Oh, hell.

CHAPTER 33

I HEARD THE FAINT SOUND OF a small outboard engine coming closer and closer. Borsack
shouted something to Vinnie, and I saw her pass in front
of the cabin door above. She waited, then told Grant
to catch the line she was throwing him. A few minutes
later, I heard her tell him to throw his gun overboard.

Splash.

"The other one, too."

Another *splash.*

"And the jacket that's full of electronic gadgets and
wires."

That didn't make as much noise. Maybe Grant just
dropped the jacket onto the floor of the outboard, hoping to get at some of those gadgets later. I sure hoped
so, too.

"Now climb up. Then put your hands on your head."

I imagined she was patting him down. If her hand
passed between his legs, she was as good as dead in my
mind. If she found the knife he usually had strapped to
his ankle, we were all dead.

She told him to walk in front of her, down the steps
to the cabin, his hands still up, in plain sight. One wrong

move, she told him, and she'd fire her gun. She wouldn't miss at this range.

When they reached the cabin where Nicky and I sat huddled together, Borsack looked at Grant, nodded, and said, "That's him, all right. Shoot him."

I screamed. Nicky started crying.

Vinnie shot anyway.

My head said it was a tranquilizer dart. They wouldn't drag Grant out here only to kill him. They needed him. That's what Borsack had told me.

My heart wasn't listening. It stopped altogether as Grant fell to the floor.

My eyes paid attention, thank goodness, and saw that Grant brought his hands up before he fell, clutching at his chest. When he landed on the floor, he managed to land on top of a dart in his hands, and he winked at me.

The dart must have hit a Kevlar undershirt Vinnie hadn't noticed, which meant she was as crazy as her father. Or so used to flabby older men she couldn't tell muscle from armor.

No matter. We had a rescuer. He had a plan. Maybe.

Borsack came and hit him over the head with the butt of another gun, just to make certain he was unconscious, and stayed that way. I winced, and turned Nicky's head to my shoulder when I saw the trickle of blood on the back of Grant's skull.

I didn't think that was part of my hero's plan.

"It's safer that way," Borsack was telling Vinnie. "He's too dangerous otherwise. Now he won't cause any trouble until we need him. Tie him up."

While she did that, he laughed, like Grandma's chickens used to cackle. "I knew he'd come. He had to."

I was scared, but I was furious, too. Why did Borsack have to hit Grant when he was already tranquilized—at least as far as Borsack knew? The anger gave me the courage to ask, "What do you mean, he had to come? His job is to study events, not sacrifice himself."

"He came for you, his mate. Didn't you know that?"

"Know what? We're not married. Not even engaged. I haven't known him a month."

"I forgot. You refused to learn, didn't you? Stupid sow. You were chosen for him, preordained, preselected, forever."

A sow, was I? I'd kick Borsack where it hurt. I'd— "No, he came because he had a job to do. And he . . . he loves me. Grant was not forced into anything."

He laughed again. "He loves you like I loved my wife, because I had to. They chose her, and it was a good choice, I'll give them that. We were a pair. Geniuses, we were, everyone said so. We made great new discoveries in the science of mind and states of consciousness. We opened our own minds until we could see Unity." He licked his thick lips. "I saw it, I swear."

"You hallucinated, old man! Those were opium dreams, magic mushroom trips, or whatever psychedelic cocktail you concocted."

"We were brilliant, I say! My wife saw Unity, too, and it was beautiful. So beautiful that her mind stayed there. She would not come back. *They* enthralled her." He tried to swing out at Nicky, sitting in my lap, but I pulled the boy aside. The smack landed on my shoulder, shoving me backward. Grant's shoulders tensed, but no one noticed except me.

"My wife stopped talking to me! She was going to lead me there, but she stopped talking to me."

"So you killed her with more drugs," Vinnie spat out at her father.

"No, I wanted her to take me with her. We'll go now.

The boy's father will take us. We'll be together, and strong, stronger than anyone, ever." He pulled my pad off the table and thrust it at Nicky.

"Is this your father, boy? And don't lie. I have a trace of that Royce truth-knowing blood in me, too, so I'll know."

Nicky nodded. "D'ref."

Borsack stroked the picture. "See, Vinnie? See what I can do? I told you I can bring one of them here!" He checked his watch again. "Soon. Soon."

I had to know. "What are you waiting for?"

"A surprise. A wonderful, glorious surprise, and more psi power than this area has seen in decades."

"Yeah, yeah," Vinnie said, obviously upset at the mention of her dead mother. "I think you should make this D'ref give you more power to control, to rule here. I want to stay. With money and influence, I can be a real star. Who needs magic when I've got talent?"

"You think your talent's gotten you this far? Think again, girl. It's my tending to the nasty little habits of people like Parker that got you noticed, that got you jobs. You'll come with me. They'll want fresh blood to mother the next generation."

"I'm an actress, not a brood mare for your ambitions!"

"Shut up. You are coming with me."

"Or else you'll kill me like you did the nannies?"

"You are the one who shot the last woman. If you stay, you'll be charged with murder. Now that they know who and what you are they'll hunt you down like a rabid dog."

They went out of the cabin, shouting at each other. They took the guns and the suitcase with them.

"Quick, Nicky," I whispered. "Agent Grant usually has a knife under his pant leg. Go find it, cut him loose.

No, cut me loose first. Then I can shove it in his back, the despicable, lying—"

Nicky was still crying.

Grant groaned, then said, "Save it for later, sweetheart. Don't scare the boy any worse."

"Is your head all right?"

"Too hard to dent." Then he uttered something that sounded like a combination of cricket chirps and birdsong and tongue clicks, and my mother's sniffs. Nicky smiled and scampered off my lap toward him.

Vinnie had taken the knife in the sheath against Grant's leg, but not the small one in the sole of his shoe. We were both free in seconds, but Grant told me to stay where I was, as if I was still tied. He lay back on the floor, so they wouldn't notice he was free.

"You're not going to kill them?"

"One knife against two people with guns? I'll save that for later, Willy, okay? I have to find out what Borsack intends to do."

I quickly told him about the telepathy block, Fafhrd's disappearance, and Nicky's grandfather, who would not be coming.

He smiled, pleased with our deviousness, so far. "I guess that means you didn't need me to rescue you."

"Go to hell, Lord Grantham."

His smiled faded. "I almost did, when we lost your signal."

How could I be mad at that?

I heard Vinnie and her father still yelling, but closer. "They are coming back. Quick, what's your plan?"

"Kill the buggers, get Nicky safe, and marry you."

As far as proposals of marriage go, that one sucked. Otherwise, it sounded good to me.

Borsack came down and kicked Grant to see if he

was awake. Grant grunted, pretending pain and befud-
dlement.

"On your feet. It's almost time." He swung the gun
toward Nicky and me. "You too."

I stood up, holding Nicky's hand.

"Weren't you supposed to be tied to the table?"

"The dog chewed the rope."

He started to kick out at Red. At which I screamed,
and Grant leaped to his feet, the knife in his hand. But
Borsack still had a gun, and I couldn't tell whether it had
bullets or tranquilizer darts.

"Put the knife down or I shoot."

I could see Grant measuring the odds. Not good.

Then Vinnie came down to see what was happening
and Grant pulled her in front of him, the knife at her
throat, her gun hand immobilized by his other arm.

Borsack held his weapon on me, but he snatched
Nicky's hand from mine and dragged the boy against
him.

Standoff, and all I had was a safety pin!

Borsack did not consider the situation a stalemate at
all. "Go ahead and kill her. She's no use to me anyway."

Vinnie screamed obscenities at her father and strug-
gled in Grant's arms. He held her, reluctant to slit her
throat, it seemed.

I guess I was glad he wasn't a cold-hearted killer like
Borsack, who put the gun to Nicky's head and cocked
the hammer. "Drop the knife."

Grant had no choice, really. He threw the knife into
the wooden tabletop, where it quivered back and forth.
Maybe he had another one in his other shoe. James
Bond would have.

"Now get on deck, all of you." Borsack swung the gun
around at each of us in turn, even Vinnie.

Maybe Grant knew what was coming, one more thing he hadn't told me. But I was too astounded to notice his reaction. Once we were all on the afterdeck, open to the sky, all thoughts of flight or fight disappeared—only awe remained. There it was, the rainbow, the colors, the magical surprise Borsack had promised.

I'd seen it once before, one summer years ago. My father woke me up and carried me out to Grandma's flower garden with a blanket, to lay back and watch the northern lights, the aurora borealis, the gods at play with paintbrushes, so rare on Long Island.

Usually the weathermen predicted the possibility, if all the conditions were right. I had no idea how Borsack knew of it, unless he'd somehow tinkered with the forecasts, which made him all the more dangerous.

He held up my pad with D'ref's picture on it. I had the second picture I'd drawn in my pocket, the one of Fafhrd on a barge, one of those ferro-cement ones that could hold tons of coal, or garbage, or trolls. That was the picture I'd keep in my mind.

"You are certain this is your father? No games, now, boy, or I'll throw you overboard."

Nicky nodded.

"Call him," he ordered, twisting the boy's thin arm. Then he turned to Grant, his gun arc swiveling, "And you tell me what he says. Remember my Royce blood and speak the truth, both of you."

Nicky spoke, sounding like a cage full of monkeys this time.

"Slower, Nick," Grant told him. "I have only studied, not spoken the language until tonight."

Nick started again, and Grant translated: "'Father, it is I, Nicholas, son of Tiffany Ryland, who you took in a tranced state, then left alone with child. A child who could not speak the language here, nor thrive. Mr. Turley Borsack wants you to come to get me. He is the human who killed my mother, who kept me prisoner for five years, who killed my nursemaids, all so he could use me to further his amb—"

"Hey, none of that." Borsack shook the boy by the neck. "Just tell him you want to go with him, before you die here. Tell him to come, damn it!" He glared at me, all the moving colors of the sky reflecting in his eyes. "You focus on the image."

"Come, Father."

The lights stopped dancing.

Vinnie scoffed. "Nothing is happening, just like I warned you."

Borsack seemed close to tears as the sky colors faded. Then he gave a high-pitched laugh like a nervous young punk about to steal his first car. "I forgot to shut down the psi-block, that's all."

He dragged Nicky with him to the captain's seat and the yacht's controls, where he fiddled with an instrument near the steering wheel that might have been a ship-to-shore radio.

Suddenly I could hear the voices from the Harbor shouting advice. My grandmother was crying. What if Borsack could hear them, too?

I shouted in my head: "Don't let him know you are listening! This has to end now."

But I tried to call Fafhrd, Fafhrd and a barge, because the water was too deep for him to stand, and he never had mastered swimming, for all his practicing.

Nothing. Borsack looked shattered.

"What now, you crazy old man?" his daughter wanted to know.

He licked his lips. "Now we wait for tomorrow and

the full moon. There will still be power to draw on then. The would-be witches of this sinkhole will help."

Something howled in my head.

"No," Vinnie insisted, from beside me. "That's just a waste of time. They'll figure out how to get to us before then. I'm taking the outboard and getting out of here while I can. I have enough money, and enough other identities hidden away. You taught me well, Turley."

"No, you cannot leave me!"

"You cannot keep me, not with your drugs and not with your domination dreams. I have wasted enough of my life."

"You cannot leave me!" he raged, pointing his weapon at Vinnie. "Not like she did."

Bang.

He'd used a real gun.

Vinnie fell at my feet. Then Borsack shrieked loud enough to wake the dead, but not Vinnie. He raised his fist to the sky, which was now dark, with the clouds rolling back in to cover the stars. Even I could tell a storm was coming, without any weather talent at all.

The boat rocked on its anchor, and my stomach roiled along with the sea. The speedboat and the smaller outboard banged against the yacht's hull, the sound almost drowned out by the rising wind. Then lightning shot out of the clouds.

Great. I was on a boat, in the middle of nowhere, during an electrical storm. Maybe my worst nightmare, until you added a psychopath with a gun. *Now* it was my worst nightmare. I picked up Red.

The next bolt of lightning was closer, forking down to the water in a straight line.

"Get below," Grant shouted, leaping at Borsack and wrestling him for the gun. It went off, out to the side where the outboard runabout rose and fell in the waves. Wood splintered.

I couldn't go without Nicky, who'd hidden under the steering column. I was ready to jump over Vinnie's body and dash across the heaving deck to his side when Vinnie pulled herself up and raised her gun.

I did not know whom she aimed at. I didn't care, either. I jabbed her with my safety pin. She fell back, the gun rolling across the deck to Grant. He lunged for it, just as another bolt of lightning struck the water.

Nicky crawled out of his niche and raised his face. "Grandfather."

"He is coming?" Borsack dropped his gun, raised both hands to the heavens and shouted, "They came for me. I knew they would! No one believed I could do it. I always believed. Now I did it."

He climbed the ladder to the flying bridge while thunder roared. "Welcome, Welcome!"

The next lightning bolt went right through him. *Thank you, Grandfather J'omree.*

And through the boat. Uh-oh.

CHAPTER 34

H AIR REALLY DOES STAND ON end near an electric charge. And the air really does smell like ozone. Until the fire starts. Then there is smoke and flames and melting plastic and panic in the crowd.

I was the only crowd, Red and I.

Grant ran over and lifted Nicky. He held the boy on one shoulder and pulled me, still clutching the dog, with him to the opposite side of the yacht. "Quick, into the speedboat."

Get into that small, open boat in the face of a killer storm? I wrapped my free hand around a cleat. I wasn't going. Sprinklers went off in the lower cabin, and rain started to pour down. "We'll be okay here."

"Until the engines blow up. Or the hull burns. Or the fire reaches the gas tanks. Come on, we'll be fine. We have to put distance between us and Borsack's boat."

Vinnie looked up. By the light of the fire, I could see blood coming from her mouth now. "No. Electronics . . . fried. Won't . . . start."

The other boat, the much smaller runabout, was filling with water fast.

"Life jackets," I cried. I put Red down to try to open hatches and cabinets. "We need life jackets."

No, we didn't. Lightning flashed again and I could see Fafhrd, on his barge, my barge, using a huge pine tree as a paddle.

As soon as Fafhrd was close enough, I took Nicky from Grant and passed him to the grinning troll. I looked at Vinnie, but she was beyond help. Then I looked for my poor panicked dog. "Red! Red!"

There was Grant, handing me the dog and lifting both of us over the side of the boat onto the barge. He jumped down after us.

"Tell me your friend Fafhrd is here, and Nicky is not dangling ten feet in the air on a pole."

My tears mixed with the rain. "It's Fafhrd! It is! I knew he'd come." I realized I echoed Borsack's maniacal claims, so I changed that to "I hoped he'd find us."

"And Nicky's grandfather came through for us, too."

"And you."

We huddled together against the wind and rain until we saw lights setting out from shore. I recognized the Coast Guard and the harbormaster, but every lobster boat and dragger, every cabin cruiser and cigarette boat from Paumanok Harbor was coming to our rescue, too. I saw a seaplane flying from Montauk to the east and a private helicopter from East Hampton to the west.

I didn't know if I heard voices in my head or shouts from the boats.

"Welcome home, Nicky."

"We missed you."

"So glad you're here, son."

And one I knew well: "I am proud of you, Willow."

Then the yacht exploded, filling the night with sparks and light.

Our barge wouldn't burn. Grant pulled me tighter and kissed both my cheeks. "My brilliant woman."

Except someone shouted that the speedboat was like to blow up next. Fafhrd decided we were not moving fast enough away from danger. He put Nicky down as gently as if he were a butterfly, then jumped overboard and started kicking and pushing until he could stand. After that he just shoved us toward the armada from shore.

They threw ropes across, then leaped onto the barge and ran to pat Grant's back, hug me, touch Nicky's cheek. Everyone marveled at the miracle of how the barge and its towboat had appeared at just the right time and place. No one commented that there was no tug in sight.

Ambulances and fire trucks waited onshore, with hands reaching out for Nicky. I wasn't letting him go, not out of my sight, not to any hospital. He was limp in Grant's arms, barely holding his own head up, his eyes drifting shut. "We'll take him to Grandma Eve," I said, and no one argued with me.

Lou took Borsack's suitcase off the barge when Grant pointed to it. I hadn't known he'd taken the case, but appreciated his foresight in that horrible moment. God only knew what Borsack had, or what it could do to the water or the fish or anyone swimming in the bay.

All the villagers lined a pathway to a fire-rescue truck. They nodded, smiled, said what a good job we'd done, and encouraged Nicky to feel better now that he was home where he belonged.

He didn't look any better to me, by the lights in the truck. We took off, sirens blaring, red lights flashing, which should have thrilled a little boy. Nicky barely moved, but he did hold my hand tight.

Grandma was waiting on the porch for us, crying because she'd been afraid for me, crying because I was safe. Once she touched my shoulder, she went back to being Eve Garland, the tough old bird. "You let the EMTs patch up all those cuts and bruises, Willow. You, too, Grant. Then go find dry clothes. I'll take the boy. Everyone else, you go on home. There's nothing more you can do."

I was staying. So was Grant. Colin and Kenneth stood by the front door, on guard, until a healer from DUE and a pediatrician from East Hampton arrived.

The medical doctor couldn't do much without blood tests and heart monitors, but he shook his head. The healer told us to talk to Nicky while she worked, so I did, telling him what a wonderful life he could have, school, friends, a whole town as family, as many dogs as he wanted.

Grandma spooned some tea into him. If her ingredients didn't help him, or the words she mumbled, maybe the honey she stirred in would.

Grant spoke, too, while the healer ran her hands over Nicky's body. No one had any idea what Grant said, of course, except Nicky, who fluttered his eyelashes at him. Grant looked sad, and I knew what he was going to say.

Grandma said it first, after a look from the healer: "He cannot stay here. We cannot care for him."

I always knew that, in my heart. I lifted him in my arms and held him close to me, accepting the blanket Grant wrapped around both of us.

"Nicky, my love, do you want Fafhrd to take you home with him?"

He gave me a shadow of a smile, touched my lips, and whispered, "Pls."

I carried him out to Grandma's porch. "We'll both think of him, then, shall we?" I asked. "So he'll come. Think of how strong he is, strong enough to keep you safe forever. And brave, brave enough to break the rules to find you. He'll bring you to your grandfather, who will love you the way we love you here."

We could hear trees crashing, as something very big hurried to us.

I brushed his hair back off his forehead. "I'll miss you, baby. I hardly knew you, but you were part of me, you know."

He touched his heart. And mine. "One life. One heart," I said.

He chirruped.

Grant interpreted: "One life. One heart. I and thou. One forever."

I tried to swallow my tears. "We better go down to meet Fafhrd before he tries to climb Grandma's wooden stairs and falls straight through."

Nicky spoke again, in his own tongue.

Grant laughed, so I demanded to know what Nicky said.

Grant touched Nicky's shoulder and smiled. "I think you could translate it as 'He ain't heavy, he's my brother.'"

"How is that possible? Nicky's mother was human, his father an elf."

They conversed a minute, half in the eldritch language, half in their minds. I could tell that from Grant's concentration, and I was jealous that I couldn't do it anymore.

"D'ref could alter his form," Grant explained, "and cast a glamour over his victims so they saw what he wished. He tricked the prettiest troll maiden in the land, a princess among her people, Fafhrd's mother. Her family insisted he be stripped of his magic for his sins."

Then Fafhrd was in front of us, kneeling, his hands out. I kissed Nicky's forehead, then laid him in Fafhrd's arms. "Keep him safe, my friend. I'll miss you, too. But I'll put both of you in my books. So we can be together. You and I, forever."

Grant cursed. "Damn, I wish I could see him, just this once."

I understood, because I envied his ability to talk to Nicky.

Nicky smiled, and whispered something to Fafhrd. I didn't notice any change, but Grant sighed. "Thank you. For everything. Go in peace."

They disappeared

Now it was just Grant and me. I couldn't hear any voices, only spring peepers calling. I guess Nicky's magic let me be a telepath for a bit, or Borsack's. Or maybe just hysteria, the way people could lift buses in a panic. Either way, I was on my own now, the way I'd always been, and more afraid than ever. Life was scary.

"We have a lot to talk about, Lord Grantham."

"Can't it wait until morning? I think we're both exhausted and emotionally drained."

"No. I'd never fall asleep tonight anyway."

We walked back to my mother's house, touching, but not talking. I made coffee. We both changed into dry clothes. I found a first aid kit; he found a bottle of brandy to add to the coffee.

We sat next to each other on Mom's sofa, which was covered with crocheted afghans to hide the dog stains. Red had collapsed onto a pile of towels in the kitchen.

"I love you," Grant said at the same time I said, "You are a British peer."

He brushed that aside. "It's only a courtesy title, carrying no seat in the Lords, no duties at court. My father is the earl, and he is young, healthy, and expected to live to a good old age."

"Expected by the seers and Gypsy fortune-tellers, I suppose?"

He shrugged. "They are usually right." He let his hand drape across my shoulder so his fingers could fiddle with my hair, twining it around his fingers. "I never mention it because people see me differently then. I wanted you to see the man, not the title. I don't have to live in England full-time, if that worries you. And I love you."

That's what worried me more. "I was chosen for you to love."

"Chosen, or chance met by moonlight, I still love you." He kissed me, long and deep, and as stirring as ever.

I pushed him away. "No. You were sent here because we were paired up, like an old-fashioned arranged betrothal to wed money and titles and land. Only this time it's talents and bloodlines and genes your matchmakers look at."

"And character. But they chose right. That is, they suggested right. No one ordered me to marry you. No one could force me to love you. I know you love me. I saw it in your thoughts when we were in danger. And the sex is magnificent. We can work everything else out."

"No, we cannot, and keep your hands to yourself. Sex is not the answer to everything."

"It's not?" he teased. "You could have fooled me."

"You don't understand. You were goddamned *chosen*

for me. Even if you call it a suggestion. We'd be like my parents' marriage, and see where that led."

"To you."

He was getting frustrated, in more ways than one. "And so what if they told me we'd be good together? We are. I did not choose to be an earl's son, or a linguist. I'd rather have inherited my mother's talents. You did not choose to be an artist or a writer; you had the gift for it. You couldn't give that up any more than you could chop off your right hand."

Which he had in his, and was kissing each finger. I wondered what his mother's magic involved, but I had to get my mind back on track. "I could have been anything."

"You might have tried, becoming an insurance actuary or a saleslady at your Bloomingdale's, but you'd never be happy."

"Who's to say I'll be happy with you?"

"Did I mention the magnificent sex?"

"There has to be more."

"Dash it, Willy, there is. I love you and you love me. You've never loved anyone else, and no other woman has ever satisfied me. Nor have I cared so much about satisfying my partner. You *are* my partner, a part of me, the part that makes me want to be whatever and whomever you need. I am already a better man, for knowing you, for loving you. I and thou, one forever, remember?" He touched the charm at my neck. "One life. One love. You're stuck with me."

"No," I insisted. "People find second loves, find that their first ones don't work after a year or two. Or fifteen, like my parents."

"Not us. We're too smart to let the wonder of it die."

"How can you know? Because it's written in the stars

somewhere? I cannot accept that. I want to be loved for myself, not because you were told to, not because some genetic genius decided we'd make beautiful children."

"Bloody hell, Willy, I was willing to die for you. I was ready to kill for you. Isn't that enough to prove my love?"

"No, you had Nicky and a world to save. I was a minor player. Listen, would you give up the earldom for me, when your father passes on? Would you give away your wealth because I don't trust rich people? Would you end your connection to DUE, which is dangerous and scary?"

"No."

"There, you see?"

He didn't bother to answer. "Would you leave the States for me? Give up your writing because being a countess takes a lot of time? Would you walk away from your parents and Paumanok Harbor?"

"Um, no."

"I would never ask any of those things of you. I wouldn't love you half as much if you weren't so loyal and true, so creative and talented, so brave when your knees are shaking."

"You felt that, did you?"

"In my soul. All I wanted was to keep you safe, and I would spend the rest of my life protecting you from danger. Love is like that, and it's all about compromise, sweetheart, give and take. We can work it out; I know we can. Look what we've already been through together. That has to form a base no one could predict or plan for us."

He made it sound so easy, and his hand rubbing my back, then stroking my breasts made me want him more than ever. "I do love you. But I need time."

"That's all right, Willy. I have to go to England with what I've learned, to teach others. I'm going to ask about having the Royce Foundation buy up the Rosehill estate to make a satellite study center. Paumanok Harbor is too unique, its citizens too valuable to the world to let anything happen to them."

"They are kind of wonderful, aren't they?" I guess I could say it now.

He took tiny nips at my neck, my earlobe. "You are the most wonderful of them. No one like you should have to uproot yourself to learn about your talents, so maybe I can convince the trustees to come to the source."

"That sounds good." And his tongue felt better.

"I'll come back as soon as I can. Or you can come visit there, see how you like it, see if you could be happy writing part-time in an old castle. We have ghosts, you know. All respectable castles do, of course."

"Of course."

"You could put them in your stories. I won't give up, Willow Tate, and I won't give you forever to decide, either. I want those beautiful children. I want you at my side always."

"I'll think about it." When my head wasn't filled with thoughts of getting him naked.

"That's good enough, for now."

So was his tender lovemaking, for now. It had to be. He left with Lou before daybreak.

They were going straight to the Air National Guard airport in Westhampton with Borsack's suitcase. They'd fly to Washington, then board a secured, secret government flight to England.

And I would go back to my apartment in the city.

I'd finish my book. I already had a sequel in mind, *Night Mares in the Hamptons*. I'd see about flying down to visit my father if I could face the plane ride. If I could, maybe I'd apply for a passport and book a trip to England, just to see.

Or I could call Van and invite him out to Paumanok Harbor for a long weekend.

A bouquet of roses was waiting when I smuggled Red into the apartment. The enclosed card had the symbols from my mother's wedding ring, along with some new ones Grant must have figured out to represent One life, One heart, I and Thou, One forever.

Under the symbols he'd written, *You and me, babe.*

Maybe I'd apply for that passport tomorrow.

Gini Koch

The Alien *Novels*

"This delightful romp has many interesting twists and turns as it glances at racism, politics, and religion en route. Darned amusing." —*Booklist* (starred review)

"Kitty's evolution from marketing manager to member of a secret government unit is amusing and interesting ...a hilarious romp in the vein of 'Men in Black' or 'Ghostbusters'." —*Voya*

ALIEN TANGO
978-0-7564-0632-5

TOUCHED BY AN ALIEN
978-0-7564-0600-4

DAW 160